Mother Country

LIBBY PURVES

Mother Country

Hodder & Stoughton

First published in Great Britain in 2002 by Hodder & Stoughton
A division of Hodder Headline

A CIP catalogue record for this title
is available from the British Library

ISBN 0 340 79390 2

Typeset in Plantin by Hewer Text Ltd, Edinburgh

Printed and bound in Great Britain by
Mackays of Chatham plc, Chatham, Kent

Hodder & Stoughton
A division of Hodder Headline
338 Euston Road
London NW1 3BH

to
Sue Fletcher

I

Spring, 1974

———◦•◦•◦———

From the street, over the bass thump of the music, he could hear the baby's harsh rhythmic wails. His mouth was dry, and his heart hammered unpleasantly. Reaching out a hand, he steadied himself on the sooty trunk of a pavement tree. Thin April sunshine filtered through the leaves, and even in his panic the young man registered pleasure at the street's air of settled and unselfconscious antiquity. London had been in his dreams for a long time, almost as much as Cambridge. 'London, England,' he said under his breath, as if there was some comfort in the words.

But the baby's cries tore through the late-afternoon air, all too audible above the soupy thud of the speakers booming from the bowels of the house. Still he stood, leaning on the tree, feeling the ridged bark beneath his hand and the odd dense weight in his coat pocket, hating his own weakness. After a few moments he found that he could distinguish another human sound from behind the scabby plaster façade. A woman was shouting.

Indistinct words ripped from her throat and soared into shrieks worse than the child's. The watcher on the pavement closed his eyes. Another voice, lower but also a woman's, seemed to be pleading or soothing. A door slammed, and the two adult voices became muffled while in the foreground the baby cried on, the note rising and grating. Fighting nausea the young man jerked his head up, scowled, squared his thin shoulders and then pulled a short crowbar from the pocket of his raincoat. Glancing furtively up and down the empty street, he marched up the four steps towards the door with its peeling paint, and without even a semblance of knocking he applied the heavy tool expertly to the crack between panel and frame, and levered hard.

There was a splintering sound, and when he put his shoulder to the door it met little resistance. He was in the dark hallway, breathing a sweet and squalid air. Hash, of course; and beyond it incense, sweat and shit and a foul chemical tang which caught in his throat. The toilet door swung open at the back of the hall, and he could see smeared tiles, a broken seat propped against the white bare pedestal, and a bucket overflowing with stained nappies. Wallpaper, fussy and floral, hung away from the walls in tattered strips. Above his head bare wires protruded from the ceiling, and a broken light-fitting leaned against the bottom of the stairs.

The music was deafening now, and without thinking he pushed his way into the room on the left of the hallway to find its source and silence it. The curtains were drawn, and he could not see his way to the beating stereo. Gingerly he moved across the room towards the crack of daylight between the drapes. The baby's cries had stopped, which confused him for a moment; but as he turned from opening the curtains to look for the amplifier he glanced down and found that he had nearly stepped on the creature.

He was looking into a pair of bright blue eyes, set in a face red and creased with bawling. The child lay on a heap of dirty shawls, its small face streaked with dirt, its tiny hands moving with a newborn vagueness belied by the bright attentiveness of its eyes. It had a nappy on, much wetted and creased, so he

2

could not see whether it was a boy or a girl. But the angry rash on the small bare thighs where they had rubbed the towelling made him wince, and aloud he said: 'Bitch!' The music was still thudding, and he turned angrily towards the cold fireplace, filled with drink cans and cigarette butts, spotted an overloaded adaptor and viciously kicked it out of the wall. The music died.

Now he could hear the women again, the low-voiced one persuading, the other slowing in her rant, slurring and stopping with a petulant whimper. The infant on the rags began to grizzle again; after standing for a moment irresolute, the young man bent to take the filthy baby in his arms.

'It's OK, buddy,' he said, straightening up. 'Poppa's here. We'll get you out of shitsville, OK? Come to Poppa.' He lowered his head until his cheek touched the baby's soft, filthy face, and shuddered with love and revulsion. 'Hey, hey . . .'

He was standing there, whispering to the baby, when the dark girl came into the room. She was tall, with a curtain of black hair to her waist and a narrow, sculpted face. Pocahontas, thought the American. There was something primitive and regal about her looks. Not, however, about her manners, which were merely primitive.

'Who the fuck are you?' she said. 'And how the fuck did you get in? And what the fuck gives you the right to pick up Sunboy? Put him down.'

'I'm Christian,' said the young man, not moving. 'Christian van Hyden. Shark's friend.'

'Oh, the Yank. She mainly calls you Bud,' said the girl. 'I'm Jules. This was my squat, mine and Neville's, till Shark and the others came. And now you've fucking well broken the door.'

'Well, yeah. Anyway, this is my kid.'

'Says who?'

'Shark said.' He kept his voice level, with difficulty. 'She told me she was pregnant, you know she's been with me for months. Long before she came up here. I've been looking for her since Christmas. This has to be my kid.' He looked down. 'Anyway, I know he is. He looks just like my dad.'

Slightly to his surprise, the dark girl did not demur. 'Yah, right,' she said. 'So?'

'So he's coming home with me. I'll look after him. She obviously doesn't.'

'She's been bad,' said Jules grudgingly. 'She had some bad gear. She's been sick, yeah? She'll be OK now.'

'Because she's just shot up, you mean?'

'I helped her. I told you, she'll be fine.'

'You people are filthy,' said Christian, levelly. 'You're not fit to be in charge of a baby, and you're not going to be. I've got a lawyer.'

The girl was standing between him and the door, and his eye was measuring the route to freedom, the obstacles, and her likely strength. He felt awkward, holding the sour-smelling baby; he could feel a tensing in its small muscles and knew that at any minute the wailing would begin again and turn his mind to mush. How could he fight her off, holding this frail thing? With an effort, he made his voice less sharp.

'Let me take him. For a bit. He's hungry. I got a place with milk, and things he needs.'

'She's breastfeeding him.' said the girl scornfully. I suppose you've got breasts?'

'He can drink formula milk. I checked all that stuff out. I'm serious, er, Jules.' He used her name, hoping to placate her. 'I only want the baby to be safe. I'm not going to squeal to the police about the squat or the smack or anything. Shark can do

4

what she likes. She told me we were finished, way back. But she can't look after a kid.'

As the dark girl looked at him her eyes, which had been hard and lively, seemed to frost over. Her mouth loosened. She had, the American thought, probably taken something herself. Christ knew what, but it was kicking in.

'I'll do it all properly. There won't be any police trouble.' Guiltily, he remembered the look on the face of the Social Services woman when he had seen her. 'Officially. I'll get custody. It'll be legal and everything. Then you and Shark can be off the hook.'

Jules was losing focus, second by second, as he watched her. She yawned, and looked around the room as if she were not quite sure where he was. The sharp beautiful lines of her face seemed to blur, and the intelligence faded from her dark eyes. Then, slurring a little, her fingers fiddling nervously with the fringes of a grimy red shawl, she said with an effort: 'He does need a bit of looking after, I reckon. The baby. Sunboy'.

'Yes. And you're all too – busy.' Christian was edging towards the door.

'Busy' she agreed vaguely. 'Don't wanna get heavy'.

'Heavy' he agreed, suppressing his rage. He was in the hall now, stepping round the broken door, nearly free. 'See you.'

Jules, unsteady on her feet, made one last effort. Frowning, enunciating with drunken care, she said:

'You need his stuff? Clothes?'

The baby, warm and damp against his chest, wore only a nappy and a too-large vest. The evening was not warm now; the sun had abruptly left, and the street was grey with a small chilly wind. He would have to find a taxi.

'Just gimme that shawl,' he said. Jules hesitated, then unwound it from her thin shoulders, standing before him in a patchwork skirt and a blue T-shirt which showed her ribs. There was, he saw with flickering disgust, a red unwholesome rash on her arms and neck.

'Clean yourself up,' he said roughly as he wound the shawl round the baby. 'Shark might not get out of this, but I reckon you could. You shouldn't be living with a lowlife like Neville. You could do better.'

She was leaning on the doorpost, swaying. 'Sunboy,' she said. 'I did help. I helped him get born, you know. Blood everywhere. Neville didn't want me to. Blood freaks him.'

'Well, thanks for that. You did well.' He was down the steps, looking up at her, the baby well tucked up in the red rag. He wanted to run, but his eyes stayed on the skinny figure with its veil of hair, unwillingly compelled. God, he thought, why was it that on the very edge of a well-deserved death, squalid in their needlemarks and lank, dank hair, these junkie women retained such erotic power to fascinate? The men didn't, the men were just filthy. But the women . . .

Jules spoke once more, her voice distant.

'What shall I tell Shark?'

The spell broke. Christian heaved the baby on to his shoulder, steadying it with one hand, and said crisply: 'Anything you fucking well like. I never want to hear her name again.'

2

2001

———◆•◆———

It was a terrible hymn for a funeral, thought Alex. Depressing tune, and words which somehow managed simultaneously to lower the spirits and make you want to giggle.

Have thine own way, Lord! Have thine own way! sang the congregation, straight-faced and conscientious, not one of them seeming to feel as he did. *Hold o'er my being absolute sway!* Alex eased his shoulders, surreptitiously, trying to banish the tension. He should feel sad, simply sad, that his grandma was gone. He should not be smirking at a hymn. Grandma would not have liked that, one bit.

But, hell, she had really gone long ago, three years back, with the last awful stroke and Keith's stuttering phone message calling him home from the Vancouver job.

'I know you're busy, son, but mebbe if she saw you – the doc says anything like that could help.' So he had walked right out of the rented apartment in the clothes he stood up in, and flown to the old folks as a good grandson should. But all that he loved and needed of Grandma had gone, long before the plane landed at Des Moines. *Have thine own way, Lord! Have thine own way!* So she had been lying with her eyes blank for three Easters, two Christmases, two tulip-times when she should have been baking and bustling and scolding and feasting the neighbours like something in a Norman Rockwell painting. Marianna van Hyden left her husband and her

7

grandson long ago. What they were burying now was something else entirely.

Suddenly, ambushed by tears, the young man dropped his chin on to his chest and squeezed his eyes shut. How wrong, how stupid, how brittle and yuppie could you get? That thing was her coffin, Grandma's coffin, with the tulips of her ancestral Dutchness ranked around it like a waxy guard of honour, blood-red and purple. This man next to him, straight as a soldier and sniffing like a child, was Grandad. Klaas Christian van Hyden, known more commonly as Keith: former city councillor, bowling team leader, father of two lost sons, widower.

If Grandad Keith could cry an honest tear and sing the goddam hymn, so could Alex. He raised his head and finished the last verse aloud: '. . . *Christ only, always, living in me!*'

Not that he believed in that any more. Not with any daily intensity, anyway. A youth of constant churchgoing seemed to have robbed him of the spiritual curiosity which his agnostically reared friends displayed. Mantras, gurus, rituals, evangelists, philosophers, therapists alike all failed to tempt him. Late-night college conversations about whether there was 'like, something greater, like, transcendent' left Alex cold. Girlfriends with a penchant for meditation, reincarnation or Feng Shui failed to engage his interest in their hobby. They took him for a spiritual ignoramus, whereas he saw himself as simply too saturated to absorb any more of it. Alex, by the age of eighteen, was a weary veteran who knew perfectly well where such talk led in the end: to the pew smelling of wax polish, the language of abasement, the dull-eyed worship, the resignation. *Have thine own way, Lord, have thine own way . . .*

At twenty-seven, he still shuddered at the weight of the religion he had quietly, tactfully, discarded a decade before.

He wriggled his shoulders fretfully, and with an effort did his duty by the commendatory prayers for whatever was left of Grandma. The tulips moved a little in the breeze from the open doorway, but still gave no illusion of life.

After the service, his arm linked with his grandfather's, Alex walked back from the burial ground and looked around his hometown with a stranger's eyes. It was a fetching sight in the early-summer sunshine, no doubt about it. A quiet, dignified little haven to have grown up in: nine thousand citizens in three thousand families; barely more than three or four of them at a time likely to present any kind of problem to the city fathers. Forty miles from the state capital and over a thousand from the skyscrapers of Manhattan, the little town was tidy, friendly, decorous and almost aggressively Dutch. For, although not one waterway wound through its logical streets and not one dyke awaited the finger of a juvenile hero, the town rejoiced in its ancestry. It sprouted red Dutch gables, garden windmills and bank after bank of spring tulips; its schoolchildren studied the Dutch masters, its churches bore witness to a painfully exported Lutheran ethic. The student Alex, who read voraciously on the subject of European mores, used to annoy his grandmother with sly jokes about opening a cannabis café to complete the illusion, and getting Mary-Jo Hoogstraten to pose naked in a shop window for the real Amsterdam feel. She would swat aside such decadent modernities.

'Wash your mouth out, boy!' Grandma used to say. 'And be proud! Your forefathers came to America in 1848, but they came for God's freedom, as surely as the Pilgrim Fathers! They were the best of poor old Europe, and here they built a better life!' For indeed, her American patriotism came second only to her reverence for immigrant roots, the older the better.

Hers, naturally, were better than her husband's. The van Hydens, she would say with a sniff, only came in 1908 as economic migrants ('though there's nothing to be 'shamed of,' the old lady would add magnanimously, 'about wanting to better yourself'). But the true glory belonged to her own family, the Kreuzers, who arrived in 1848 'on a terrible ship, your great-great-great-grandmother pregnant and sick, but all of them rejoicing in freedom and deliverance. Then they worked the land in Illinois – though by the bye they were professional people back in Europe' – here she would sniff –' and at last they came here to Marion County, with enough money saved for the farm.'

The farm, long since gone from the family, also played a great part in the mythology of Alex's childhood. Once a year, on Great-great-great-grandfather Kreuzer's birthdate in July, his grandparents would bundle him into the station-wagon and drive out into the flat, featureless cornlands that waved like the sea, mile after mile in every direction, broken only by the stark industrial shapes of silos and elevators. When they reached a certain bleak red farmstead, surrounded by a dispiriting scatter of hot broken concrete lumps and machinery, they would stop the car, get out, and stand for a moment while Grandma said: 'That was the farm that made our family fortune, boy. Never forget it.'

It must, he thought from the perspective of an adult wage-earner, have been a damn' good fortune. Old Kreuzer's son came into town, built a fine brick hall with curved Dutch gables, and gave it to the community as one of its first meeting-places. His son left the farm to a tenant and increased the family fortune as a grain-dealer; in time he led the council, anglicizing his name to Kroozer. At last the line petered out into mere girls, and pretty Marianna Kroozer met tall, awkward Keith van Hyden at a dance given for the returning soldiery in 1945.

He had been in France and seen action on the beaches, but more importantly to her, he had been sent with a liberation party into Holland. Keith had breathed the ancestral air, had walked the streets of Leyden and shaken the hands of Dutchmen who had resisted the Nazis. 'It's all so small there, honey,' he used to say. 'So, so sweet 'n' small, like a dollhouse.' They married in May, 1946, in a church full of tulips and solemn, metrical Reformed Church hymns; she bore their eldest son Alexander just in time to ensure that he would be drafted to Vietnam at twenty-one and sent home half-crazy in 1968 to frighten the hell out of his parents and his little brother.

Here a familiar darkness rippled at the edge of his thoughts, and Alex terminated them, sharply. His grandfather was saying something.

'I never thought it'd be me burying her,' he said. 'Never thought it'd be that way round.'

'She didn't know much, Grandad,' said Alex, 'towards the end, I mean. She just kinda faded, right?'

'Right,' said Keith. They had reached the house. The little windmill in the front garden was still, the drum behind its sails wedged with a neat rubber triangle out of reverence for the dead. The old man fumbled for the key and then, remembering the arrangements of the day, pushed the door open instead. Three neighbours, sharp-faced kindly women of Grandma's generation, had slipped away early to lay out a funeral tea on the long dark table. Everything was ready. Alex stepped aside as the first few mourners came chattering in behind them; Keith went to the kitchen and drew himself a long glass of water, then came back towards his grandson, drinking it. He was always, Alex remembered with a heave of affection, a tremendous water-drinker. The old man grimaced at the way the room was filling up.

'Into battle, son,' he muttered. 'She'd-a-wanted things done right.' Alex grinned at him, and their perfect mutual understanding lightened the sombre day. Neither had ever taken much pleasure from Marianna's 'gatherings', and this was set fair to be a classic, even without her presence. Women poured in, trailing reluctant menfolk. chattering, patting their grey or blue hair, inspecting the slices of ham and the sandwiches and cookies with sharp professional eyes, sipping tea, boasting modestly about their children's achievements in college and employment.

'And you're doing well!' said Mrs Hoogstraaten to Alex, in a tone that brooked no disagreement. 'Computers!'

'Yeah, well. Computer *systems*,' said Alex edgily. 'It's OK. It's a living.'

'It's the *future*,' said Mr Hoogstraaten, with the conviction of a man who has lately mastered his first PC and taken to sending argumentative messages to discussion boards about the Iowa police department. 'It's a computer world now.'

In places where Alex worked, the very word 'computer' had been out of style for some years, so woven into the fabric of their lives was the silicon chip. He supposed that an Eskimo, equipped with myriad words for types of snow, probably never said 'snow' either. There was just too much of the stuff to bother naming it in such a vague way. Mrs Hoogstraaten began telling him about Mary-Jo's wedding, in tones which made it very clear that he had missed his best chance there. Alex listened and painfully suppressed a yawn, of the type he thought of as an 'Iowa yawn', for reasons that were not entirely onomatopoeic. Back to town tomorrow. He had offered to stay with Keith for a while, but the old man gently declined.

12

'You came back when Marianna was took sick,' he said. 'We were both glad of that. I reckon she knew sure enough that you were there. No need to stay now. I got good friends in this town, and you got a life to live.'

So in the morning, Alex would fly back to Boston and his spare, neat, expensive apartment above Water Street. He felt brief guilty pleasure at the thought of his solitude, his books, his private and controlled and wholly Hoogstraaten-free life. Hours later, when the guests had gone, the ladies taking their dishes and plates with them and leaving the small house spotless, he said diffidently:

'Grandad, is it OK if I go in the loft and get some of my books and stuff?'

The old man nodded assent. He was slumped in his chair, thankful for the silence, but when Alex had rooted around in the kitchen drawers and come back with the key to the trap door he roused himself and said: 'There's some stuff you should have, anyway. Red box. Your grandma made me put it up there when you went to college. I wasn't happy about that, boy, thought you should've had it then and there. But hell, the women!' He attempted a smile.

On one level Alex was wrenched by simple pity. He knew other old men like his grandfather, widowers trying to handle the new silence and freedom. But more urgently, he felt a leap of private excitement. The red box could only be a repository for one thing: family history. Not the Kroozer history, which lay all around them in the house, in prints and china ornaments and old farm documents tastefully preserved in acrylic bricks as paperweights. Marianna had never hidden any of that away in a red box to put in the roof, out of his sight. The box might – must! – contain something of his more immediate history.

13

'Is it about my dad?' he asked. 'And when I was born, my –
He could not quite say 'mom', or even 'mother'. Not to Keith;
the interdict on that subject, laid down by Marianna ever since
he could remember, still hung too strongly in the air of the little
house. It was a localized inhibition: Alex had never, he thought
with a twist of his mouth, had trouble using the word to
girlfriends. Easily enough he would say to them: 'I never knew
my mom. She was English. She was a junkie, and she died
when I was a baby, so I came to live in Iowa with my dad and
grandparents.'

This revelation over dinner usually preceded the first sexual
encounter with a girl; it was not, thought Alex, mere imagination which made it seem that girls clasped him all the closer
(poor motherless boy!) for knowing it. He had come to wince at
that phenomenon, enough indeed to avoid girls for almost a
year now. He disliked himself for using the line, disliked them
for responding with such unwholesome excitement, and felt
even more uncomfortable when he realized how very few of
them probed further by asking: 'And your dad?' Girls, he
thought bitterly, were only interested in the mother. Perversely,
though, his reply to the dad question was a terse: 'He died
when I was only two. I don't remember anything about it.'

No girl had ever had a straight answer to a question about
precisely why Christian van Hyden died so young. The
circumstances of his death were known in this town, all right,
by the likes of Mary-Jo Hoogstraaten; they got the story in
hushed murmurs from their gossiping old witches of mothers.
Alex took good care not to bring any outsider girls home to
find out about it.

He felt a sudden bad urge to question Keith. 'My dad,' he
began again, helpless to stop himself. 'You told me about
Uncle Al, and what happened, but I never—'

The look on the old man's face, a weary grief, stalled him and he put up his hands. 'Sorry. Sorry. It doesn't matter. I'll go to the loft'.

The red box was not hidden; it stood a little apart from the old trunks and debris under the roofbeams, kept from him all these years by no lock more potent than an old woman's implacable will. It was a little bigger than a standard shoebox – a boot box, perhaps – of scuffed and fading cardboard with *SMARTIQUE* stencilled on the side, and the outline of an elegantly pointing toe. Alex, who liked his filing tidy, logical and preferably on a flat screen, felt his fingers flinch away from the dusty homeliness of the thing. After a moment he made as if to open it, but changed his mind and brought it away from the dim, cluttered space, carrying it down the ladder under his arm with the two books he had been looking for. On the landing he hesitated, then with a deliberate act of will turned and left the box alone in his childhood bedroom, under the Superman painting-by-numbers oil that he had done when he was nine. He went back to his grandfather, giving a fair impression of a young man without worries or impatience.

'Hot drink, Grandad?' he said. 'Help you to sleep?'

When Keith had finally gone to his room with hot milk, Alex poured himself a Bourbon and brought down the box. The house was deathly quiet, only the Dutch clock ticking like a bomb on the bookcase. He opened the lid, and at first sight he thought that it held only photographs, like so many of the other boxes his grandmother accumulated. A young soldier in uniform grinned up at him, fresh and untroubled by war. The same soldier, out of uniform now, occupied a sheaf of other pictures – coupled with a younger Keith, a smiling Marianna, and in several cases with a slighter, younger version of himself. The brothers – they could not have been otherwise – were arm-in-arm, or play-fighting, or simply standing together at ease.

Then there were two black-and-white portraits of the younger boy, sentimentally softened in the processing into a rounder-faced version of Alex himself. *A mommy's boy*, thought Alex with an involuntary grimace, then hated himself for traducing his vanished father. He glanced across the room to a silver frame on the wall: the face which looked out at him, a more familiar icon of Christian van Hyden, was harder-edged, thinner, tougher, older than these mommy-dream pictures. He preferred it.

At the bottom of the box, fitting it as exactly as a false bottom, was a cardboard folder, which he prised out carefully. Beneath it, lying on some kind of red cloth padding, lay a thin brown leatherette diary marked 1974. Before he laid a finger on it, Alex opened the folder and found three photographs more carefully stored. He stared at these for a long time.

In the first, the younger brother stood by the windmill in the front garden, holding in his arms a baby whose face just showed inside a woollen shawl. The father glowed with pride of possession; Alex's heart jumped painfully. He had seen this picture before, years ago. He was eight, acting up and shouting unkind accusations at his grandparents, saying that nobody loved him or wanted him and everyone was against him.

Pretty standard stuff, he thought now. Normal eight-year-old brattiness. But Grandma had left the room, white-faced, and returned some minutes later with this little slip of a photograph. 'Your daddy loved you. He loved you enough to bring you alla way from England so you could be safe. An' we loved your daddy.' She had held it up to him, then snatched it away as if he was not worthy to hold it. He had not seen it since.

The second photograph showed Christian again, kneeling by a bathtub supporting a grinning baby with his big hands. It was crooked in the frame, and the flash had been too harsh, but life and love reflected off it like streaks of winter sunshine.

The third photograph was of a child of about two, in winter clothes, against a desolate background of flat bare fields, with just a corner visible of the familiar church at the town's edge. The infant held a wreath in his small hands; Alex, who told every girlfriend in his life that he remembered 'nothing' of his father's death, could hardly bear to look at it.

There were no pictures of his mother or her country. Only these various dark-haired, squarely handsome van Hydens. The hope which had sprung when Keith mentioned the box died, abruptly.

But the diary, Christian's diary, still lay in the box, nestled on the silky, faded red shawl. Suddenly weary, Alex picked it up, threw the jumble of photographs and folders back into the box, and with the limp brown book on top of them carried it all to his bedroom. He would read the diary – if it truly was a diary – in the morning, with light and hope and reality all around him.

Not now. Not in the night, in the grieving house. The stair creaked as he went upstairs, and he heard a low weird groan from his sleeping grandfather's room.

3

———◆•◆•◆———

In the event, Alex woke long before it was light. He flicked on the spaceship lamp and lay there, tired and idle in his childhood bed, looking up at the smudged Superman on the wall. The red box lay by his bed, the diary balanced on top of it. He rolled on his side and contemplated it for a while, then heaved himself upright, punched a pillow behind his shoulder, and balanced the limp brown book on his knees.

'So tell me, Dad,' he addressed it softly. 'Tell me about England!' He paused, then continued, still aloud: 'And tell me about Moira. Shit, Dad. I'm twenty-seven. Old enough to know.'

He knew her name: it was on the birth certificate which Marianna had, with deep reluctance, allowed him to have when he got his driver's licence. *Moira Charlotte Grayson* had given birth to him, said the bald official print, on 3 March 1974, in London. Father's name, blank. He had been momentarily distressed by this, but Marianna said hurriedly, almost snappishly: 'That don't matter. Your pa came to get you soon 'nuff. Your ma wasn't well.'

He was irritated by the euphemism, since Keith had told him clearly enough, ten years earlier, that his mother was a 'poor unfortunate drug-dependent lady' who had died, and that it would be distressing to his grandma if he mentioned her. Grandma, as they both knew, had a morbid terror of drugs and junkies, fuelled by her avid reading of magazines. She also had theories about Bad Blood which Keith, not unnoticed by his grandson, had been heading off with some skill in family conversations for years. 'If'n you need to talk about your ma, boy, come to me,' the old man had said. 'But better not, maybe. Let her rest, poor lady.'

Once or twice since, Alex had thought of approaching Keith to take him up on this reluctant offer, but always drew back. Why, in any case, would Keith know anything about Moira Charlotte Grayson? The only one who could have told the story properly was his own father Christian, and he was long since gone on the same dark journey.

So Moira Charlotte's son had, for years, studied her country instead. From boyhood he devoured TV films about England, whether flickering black-and-white period pieces, war movies or sumptuous Edwardiana from Merchant Ivory. He sat devotedly in front of Masterpiece Theater on television, and while schoolmates giggled at the quaint clipped accents and crumbling antiquities of *Brideshead Revisited* or *Jeeves and Wooster*, Alex hugged to himself the knowledge that these things too were part of him, his birthright.

'I'm half-English,' he said once in the schoolyard, and was thumped and disbelieved as surely as if he had claimed to be half-Vulcan. The first time he ever met anybody from England was at college, when a young lecturer arrived for a term to teach history: Alex was so overwhelmed he could barely speak in Mr Grindley's class.

As he grew older, encouraged by Mr Hammerbawm at the college, he had dived and swum ecstatically through the canon of English literature, relishing the density, the antique language, the layers of meaning and beauty. He discovered Henry James at sixteen, and puzzled over the riddle of American innocence and corrupt European experience, but the continent of Europe in general failed to intrigue him in the way that Britain did: especially and particularly England. Absorbing his native land through culture, he tuned out any news of its contemporary doubts and weaknesses and enjoyed only its glory. Alone in his year he was a boy who could spot Shakespearian references in Milton, and Miltonic echoes in Wordsworth. Certainly he was the only one in his college dorm whose posters were prints of Holman Hunt's *The Light of the World*, the *Death of Nelson*, and Turner's perspective of Richmond Park. He read T.H. White's version of the Arthurian legend, which led him to Malory and to C.S. Lewis; he blinked away tears at vintage World War II films about gallant airmen and Blitz courage. Growing up on the great hot Midwestern plain, saluting the American flag each day, always he felt a deep romantic connection to the little country in the salt North Sea: to the magical and sacred, heroic and democratic, happy and glorious realm of England.

He startled his English professor at Harvard – a bright young woman from Glasgow – by his passionate, and in her view absurd, adherence to G.K. Chesterton. *The rolling English drunkard made the rolling English road!* Miss Mackenzie ridiculed his taste, and gave him some sour-hearted social realist novels to read instead. Alex skimmed them, made the right college-intellectual commentaries on them, but in his bones knew that they lied. The other England, the country in his heart, basked on untroubled by cynicism: green and golden, ancient and majestic.

'So just go there!' said red-headed Miranda impatiently, sprawling on his bed as long ago as 1995. 'So you're half-English – so go and have a look at it! I'm telling you, I went there in the summer of my sophomore year and it's just cold and grey and full of broken stuff. Windsor Castle was neat, but London is a pisser. And it costs! And they don't like Americans, be sure of it!' She had rolled over, turning perfect breasts to the ceiling, and added, '*Italy*, though . . . wow! Do Naples and Venice and Rome! Now that *is* something.'

But Alex had never been to his mother's country, never dared. 'Why?' asked friends idly enough, and with great seriousness he always replied: 'Because I don't know where to go to. If I went, the point would be to find my mother's family or her friends, and get to know my English relatives. I couldn't just be a tourist there. Like everyone else.'

'You know you were born in London. Go to London.'

'London's big. It'd be stupid. I want to know where her folks lived, and everything. I want ancestors I can actually find. I reckon Grandma knows more'n she lets on, but she thinks Britain's just full of sin and drugs.'

Miranda, and all the others, thought this point of view very stupid, so over the years it had turned into a joke. Only one girl – a lofty Bostonian called Isabelle – had accused him outright of cowardice.

'You're just scared to go. You're afraid it'll be a let-down.'

'No, I'm not. I just want more information.'

'Well, go there and get it. Go to the Records Office, or whatever they have. Find your mom's birth certificate. All that stuff. See where her family lived.'

Alex was silent because he knew that she was right. A determined seeker for roots would have been on a cheap flight years before.

'You're just worried how you'd deal with it, OK?' said Isabelle. 'With her being dead, and the drugs and all, and her folks might not want to be reminded. But if you gotta go, just go. I'll come. I'm a whiz in records offices.'

He did not want to go with Isabelle, who was tall and grand and already bossed him around more than he was happy with. He made more excuses, and they broke up a month or so later. And gradually, over the years, as professional success soothed and flattered him and America gave him an adult role, Alex van Hyden's fascination with all things English began to lose its edge.

But now he had the diary. The diary changed everything. It spun him back down the years to his childhood bewilderments and adolescent broodings. The little brown book, he saw from the date, had been around when he was a baby, when his dad was alive. It had been in the hand of that determined young father, younger than he was now. It had flown out with the two of them on a plane to Des Moines, and come to rest in the dull, safe little house with the windmill.

Suddenly he could see a clear vision: the man in the photographs, his father, trying to manoeuvre an inflight case out of the overhead locker while supporting a small baby on his other arm. How did he manage? Did he put the baby down on the airline seat behind him? Did he, Alex, wake up and cry? The detail almost overwhelmed him. The brown book had been there. It had seen all that stuff. Even if it was empty, every page blank except for appointments and flight numbers, it was a witness to his strange beginnings.

At last, in the pool of lamplight, Alex opened the diary. Its pages were a little yellowed with age, but of thin, high-quality paper. Scribbled on the inside cover: *Christian van Hyden, Caius College, Cambridge.*

It had been, he saw with initial disappointment, designed as an appointments diary, with a week to a double-page opening. However, as he turned the pages he saw with a rush of excitement that the owner had disregarded the ruled lines separating the days and used it as a scribbled, narrative journal with only the occasional date or appointment marked in its proper place. None of the entries was long, but the writing was small and clear, the blue ink sharp and fresh.

27 March – I got the little guy! After all that shit, I got him safe. He's mine OK. He looks like pictures of Al when he was born! Shark was out of it, full of junk, I didn't even see her, just heard her wailing in the other room.

Doctor N. says the boy might have to detox. He says that junkies' babies get born already addicted. Christ, assholes, to do that to a baby! He cries a lot, high wobbly shrieking. I can't think too good.

29 March – Saw lawyer. Told him everything, all the details, about how filthy the house was and how she's totally useless. I think he's good. Baby doesn't sleep. Mrs O. is being great, teaching me stuff about diapers.

Love the little guy but this is scary. Can't stay at college now. Bit scared to tell Professor M.

Alex blinked. He had always wondered, during his own days at Central College and then Harvard, whether Christian had given up his studies in Britain in order to bring him home. He had wanted to talk to his grandparents about it, but knew how much they hated to speak of their two dead sons. Now he knew. Poor kid, losing Cambridge and all! But how would a guy on his own, in a British college, bring up a baby? In 1974?

He read the entry again, noting especially: '*Saw lawyer. Told him everything*'. Another question of his youth was being answered, more fully in the next entries.

4 April – Looks like we can get a court hearing real quick, this week even. Lawyer says guys don't usually get custody, but with Shark out of it, shouldn't be a problem.

Out of it? How, out of it? Dead?

I need to get Alexander home to his grandma. Freaks me when he throws up. Mrs O. says it's OK though. They all do it, it's not the junk. He's smiling, I think. Mrs O. says not, but I say yes.

5 April – Didn't sleep. Mrs O. being brilliant, I love her. The little guy screams a lot, really high and weird, the doc says he's still going through some withdrawal. Shit!

I spoke to the Pocahontas girl today at the house. She gave me a lot of feminist crap, but I told her I saved Alex's life taking him out of that shitheap, and she went kinda quiet, like she couldn't argue with that.

Saw Shark. Asleep, looked like she was dead. I reckon Pocahontas is worried. Her guy does heroin too, and she keeps saying he's OK and it's just some liver bug that Shark's got, but I think she thinks the same as I do.

9 April – We got a hearing! Amazing: Pocahontas (NB: Julia Tainton Morrowack, 763 4988) is giving evidence. For us! Can't believe it. Thought she'd speak for Shark. Lawyers have got their tails right up now. Especially Les, the fat one.

14 April – I am the legal custodial parent of Alexander Grayson, shortly to be known as Alexander van Hyden. His mother is now officially an 'unfit parent'. You can say that again!

Checked out the birth certificate. Amazingly it's got none of the Sunboy Moonflyer crap on it. The Morrowack broad says it was going to, but in the end when the hospital woman came round to register him Shark just said Alexander, for her brother.

And my brother! How's that for a weird coincidence? Al will be pleased. Had a letter from Mom, she thinks he's getting better. Had a bad drunk two nights ago but he's said he's going for a job at Firestone in Des Moines.

Anyway, the little guy's getting fatter. He doesn't cry in that funny high way any more. Doc says he's probably clear now.

Took my gown back to college store, got £6 for it. A bit sad. But home now, with baby Alex.

NB: Flight BA 4569, 5/17. Heathrow, nb ring re babyseat. Sort out passport at US Embassy.

17 May – On the plane. He's asleep, thank Christ. Tried to ring Morrowack to say thanks properly, but phone just rang and rang. Probably better. She must feel like shit anyway, saying what she did. Lawyer Les says it made all the difference. Wrote to her to say thanks and goodbye.

I heard from Danny that Shark is in hospital, Fulham Road. I tried to see her, just to sign off. Shit, we made a baby together. That should mean something. Not allowed in. The nurse looked at me like I was her dealer, said, 'She's dying, you know. I don't know why you're so surprised. It's what junkies do best.'

Shit. Going home. Grandma says the tulips are good. Little Alex might like that, he looks at moving coloured stuff now.

Unbidden, a vision of nodding tulips danced before Alex's eyes. They must, indeed, have been among the first things he ever watched. He turned the page, hoping for an account of his arrival and welcome in Iowa, but to his dismay the rest of the book was blank.

He turned page after page, fretfully, until one of them

seemed to stick. He tugged at the paper and felt resistance. Something thicker lay between the fine pages. More gently he eased it open and saw, wedged hard into the binding of the diary between two late pages, the outline of a photograph hardly bigger than a large stamp, of the kind that used to spew stickily from drugstore photo-booths in his childhood. The paper had adhered to its front through years of damp attic winters. Holding his breath, with infinite care Alex eased the surfaces apart. Some streaks of monochrome picture remained on the blank diary page, but they were only streaks of the subject's tousled blonde hair and of the curtain backcloth. The face on the photograph remained clear, with big pale eyes fixed on him and a slight, enigmatic smile.

There was no name. There did not need to be. He was looking into his mother's face. His first reaction was to think how young she was to be dead for such a stupid reason. The next was pure feeling: he shook to his very bones, and tears of angry self-pity rose to his eyes and spilled down his cheeks, a sensation so unfamiliar that the shock of it laid a second distress on him. Boys, in his grandfather's world, didn't cry.

Thrusting the diary back into the box he felt the red cloth. Half-blinded by the tears, he pulled it out roughly, scattering photographs, and mopped his face with it. It was some soft heavy cotton, with a faint, figured oriental pattern on it. Although it was as clean as any piece of cloth must be in Grandma's house, there clung to it a faint strange smell, as if it had once been perfumed with incense. The comfort of feeling it near his face made Alex go on clutching it after the burst of tears had gone. After a while, he slept.

4

'"Morning, boy," said Keith into his grandson's dreams. 'Hey, what is that? Wow, I haven't seen that since you were a baby.' Opening his eyes, Alex saw that the old man was standing by him with a mug of coffee, his free hand fingering the red shawl which dangled from the bed. 'You used to hang on to that. Marianna said it was a dirty old rag, but your daddy wouldn't let her throw it away. She must've put it in the box later on.'

Alex shook his head, confused. 'You're up!' he said stupidly. 'I was gonna bring you coffee and stuff. You didn't have to—'

'You got a plane to catch,' said the old man. 'It's after nine. I had an idea to drive you over to the airport and go see Vernon on the way back. He's fixed the new fishing lake. They're putting the young ones in today.' He looked younger, spry and lively; last night's air of weary grief had evaporated entirely. Alex remembered what one of the neighbour ladies had said to him, sympathetically bustling as she cleared up. 'It's been a big strain on Keithy, her being sick for so long. You wait and see, he'll be a changed man now he's laid the poor soul to rest. It's always like that.'

Alex wriggled upright in the bed, feeling years older than this energetic old man: stiff and jaded and still obscurely threatened by the tears of the night. The messy red box

29

was still on the floor, photographs spilt around it. Keith glanced down at them.

'Family history,' he said with little expression. 'You know, boy, sometimes I think your grandma went in for a bit too much of that. Always either showing it off or hiding it away. You can only live your own life.'

Alex reached for the coffee and gulped at it gratefully. 'Siddown, Grandad,' he commanded. 'I want to ask you stuff.'

'Family history stuff?' said Keith, sitting on the end of the bed. 'OK, boy. Whatever you need. I suppose I owe it you. But, remember.' He looked hard and a little warily at his grandson, as if seeing him for the first time in years. 'The great thing about history is that it's over. Can't hurt you, can't help you. And there's only so many times you can dig it over.'

'OK,' said Alex. 'But I read my dad's diary last night. It was weird, seeing it in his own writing. I just want to know what happened when he got me, and brought me home.'

A look of almost sly relief flickered across the old man's face. These questions, clearly, were of a kind he was happy to answer.

'Well,' he began, 'darned kid didn't even tell us there was a baby. He didn't even tell us there was a *girl*. I was at work, and he rang up your grandma from Des Moines Airport at nine o'clock in the morning with baby-crying noises behind him, and asked her to drive over and get you both.'

Alex was silent. This version, with sound effects and airport telephones, was something he had never heard. Grandma had repeated only the soothing vague childhood story, of how his poor mom had died when he was little, so his daddy naturally brought him to the grandparents who loved him. Nobody had ever mentioned the element of sheer surprise involved.

'Did Grandma drive out to get me, then?' he asked. 'It must

have been a hell of a shock. I mean, was she OK to drive?' It had long been axiomatic in the family that although Marianna was a perfectly competent driver, she needed time and a couple of prayers to 'collect herself' before any journey that took her out on to the highway.

'No, Al went to get you,' said Keith. And added hurriedly, 'You gotta remember that he was A-OK some of the time. He couldn't hold down a job after he got back from Vietnam, and yeah, there was the drink and the bad stuff. Yeah.' He paused, not having meant to go so far down this avenue. He gave Alex a sidelong glance, but the young man gave no sign of wanting to pursue him down it. Keith resumed.

'But it was one of his good days, so Marianna gave him the keys of the Chevy. And when you arrived you were all three laughing and happy, like it was a big joke. Surprise baby.'

Keith paused again, and Alex, sitting quiet and tousled in his bed, waited for his grandfather to determine the next stage of the story. Taking the silence for disbelief, Keith repeated: 'A big joke. You all laughed. That's as true as I'm sitting here. You oughta know that. I don't want you to think it was always bad with Al. After we'd lost both our boys together, it was natural your grandma didn't want to talk about them much, not after she got over it. She said she'd talked to the pastor and it was better for you that we put it in the past, because she and I would be like parents, and let you grow up normal.'

'You were my parents. I did grow up normal,' said Alex quickly. 'You did great. Look at me!'

'I was glad when you found out about Al,' said Keith abruptly. 'Marianna wasn't. She was angry with the Hoog-straaten girl. But I thought you had a right to know.'

'Grandad, it's OK,' said Alex. 'It is. Forget Al. I'm a man now. I studied politics for three semesters. I know about the kind of thing that happened. I did a paper on Vietnam. I'm cool about it. Shit happens.'

The old man looked at him, speculatively. 'If you say so. Is that all you want to know? Just about the day you came?'

Alex hesitated. It was rare for his grandfather to talk about the past this freely. He stalled for a moment.

'What did *you* think about it, when you got back from work?'

It was the right question. Keith laughed, a laugh far younger than his years. It was a joyful sound in the still, sorrowful little house.

'I fell into my chair,' he said. 'You never saw a man smacked flat like I was. I thought Christian was settled down for his studies, an' I was just getting used to the idea he was so far away. And, yeah, I was getting used to bragging to Vernon and the guys about my son at Cambridge, England. I was even keeping my spare reels and catch-nets in the corner of his room.' He glanced round. 'He slept in here then, did you know that? You took it over when you were outa your crib. Anyway, it was a good shock to get in from work and find him standing there with you, wrapped in that red rag like an old pudding, and saying you'd both be living at home now. I was flat, boy, flat!'

Emboldened, Alex shot in the next question.

'How much did he tell you about my mother?'

'Not a great deal, boy. He told us she'd been in hospital when he left, and that the drugs were killing her. Said he hadn't had any trouble getting the right to look after you in the English courts, that it was real quick and easy.'

'Because of her doing drugs?'

'I suppose so. I could never like to think about you being in that house he got you from. He said it was real trashy and dangerous, and you were just on the floor on some rags, no crib or nothing.'

'So she wasn't dead when he left? Till last night I always thought—'

'It was very soon after. A few weeks.' Keith frowned, remembering.

'He made a call to England. To someone he told me looked like Pocahontas. A girl who'd helped him get care of you. It was her who told him your poor mom was dead. Overdosed. Your grandma had them say prayers in church for her.'

Suddenly, Alex had had enough. The chronology had never been plain to him before, being blurred by the careful kindness of Marianna. In the version he had told the girlfriends, his mother had died of drugs before he was rescued and brought home by his father. The diary, and now Keith, confirmed a more harrowing sequence. There was a fight over him; his father won, and only weeks later Moira Grayson overdosed. A familiar black ripple of horror moved at the edge of his thoughts, and he closed his eyes with the effort of pushing it away.

Keith read his mind efficiently enough. 'It was a heroin overdose,' he said levelly. 'I know what you're thinking, but you're wrong. It wouldn't be losing you that made her do it. She was doing it all the time, for kicks, and what killed her was just more of the same. Heroin. You live in the big city. You know what drugs do to folks. P'raps she hardly knew she had you. No, your daddy did the right thing, taking you right out of England and all that lousy gang.'

'You and Grandma never talked about it,' said Alex with a touch of petulance.

'There's lotsa things it's better not to talk about,' replied Keith. 'Like I say, live your own life. Now, get on up. I'll fix breakfast, then you got to get back to work, and I got Vern's fish to see to.'

When he had gone, Alex held the shawl to his face for a moment, trying to identify its faint incense smell, then put it in his case. He hesitated over the diary, but finally kept it and the best photograph of his father, stashing them in the pocket of his computer bag. Handling his clothes and luggage made him feel better, more like his adult working self. He called the Boston office on the mobile and told them he would be in before the end of the day to catch up. A tinny, distant whoop of satisfaction put heart into him. He ordered himself to let history slide away into the past: Dutch forebears, old tragedies, dead passions, fading memories, all of it. Keith drove him to the airport and the great silver bird lifted him eastward, away from the plains.

5

'Hey, d'you have a good break?' asked Janis, bouncing into his corner of the office with a sunny cheerleader grin. Then her face fell, its rubbery freckled surfaces composing themselves into an expression of bottomless woe.

'Oh, no! Oh, wow, it was a *funeral*, wasn't it? Doh!' She slapped her brow and her russet curls jiggled with the impact. 'I am so, so tactless – I gross myself out sometimes! But was it, like, OK?'

'It was fine' said Alex, adding kindly, 'Grandma'd been totally out of it for two years, since she had her stroke. It was a release. Everything's fine. Grandad was more cheerful this morning than I've seen him in ages.'

Janis performed some more grimaces of embarrassment, topped them off with another abrupt grin and, with a theatrical twirl, bounced off. Alex sipped the froth of his cappuccino and surveyed his desk with real pleasure. It was eight in the morning. Yesterday's plane had been delayed, and he had reached Boston only in time to get jammed in the rush-hour tunnel traffic under the bay. Calling in to the office, he found that Johnny Parvazzi had gone home early in order to see his son's nursery spring festival, in which small Rudy Parvazzi was playing – so Janis gigglingly informed him – the part of a singing beansprout.

'Any point my swinging by?' asked Alex once the cab

struggled clear of the tunnel. He was relaxing, feeling his adult working identity settle gratefully round his shoulders. 'Did Johnny leave anything I ought to look at tonight?'

'Nope,' said Janis. 'Marty took the Edmonton discs home yesterday and he's had a day chilling over that – no calls, no visitors, no sex – and he says he's fixed it. Johnny's called a conference for nine. You got two queries from Montana, but they're basically cool. And there's some new job that Johnny's being all secretive about, and says he'll roll out at the meeting tomorrow. There'll only be Mahmood not there, and I guess he'll tell him later. You get some sleep. Reboot your head in the morning!'

Alex redirected the cab, and when it pulled up in Water Street he almost bounded up the three flights to his apartment. It was as tranquil and tidy as he had left it, tiny and immaculate beneath its sloping garret roof. He unpacked his bags, and when he came across the diary and photograph, put them carefully but firmly into the folder which hung furthest back in the rosewood filing cabinet, marked 'Birth Cert'. Everything else he shook out, hung, folded or returned to its set place. He grimaced at the shawl, but threw it into a drawer. The books on the well-dusted shelves seemed to look on approvingly, glad to have their master home. Before he settled in his cherished leather chair to watch the evening news, Alex hesitated for a moment in front of the desk which bore his Mac and PC side by side.

In the end he did not switch on either of them, but went yawning to bed and slept dreamlessly, barely ruffling the covers. He had checked his emails at the airport; there was nothing that needed instant attention except an invitation from Isabelle to dine in lower Manhattan and meet her newly acquired fiancé.

In the morning, Isabelle was a hot topic of conversation in the office. She had worked there as a clerk for a few months before drifting off to the front desk of an auction house, but she belonged to the kind of well-drilled networking Boston family which never loses touch. At eight-thirty, when Alex had handled his mail and email, Janis stuck her head round the door again and said, 'Johnny's here. On the line. He's conferencing with Mahmood and the guy in the New Orleans company now, then he's coming through. Apparently Rudy was brilliant in the beansprout song. Remember to ask. Anyway, he says we'll meet in your room, 'cos Marty's filled his up with junk hardware from his mail-order cookie job.' Then, with even more enthusiasm, she got down to the gossip. 'And, hey, Isabelle's marrying a ten-room house in the Hamptons *and* a private helicopter, did you know that?'

'Good,' said Alex, peering at his screen. 'I knew she'd do well.'

'You'd have been a better catch, babe,' said Janis, with a lascivious wink. 'A big stiff wallet isn't everything.'

'I could sue you,' he said tranquilly, erasing a line of mail, 'for sexual harassment, suggestive obscenity, and also for causing me post-traumatic stress and actionable humiliation by pointing out that Isabelle dumped me.'

'You dumped her!'

'No, I'm a gentleman,' said Alex. 'I used telepathy. I *willed* her to dump *me*.'

'I never knew that!' said Janis, delighted. 'Wait till I tell Marty!'

'You never knew it, because it is not strictly your business,' said Alex. He swept his mouse across the mat, clicked, and stood up as the screen went blank. 'OK. Meeting. Let's do chairs.'

Candoo Solutions was five years old; Alex's years there had been the happiest and freest of his life. Johnny Parvazzi, fresh out of Yale, had founded the company with Marty and Janis Lane in order to capitalize on Marty's extraordinary talent for cutting through the confusions and contradictions which almost inevitably built up in company software. On a work placement in his final year of business school, Johnny had found himself in the office of a finance company whose daily work was disrupted by dozens of system crashes. After the original installers and designers confessed themselves beaten, the company riskily answered a small-ad and found Marty Lane, who called himself a 'system doctor'.

He arrived, bearded and bandanna-ed, with filthy fingernails and a startling vocabulary of curses. This figure of corporate nightmare moved in for three days, sat alongside the highest and lowliest users of the system in a crouched, farouche silence, then identified the problem as originating from one very senior user's habit of switching between two programs without going through the prescribed protocol. The complication was that the user had not even been online at the time of most of the crashes: the connection was subtler than that, working its sinister curse through the computer's international time-zone program. It took Marty half a day more to untangle, and earned him a fee which Johnny – who knew how seriously the problem had been threatening the company's very existence – thought appallingly low.

So he took Marty out for a drink at the end of the day and told him that with his talent he should be a company, not a small-ad mercenary. He offered to find more problem-solvers for Marty to train and use, and pledged himself to run an office and take on the burden of hideously tangled tax affairs to which, after a fifth shot of tequila, Marty somewhat tearfully confessed.

Then Johnny found a bank loan and persuaded Marty's exuberant girfriend Janis to abandon her doomed attempts to become a cabaret singer and run the office. He had an instinct that only she would ever be able to keep Marty to any sort of discipline where paperwork and timesheets were concerned.

They called it 'Candoo Solutions' so that everyone could answer the phone with 'Hi! Can do!' which suited Janis' style very nicely. Oddly enough, though, once her days were soberly occupied in the commercial arena her singing career improved as well. She now had a regular slot three nights a week belting out 'Cry Me a River' and 'Reason to Believe' in a waterfront restaurant.

Alex had joined when the company – still a little band of friends – was two months old, and cheaply housed in a condemned and chaotic 1960s bunker near the docks. When he met Johnny he instantly made the necessary leap of faith, left his dull first job and threw in his lot with them. The faith was mutual: like Marty, although with less eccentric brilliance, Alex had a gift for understanding how problems arose in complex computer systems, and already knew enough about the most common software to feel his way to a simple solution.

'It's always a simple solution,' Johnny had told him. 'Marty says that more often than not it's taking out some facility they don't need anyway, but that got sold to them by a salesman who didn't bother to understand the company and its kind of users. System buyers get snowblind with all the offers, and opt for extra bells and whistles on everything, and next thing they know the whole thing's tangled up and crashing and the customers are bleating, and they panic.'

'Why can't they work it out themselves? They use the system most,' asked Alex.

'Because they're thinking about the product, not the system, and they're just so upset at losing business every day they're on the deck, sobbing. So we go in, all calm and serious like a doctor – or in Marty's case witch-doctor – and we look up the company's ass and jiggle its balls about a bit and ask seriously embarrassing questions. Next thing they know, everything's pretty again.'

Candoo rapidly became known beyond the city of Boston, and as it became respected, it raised its prices and designed some elegant, minimalist advertisements. Two more trouble-shooters were recruited: Mahmood, and Ellie, a part-timer with baby twins. Janis got an assistant, then another. The accountant was happy. They moved downtown, so Alex could walk to work and Marty could use his microscooter. Apart from the clerical workers who helped Janis, nobody ever left.

Johnny devoted his energies to spreading the company's reputation, and to his immense delight pulled in two Canadian contracts in quick succession after the Year 2000 changeover. One of the Y2K problems proved so intractable that Alex spent three happy months seconded full-time to a Vancouver finance company whose IT manager had disappeared after making a backyard bonfire of all the systems records and introducing a virus which emailed daily insults to clients. Candoo had little experience with deliberately introduced viruses, specializing in accidents and user incompetence, but after many late-night conferences with Marty and one brief visit from the master, Alex solved the problem without committing the company to the vast expense of new hardware. Johnny paid him a $1000 bonus on the spot.

The work fascinated Alex van Hyden: it suited his talent, his analytical powers, his liking for order, and not least his natural kindness. He liked helping people who were distressed and disoriented by the capricious betrayals of their vital computer system. He liked transmitting confidence and hope. He liked the problems, and the eureka moment when the synapses of his own brain suddenly reached out, embraced and fully understood the man-made system in front of him. He liked knowing that his own intelligence, fed by blood and the sordid processes of animal digestion, could still outrun the sleek shiny brilliant machines at his fingertips. He liked getting glimpses into different companies' working worlds and feeling himself part of the bloodstream of American commerce. Reared in a slow town by elderly grandparents, he loved being part of a young company whose members were also one another's closest friends. And he caught from the others an enthusiasm for the very newness of his trade.

'We're like the first car mechanics,' Marty would say happily. 'Or the guys who sorted out glitches in Caxton's printing press. Imagine the buzz, being the first to solve a new kind of problem the world had never seen!' On the company's fifth anniversary Janis wrote a song in its honour along these lines, and performed it *con brio* in a downtown bar. The story made the diary columns, and still more business resulted.

Today Marty appeared, noisily, just before nine. The meeting convened, Johnny Parvazzi lounging on Alex's reclining chair, Alex himself with his elbows on his desk, his hands fiddling with one of the stretchy rubber stress-balls which Janis distributed and regularly replaced when chunks were torn off them. Quiet Ellie sat cross-legged on the floor, her ebony face lean and chiselled as a Kenyan statuette. Janis leaned against the wall with an expression on her face that suggested she was running through her pelvic-floor exercise routine, and Marty sat slumped astride a hard chair, his straggly beard draped ridiculously over its back.

'OK, Mahmood's still in Louisiana, till tonight he reckons,' said Johnny. 'But he's got his next month mapped out anyway, doing their Manhattan office. Marty, you happy about Edmonton?'

'Flyin' out tomorrow. I reckon I got it. They should not have been using the X345 printers. It's that simple.'

'New printers?'

'Not if I can help it. Janis, do we have a cost-save clause with Edmonton?'

'Twenty per cent,' said Janis, without hesitation. 'Twenty-five if we fix it in two weeks without any new hardware.'

'So, no new printers for Edmonton. I can write a little line of code I dreamed up in the shower. Cool.'

Johnny smiled benevolently at his protégé. 'Look on your dressing-room door, Marty, you'll find that there's a star. Alex, you're clear right now, yeah?'

'Yeah,' said Alex. 'I emailed PiePost today, that's all cleared up.'

'No more sad old pies turning up a month late,' said Janis. 'Jeez, imagine! In New Mexico heat!'

'Do you want me to join Ellie on the realtor problem?' asked Alex.

A real-estate company had been suffering repeated crashes whenever it used its scanners for house pictures. It was a company of just the size that needed Candoo: too big merely to buy new kit, too small to maintain its own IT manager, and too mean to sign up for the suppliers' service contract.

'No,' said Johnny. 'Ellie, you're fine with this?'

The silent, intense woman on the floor inclined her head, once, in the briefest of nods. Johnny continued.

'Good. 'Cos I've got two surprises. One – the guy from Microsoft, Abby, is going to join us after all. You'll like him. He's taking a pay cut to come here. I schmoozed and schmoozed him after the spring festival. He's got a kid just about Rudy's age and he's not getting on with his manager.'

'Cool,' said Marty. 'Abby's good. And he knows the new-generation stuff. We can have a brainstorm, all of us.'

'There's the other thing,' said Johnny. 'And whaddya know? It's a job for Alex the Pie King.' He spun the chair and pointed. 'Our anointed ambassador. As of yesterday, Candoo Solutions goes international.'

'Hey, what about Canada? We *are* international,' said Janis. 'And Mexico.'

'Canada doesn't count. Too easy. But put it another way, we've gone oceanic. Transatlantic! Global!' said Johnny. 'Britain calls!'

A pleased buzz went through the meeting. Even Ellie murmured 'Cool!' and Marty, a little nettled, said: 'You never told me that.'

'Wasn't definite. Now it is. As of last night. Not a big job, by the sound of it, but a start.'

'Haven't they got their own troubleshooters in Britain?' said Marty.

'Not as good as us. Besides, it's all-US kit, and a system cloned off the American parent. And little pink tapping Brit fingers are screwing it all up. It's a mail-order clothing company, just like the one you did in New Jersey, Alex. Same system.'

With the perplexities of the little bedroom in Iowa far behind him, Alex was so wrapped up in his working world that he asked three or four technical questions about the company's problems before the truth hit him.

This was not a routine trip to New York or Chicago or Canada or Los Angeles. He was going to England.

'Tomorrow,' said Johnny. 'Tomorrow would be good. Janis, flights?'

6

When the meeting had dispersed, Johnny stayed behind in Alex's room and said: 'Everything all right? I would've asked you first, but it's such a blast that I wanted to splash it – British clients! Hey! Are we bigshots, or what?'

'Well, OK,' said Alex. 'You sure it's one for me, not Marty?'

'Listen, man, it's a piece of piss!' said Johnny, spinning the chair. 'I could do it myself, almost. Same sort of glitch as the New Jersey company, only with *aw'fly British excents*. I spoke to their IT manager. He's just one scared bunny, but I reckon he was never so hot. The expenses agreement is fine. Janis will sort you a good hotel. It'll be a blast.'

Alex bit his lip. Although it was some years since he had been urged by the scornful Isabelle to go to England, dig up his roots, shake the dirt off them and stop dreaming, deep within him lurked a childish idea that when he did at last set foot in the country of his birth it would be a solemn and momentous occasion. Not just some scrambled business trip to sort out someone's problems with mail-order pants.

Johnny looked at him, faintly puzzled. In five years, Alex had never shown such hesitancy over a trip. He wondered, fleetingly, whether his second most experienced trouble-shooter was in secret talks with another company. With another spin of the chair, he dismissed the idea. Alex was straight. One of the good guys. If he was sniffing around, he'd say so or leave straightaway. Another thought occurred to him.

'Looks like you don't wanna go?' he said. 'You in love or what? We might fix a trip over, for the girl. You go economy, that leaves slack in the budget for her.'

'No,' said Alex. 'There's no girl.' And after a moment, because his boss was also his friend, he went on: 'Johnny, I was born in London, England. Did I ever tell you that?'

'Isabelle did,' said Johnny surprisingly. 'Kept going on about how she was going to take you there and make you dig your roots. Man, that was one bossy broad!'

'Yeah,' said Alex. 'But maybe I should've done what she said. Not just sat thinking about it and reading English poetry and stuff. Now I feel kinda creepy, about going there just on a working trip.'

'So stay on,' said Johnny expansively. 'Take your vacation. Go look at old stone ruins. Dig up your ancestors' bones and bring 'em home for the dog! See the Queen!'

'Could I do that?'

'See the Queen? Easy. Anyone can see her. She rides around on horses and stuff, you just hang out by Buckingham Palace.'

'No – I mean, could I really stay on? Take vacation time? It's not much notice. For the company, I mean.'

'We got Abby joining. Marty thinks he's good. We've got a bit of slack in the schedule anyway. Marty's hanging loose if there's an emergency, he's finished with Montana already. Man, go on – take your vacation! You only had a week last year, apart from Thanksgiving.'

'I just had another four days, for the funeral.'

'Funerals don't count.'

Alex dropped his head on to his hands. 'Oh, shit!' he said. 'It would happen *now*.'

Johnny tired of the discussion, since it was clear that Alex would go. 'Tell you what,' he said, swinging himself upright and beating his chest briefly in the manner of Tarzan, 'I'll call Isabelle to come back and go with you, with her spade. So who gives a damn if she misses her preppie wedding?'

Alex looked up again and laughed properly, as Johnny had meant him to. 'OK,' he said. 'You win. I'll go if you promise not to set Isabelle on me.'

Janis found him an evening flight. The next day, after a long session with his colleagues where they updated one another on the latest vagaries of common corporate software, Alex went home at four o'clock, walking through the brown familiar city with both his laptop computers slung over his shoulders and in his pocket a diagnostic program that Marty wanted him to try out. Glancing round the little apartment, which yesterday he had been so glad to regain, he wondered what to pack.

'Brits like collars and ties,' Johnny had warned him. 'Think Harvard Law School. Think bean counter. Think boring.' Obediently, Alex packed two lightweight suits. It'd be spring by now: he knew his Browning.

Oh, to be in England, now that April's here!

No, hang on – it wasn't 'here', it was 'there', surely? Rhymed with 'unaware'? He dropped his shirt into the case and went to the bookshelves built beneath the high platform bed. The sun was dropping fast now, and gold struck through his western skylight as he turned the pages and stood for a moment, reading.

Yes, that was it, 'April's there.'

And whoever wakes in England
Sees, some morning, unaware,
That the lowest boughs and the brushwood sheaf
Round the elm-tree bole are in tiny leaf,
While the chaffinch sings on the orchard bough
In England – now!

Now! A faint pricking of simple excitement touched him for the first time. Why be apprehensive, why mistrust this happy coincidence? He would go, he would spend the extra time. He read on:

And after April, when May follows,
And the whitethroat builds, and all the swallows!
Hark, where my blossomed pear-tree in the hedge
Leans to the field and scatters on the clover
Blossoms and dewdrops – at the bent spray's edge –
That's the wise thrush; he sings each song twice over,
Lest you should think he never could recapture
The first fine careless rapture!

Alex smiled, and closed the book. That was it. Precious isle, silver sea, blessed plot . . . yeah, he admonished himself, forget the sadness! Don't think about the dirty house and the defeated woman and the druggies and the sorrowful puzzle of a lost babyhood. He was going to see England, for its own sake. He would not waste effort on a mawkish search for relatives who might not even exist. With the time he'd got now, he could go to Scotland, and Wales – and Ireland!

He reached for other books, poems by Yeats and R.S. Thomas, and stood for a while longer, turning the pages of each in the golden twilight. Then with a sudden jump of realization he looked at the clock, flung some more clothes into his case and closed it. He wondered whether to take the books; but no, England would be full of wonderful books. He must leave space to bring back more for his library. He took a paperback Dickens for the plane, set the alarm, locked the apartment and scuttled down the stairs, bumping the case at every step.

In the hallway he stopped, his heart suddenly hammering, and left the case while he ran up again, unlocked and disarmed the alarm with impatient fingers, and went to the filing cabinet. He had locked that too: he had to fumble with his bunch of keys to open it, and his hands grew damp. He plunged his hand into the back and pulled out his father's diary. A few minutes later, in the back of the cab, he stashed the limp brown book into the side pocket of his laptop bag, zipping it securely inside next to Marty's new diagnostic disc.

'OK,' he said aloud. 'England!'

'Jeez,' said the cab driver. 'Whatcha wanna go there for?'

'Business,' lied Alex. 'Only business.'

It was dark by the time the plane left; he looked curiously around him in the half-empty cabin, marvelling as he always did at the curious tranquillity which overcame people strapped into a hurtling 600-m.p.h. steel tube with a hundred total strangers, high above the face of the earth. He would, he realized, have preferred to approach the ancient island of his birth in some more measured way. On a ship, perhaps. He smiled at the thought, for despite the romantic streak he was not without a sense of irony. What you want, boy, he admonished himself silently, is to step off the *Queen Mary* in a homburg hat alongside Trevor Howard, and look around you for some chick with a black net over her face.

Whereon, right on cue, an English stewardess stopped beside his seat and said, in crisp cut-glass tones which might as well have come from behind that 1940s net veil: 'Fish or meat, sir? Have you seen the menu?'

She sounded like an English Isabelle. Alex wriggled in his seat with delight, and just to hear her accent again, said: 'What's the meat again, ma'am?'

'*Boeuf Bourguignon*, sir. It's very nice. The pilots both opted for it, and they should know.'

'I thought they each had to have different food, in case – um – like in that movie, you know . . .'

'I know the one. *Flight into Danger*, wasn't it? With the food poisoning? Yes, you're right.' She smiled a regal smile beneath her neat blonde bob. 'They do. I only said they both *opted* for it. The co-pilot had to have the salmon. Not that we've ever had a *single* case of tummy trouble.'

'I'll show solidarity with the underdog. Gimme the salmon. Please.' She smiled at the 'please', and slipped the tray neatly in front of him.

Next to him a stout man with a Chicago growl said: 'That beef ain't British, I hope?'

'Argentinian, I believe. I can check for you,' said the Englishwoman smoothly. Alex cringed as his neighbour hammered the point home.

''Cause I don't want to catch no mad cow or hoof and mouth disease,' he said. 'Gimme the fish.' He did not say 'please'. Alex directed a placatory smile at the stewardess, but she seemed impervious to boorish ways, and moved on smoothly through the plane.

He could not eat his fish. A wave of sick excitement coursed through him, and he leaned back instead and closed his eyes. He had flown over North America, often; had seen the endless prairies and the Great Lakes, skimmed over the crinkled Rockies, started a flight with a turn over the shimmering Pacific and ended it gliding down towards the grey indentations of the Atlantic coast. Vast as it was, all of America was home, from sea to shining sea; and Canada hardly less so. But now for the first time he was far out over the empty and emotionless ocean, heading east for an older world. In the morning, so he imagined – England's afternoon – he would see beneath him tiny patchwork fields, ancient castles, higgledy-piggledy medieval town-plans, quadrangles, tall spires brooding over fertile water-meadows . . .

His eyes were still closed, holding the dream, when the man from Chicago leaned across and said: 'Hey, if you don't want that fish . . .'

He nodded, gesturing to offer it to the man, his eyes still half-closed. *There'll always be an England, where there's a country lane* . . . What film had someone sung that in? Something from the war. *And did those feet, in ancient time* . . . William Blake. *Green and pleasant land.*

All the dreams of his lonely childhood gathered round him with gravely rustling, softly iridescent wings. *England's pastures green.* From the high school library window he had looked out over the vast flatness of his Midwest home and thought of shady pastures, Constable landscapes, castles and banners. In church at Easter, kneeling beside Grandma by a bank of garish tulips, he had sung *There is a green hill far away* and seen not Calvary but his imaginary England. Tomorrow he would land in London: *Sweet Thames, flow softly* . . . a noble river flowing through a noble city, a dignified grey lady edged with the red of double-decker buses.

He opened his eyes, to see the Chicago man contentedly munching his unwanted fish. He felt no irritation any more.

He was right to go. He was glad to go, and with a rush of feeling he decided that he was glad, also, that there was honest work to take him there. He wasn't going as some wretched lost soul or tacky ancestor-worshipper. He was going to England to help some English people to get their work straight and keep their jobs safe. The baby who'd left with nothing but an old red rag was going home as Superman, the solver of problems, to pay back a debt he hardly even owed.

Thus the spires, the meadows, the alleys and the green hills of England would be all the more truly his. He smiled at his fat neighbour, offered him his plastic-wrapped cheese with a flourish, ate the bland dessert in two mouthfuls, and fell into a long untroubled sleep.

———◆◆◆———

Fog lay thick over Heathrow. The aircraft was stacked for half an hour; far above his native land, Alex circled blindly with his fellow-passengers and forbade himself to be disappointed. A middle-aged English couple behind him, who had been silent all through the flight, exchanged irritable banalities.

'Unseasonal, fog in April.'

'Global warming, dear.'

'So they tell us.' The man's voice fell curiously on Alex's ear: flat but irritable, confident but without pleasure in itself. It sounded a note that Alex had never heard before: prosperous yet depressed. The woman was – twittery, thought Alex. Too anxious to please, as if the whole career of her life had been to keep Mr Grouchy from getting any grouchier. He listened despite himself, and reflected that apart from a few students at Harvard, and Mr Grindley, he had hardly ever heard ordinary English people speak. Only actors and rock stars and politicians on TV.

'It's a nuisance for Sarah,' the woman said in her high bright little voice. 'But she'll have the car in the Short Term parking, I darcsay.'

'Disgraceful prices! Well, she can spend another fortune in the Sock Shop like she usually does, on all those fancy tights.'

'She has to be smart for her job, dear. And it's nice of her to collect us and drop us at the station, it saves us going right into London. So silly, I always think, Waterloo being so far over to the east when the trains are going to run south-west! If you think about it. Silly.'

'Bloody fog!' said the man, staring out of the window at whiteness. 'D'you suppose the Connex trains are back to normal?'

'There wasn't anything in the American news about their not being.'

'Bloody wouldn't be, would there? They're so *insular*. No interest in the rest of the world.'

Alex, stiff and weary, suddenly felt like snapping at them: 'We're not insular, we're half a continent, and what's a Connex when it's at home?' Instead he yawned, wriggled his stiff legs and glanced sideways at the fat Chicago man.

On cue, his neighbour woke, burped, glanced out of the window and said: 'Fog.'

'Yeah,' said Alex, just to hear the sound of his own voice. 'Pity. I wanted to see England from the sky.'

'Your first trip?'

'Yeah.'

'Don't get your hopes up, boy. It's a weary little country. Cramped like a bird-cage. Can't quite live up to its publicity.'

Alex looked more carefully at the man, and saw lines of unexpected intelligence in his face. The previous night's exchange with the stewardess about catching mad cow disease, and the man's appetite for double airline meals, had made him assume that this was some xenophobic hick. Now he noticed what looked like a sheaf of academic papers stowed in the magazine pouch.

'You been to England often?'

'Too damn' often,' said the man, wriggling in his narrow seat. 'I do some lectures at UMIST. Manchester University. Low-impact automotive technologies.'

'Uh-huh,' said Alex. 'But you don't rate Britain?'

'University's good. Can't see how, on the kinda money they give their professors – but they got good people. Jeez, though, what a country!'

'Why?'

'Worn out. Depressed. Defeatist, I'd say. Needs some kinda therapy.'

'Why?' he asked softly, hoping that the couple behind would not hear, but the man boomed out his answer.

'Brits don't know what they're about. Talk themselves down. I guess they just lost the plot when they didn't have India or Queen Victoria or Churchill, or Germans to fight any more.'

'It's a beautiful country, though, huh?'

'Yeah, if you ignore everything they built in the last seventy years. And if you can see through dirty concrete.'

'Aw, c'mon!' said Alex. 'It's, like, the centre of world history! It's England! Everything started there: the *Mayflower*, democracy . . .' He faltered, realizing how naive he sounded. 'Well, it's got a history,' he concluded lamely.

'Democracy is Greek,' said the man. 'And to hell with the *Mayflower*, my ancestors came from Stuttgart in Germany. Yours?'

'Leyden, Holland,' said Alex unwillingly. 'It's all Europe, though.'

'Tell that to the first Brit you meet,' said the big man, grinning. 'Yeah, that's a good idea. Tell them they're just part of Europe. They're terrified, boy. They reckon if they have the same *coins* even, they'll lose their souls and turn into Brussels sprouts. Like if a Yankee turned into a Texan by using the same dollars. Jeez!'

'We're all Americans.'

'They're all Europeans. They just can't see it, poor stupid bastards.'

'It's no more stupid' said Alex, 'than us being scared of getting hoof and mouth or mad cow from their beef.'

The man gave him an amused, sidelong glance, fully acknowledging the dig.

'Yeah, I guessed you didn't like me winding up that English stewardess,' he said. 'I just love to do it, you know? I love hearing them try to be polite. She oughta have told me not to be an asshole, but I love watching 'em think it, and not say it. Hey!' The same stewardess was moving through the cabin, glancing at their seat-belts. 'We're going in. Welcome ta England!'

Alex thought that he could feel waves of disapproval coming from the English couple in the seats behind. As wisps of white mist streaked and billowed past the hurtling windows, he strained through them to catch sight of the ground. But there was nothing: nothing until the airport buildings and runways, the bump of the wheels and the hazy lights that blinded through the fog. His companion took out a business card and scribbled a UK telephone number on the back.

'That's me,' he said. 'Marvin Gottschalk. I'm there for three weeks. If you come up that way, and want a rest from Brits sneering at you and thinking the worst, call me.'

Alex returned the courtesy, saying, 'There's only the mobile number, I might be travelling.'

'Well, good luck. Did you know their whole railway system, like, collapsed over the winter? They had this one crash, and now everything's running half speed?'

'It said on the websites that it's OK now.'

'Yeaaaah . . .' said the man. 'And Bill Clinton never cheated on Hillary, and there *is* a Santa Claus'. He unfastened his belt.

'Cabin crew, doors to manual,' said the loudspeaker. Alex van Hyden was in England at last.

The impersonal airport rituals passed, and with his bags he followed the signs to queue for a taxi. Their chunky black squareness delighted him, and he watched the line of passengers ahead of him dwindle in a pleased, tired haze. When it was his turn the cab was bright blue with advertisements on it, and he felt oddly cheated. He glanced at the itinerary Janis had given him and leaning into the internal window said: 'Do you know the Melbourne Court Hotel?'

'Stockley Street? Behind Buckingham Gate, is that?'

'Probably. I don't know London. How much will it cost?'

'Thirty, bit more – depends on the traffic, squire. It's on the meter.'

'OK.'

He climbed in, and watched the new land beginning to slide past. He could have got the train or the subway; thinking of the stories his backpacking college friends had told him about their adventures in Europe, he suddenly felt middle-aged at twenty-seven. It was shaming, to be travelling outside North America for the first time at his age and on expenses. He stared out at the dull environs, the road signs and crawling traffic on the airport approaches, and blinked rather rapidly. The fat engineer's words about dirty concrete and depression had sunk in, and so had the colourless, irritable dialogue of the English couple behind. A sadness settled round him with the pale fog. He had no mother. She was long dead. What he was visiting, this gloomy, grimy, sour-spoken little island, was her grave.

The cab gathered speed and, cheered by its progress, the driver began chatting, throwing remarks over his shoulder through the open glass partition. Alex clung to the handle by the door, leaning forward to catch his words and try to comprehend them.

'You been here before?'

'No – first time in England.'

'You American? Or Canadian? We haven't had many tourists from your part of the world this winter, not with the foot-and-mouth.'

'I'm American. I'm not on holiday, it's a working trip.'

'Gotta keep working, eh? Another day, another dollar. That's what I tell my wife. "He who does not work, neither shall he eat" – know what I mean?'

'That's the Bible.'

'Certainly is. Only thing is, a lot of these spongers – know what I mean? Asylum seekers, refugees, hangers-on – they reckon they can come here and live off our taxes and never do a stroke of work. Or if they do, they don't pay any taxes. Look after number one, know what I mean? Now my son's in his first job, and do you know how much tax he's paying? I'll tell you—'

Alex closed his eyes, and let the driver ramble on. He had lived long enough in quarrelsome, factional Boston to feel no particular surprise: there was something about the cab trade all over the world, he supposed, which attracted the opinionated. It was a warm, sit-down soapbox with a captive audience in the back: these advantages clearly made up for the drawback that you had to preach over one shoulder to a disciple you couldn't quite see.

'– and it's not as if the public services were any good. Dunno what Gordon Brown spends it on, but the roads are diabolical, the kids don't learn anything at school, just run wild, and my mother-in-law's been waiting two years for a hip – *and* we have to get nurses in from Bongo Bongo Land or wherever. And then they put these Afghan illegal immigrants into hotels, no expense spared—'

Alex could stand it no longer. 'Tell me,' he said, in a loud firm voice, 'something good about England. Go on, just one thing.'

The cabbie was entirely unfazed by this direct assault.

'Best television in the world,' he said. 'Not as good as it used to be, mind, it's all smut after half-past ten, but you Americans never did anything as good as *Steptoe and Son*.'

'I saw that!' cried Alex. 'I bought a Heritage Videobox of classic British TV comedy when I was about fifteen. Isn't that the one with the old guy and his son, and they're kinda recycling things?'

'Thassit. And the young one always wants to get away, make somefink of himself, like.'

'And the old guy always drags him down!'

' "Haaaa-rold!" ' squeaked the driver, in a fair imitation of Wilfred Brambell. ' "Where's my tea?" Gor, fancy you knowing that. What else was in the videobox?'

'*Fawlty Towers*!'

' "He's from Barcelona—" '

' "– we're training him!" '

In perfect amity, forgetting the iniquities of asylum seekers and Chancellors of the Exchequer alike (and, temporarily, forgetting the way to the Melbourne Court Hotel), driver and passenger passed the next twenty minutes in remembering their favourite situation comedy moments.

'Mind you, squire, I didn't like that Jennifer Saunders *Absolutely Fabulous* thing. That went too far. My wife said . . .'

'Did you like Hancock? He was in the box.'

'Hancock was the guv'nor. Mind you, better on the radio.'

'He was on the radio?'

'You joking? 'Course he was—'

Janis had excelled herself with her hotel researches: she had spent much of the day giggling over Internet sites and blanking her screen whenever Alex came past, and now he saw why. The hotel she had chosen for his first night was a piece of Disneyland England: an imposing, turreted, redbrick Mary Poppins fantasy set well back from the pavement: when the cab had chugged away and Alex ventured through the hotel's oddly small revolving door he found himself in a 1930s film set, standing on a tastefully threadbare Persian carpet, looking up at curved internal balconies and a sweeping staircase. The effect was slightly marred by a large green sign announcing, in laboriously pegged white letters, that the Federation of Engineering Associations was meeting in the J.M. Barrie Room and the Seminar for Independent School Governors in the Astor Suite. But the effect was magnificent, and English, enough for Alex to smile in affectionate recognition of what Janis had prepared for him.

'It'll be a chain, kinda motel place, when you get to Essex,' she had said, snapping the picture off her screen for the fourth time. 'But when you get off the plane, Johnny says it's gotta be either Buckingham Palace or the Tower of London. I'm working on it. You get the train to Brentwood the next morning.'

The receptionist said coolly: 'Can I help you, sir? Do you have a booking?' and Alex tore his eyes from the riot of curly balconies and pulled out his documents.

'The lift,' she said eventually, pushing a keycard towards him, 'is through the double doors over there. Fifth floor. Follow the signs.' He glanced around to see if anyone was going to carry his bags, but there was nobody in sight.

'Can you manage your bags, or . . . ?' said the girl, still

glacial. Alex picked up the clear implication that a fit young man like himself ought not to use bellhops.

'I can manage,' he murmured, and spent the next five minutes manoeuvring his case and laptops, with some difficulty, in and out of the tiny lift. 'Charm!' he muttered. 'There's a price tag on it.' But his cramped, featureless little room looked out on a jumbled roofscape, with the thinning fog gilded by sunset. He threw open the window and stood for a while, looking out at it, until the chill crept into his bones and he retreated to the shower. When he was warm again he felt disinclined to eat and too weary to go out. He lay on the bed, pulled the quilt over him, and slept.

His last thoughts were about the cab driver: how, he wondered, could a guy be so harsh and unimaginative and hawkish about refugees and Social Security claimants and black nurses, and yet so fond of the gentle, ruefully self-deprecating comedy of *Steptoe and Son*? How could you rant on as meanly as that and still get the joke of Tony Hancock?

When he woke, it was dark. The streetlamps far below his window filled the room with ghostly orange light: for a moment he struggled to remember where he was. The green light on the TV at the foot of his bed said 0200. He glanced at his watch, still on Boston time, and realized that he was ravenously hungry. Upright, yawning and unsteady on his feet, he scanned the Room Service menu and noted the purple italic message 'Sandwiches only 11p.m.–7a.m.'. The list of sandwiches gave no indication that any of them might come toasted. He shivered and resolved to find hot food.

Outside, the fog had almost lifted, leaving only a fuzzy halo round the pale moon overhead. The street was absolutely silent; when he had been walking for a few minutes Alex understood that this was not a residential area, apart from its stately self-contained hotel. A subway station marked ST JAMES' PARK and USE OTHER ENTRANCE 2200– 0700 lay barred with a folding iron grille. He turned the other way, past offices and anonymous buildings which instinct told him had something to do with government. His light chinos and cotton sweater left him shivering, and he wondered whether to go back to the hotel for his jacket. Then he balked at the thought of crossing that silent, ornate foyer again under the cold eye of the porter and walked on instead, hunching against the sharp little wind. He was drawn towards what seemed to be an open space, with an indeterminate large building at the end of it. A square, perhaps, somewhere with an all-night burger stand . . .

There were statues. A man in an apron, leaning on a lion. And a woman with a scythe, like a female version of the Grim Reaper, threatening another lion. He stood by the monument, disoriented, and took a moment to understand where he was: right in the heart of every tourist photograph, by the railings of Buckingham Palace. A car shashed past on the wet road. Alex stood irresolute on the deserted Mall, then began to walk down it, with the bulk of Buckingham Palace looming behind him. He looked at the hotel's little schematic map: at the other end of this avenue there would be Trafalgar Square, and a rail station. Food. Feeling in his pocket as he walked, he pulled out his mobile phone and dialled a number.

Keith, yawning in his chair, stretched out a wrinkled hand for the phone.

'Hi, Grandad!' said Alex. 'I'm in London!'

The old man's voice crackled warmly back at him.

'Well, how about that! Where?'

'Outside Buckingham Palace!'

'Is it night there?'

'Past two in the morning. I got hungry, so I went for a walk.'

'A lot of folks about, I suppose?'

'Not a soul. Not one single soul. I got the place to myself.'

'Say hi to the Queen from me. She got a light in the window?'

Alex twisted his head round as he walked, then stopped and looked harder at the great shape of the palace.

'Yeah,' he said. 'There's a light!' Then, ashamed of his childish moment of wonder, 'Probably a security guy.'

'No,' said Keith. 'That's your Queen of England, reading late. How about that! Just you and her awake, in the whole of London.'

'Anyhow, you OK?'

'Fine. The fish went in great. Next season, we'll have good fishing, me and Vern.'

'I love you, Grandad.'

'You too, boy. You be careful.'

Alex walked on, grinning, to search for burgers in the drowsing city.

8

---·•◆•·---

'The Yank's coming today,' said Martin Sayeed of IT to his friend Eric from Sales. 'In the end, I think I'm glad.'

'You had your doubts, then?' said Eric, switching on his computer monitor. It glowed for a moment and then showed a twirling, sculptural shape which resolved itself into the words 'Clobber. com'.

'Well, it's a bit embarrassing,' said Sayeed. 'Hauling a guy all the way from Boston. I reckoned I could track the fault down myself, with the software suppliers, but Dorman said it couldn't wait. He's a great believer in hired guns.'

'Hmm,' said Eric. 'D'you reckon it's fraud? I mean, deliberate stuff?'

'Has to be,' said Martin Sayeed, wriggling his shoulders uncomfortably. 'I reckon it's a fault in the firewall. Sabotage, even. They wouldn't have wanted it to crash – it's the crashing that's alerted us.'

'Steady on!' The older man turned away from his screen to stare at his friend's dark, worried face. 'Nothing's gone missing, has it?'

'How can you be so sure of that? Just because the computer record says there's nothing unaccounted for – and what kind of fault is this?'

'Computer fault . . . see what you mean. God!' said Eric, shuffling through a pile of dockets on the table beside him. 'In the old days you could just go to the bloody warehouse and count boxes.'

'Anyway, like I say, I'm glad he's coming. Shifts the burden a bit.'

'Yeah.' Mr Sayeed wandered over to the window and stared out across the bleak industrial estate. 'Cab coming now. D'you suppose it's him? He flew in yesterday, it could be.'

Minutes later, the two Englishmen were cautiously contemplating a tall, lean young American. Eric, whose business it was not, stayed only long enough to form an impression: very young, eager to please, unsophisticated, intense, a touch geeky. When he had started out in the mail-order clothing business back in the late 70s, he thought, it had not been so pathetically dependent on the kind of twelve-year-old prodigies who these days ran the computer side of things. Then you opened envelopes, filed dockets, and if you were especially racy you used the telex. Computers were for playing Space Invaders on. Now they had invaded everything. He took his leave, with a significant glance at the IT manager and a mouthed 'good luck'.

'OK,' said Martin Sayeed to Alex, who was still hovering a touch awkwardly near the door. 'Shall we sit down, and I'll run you through the problems we've had?'

Within ten minutes he had revised his impression of the visitor. Alex clearly understood the nature of the business, and asked some unnervingly detailed questions about incidents when the server had gone down, crashed and frozen, and lost the company the rest of the day's work. He seemed particularly interested in the system for handling phone and internet orders through outworkers.

'You don't run a callcentre, then?'

'No. We had a small one, about twelve positions, but we

found all our best workers were the ones who wanted the most flexible hours.'

'The women?'

'S'right. Women with young kids, or old parents, or husbands who didn't really like them going out to work. Asian women, quite often. They're very, very good. So we took the homeworking route, and tooled up thirty of them with phone lines and connections at home, from a dedicated terminal. They opt for their hours each week online, and the server meshes it all together.'

'Do you get problems? Giving them so much choice?'

'We get a bald spot in the phone operation at about seven each night, when they're all doing family suppers and the customers start ringing up with orders after their teas. Or else the yuppies are ringing on their mobiles on the way home from the wine-bar. We're pretty upmarket. Obviously the online orders aren't a problem, the girls pick it up overnight, we've got a lot of mums who like to do the late shift. But at seven o'clock we get round the bald teleordering spot by paying time-and-a-half.'

'And you haven't taken on any new operators just before the crashes?'

'No. And it's not them.' The IT manager pushed his thinning hair back and shook his head, defiantly, his hand still on his brow. 'The MD decided straight away that it must be, but I stand up for my girls. They're great. I've interrogated the server, and there aren't any bad traces from operators. I tell you, it's almost certainly a breach in the firewall. Someone from outside's hacking in.'

'Any suspicions?'

'Could be theft, could be a competitor. Worst of all, could be someone trying to steal our customers' credit-card details. I can't see that it would work, but it's the nightmare we all have.'

In five years, Alex had learned a great deal about the psychology of business executives. There was, as Marty said, always one thing they were scared of, and that was the one thing they would focus on. It amused Marty Lane greatly: 'They're all looking one way with a shotgun, waiting for the wolf, while Mr Bear wanders around behind them smashing up the office.' Sayeed's anxiety about hackers, thought Alex now, might have compromised his vigilance over his employees.

'Any stock missing or unaccounted for?'

'Not according to the system. And I'd like to believe the system. We have good spot-check systems.'

'Do the operators do their own thing on your home terminals? Out of hours?'

'Absolutely not. We put in a system called EcomGuard to make sure they can't.'

'Right,' said Alex noncommittally. 'May I interrogate the user records on the server first?'

'Sure.'

Beginning his task, with Marty's new program running alongside him on the laptop, Alex let the comforting mantle of his expertise settle round him. He knew this trade: this particular job, he judged, would not be a hard one. Sayeed was competent, but not brilliant. EcomGuard was not a program he had encountered before, but he suspected it would be flawed. Most commercial security systems which got bolted on as an afterthought were, in his view, disruptive rubbish. Either it was the safety system itself that caused the trouble, or else a rogue operator getting round it. He worked on, patiently checking lines of code and replying to them with Marty's program.

At eleven, Sayeed brought him coffee with his own hands, and sat next to him.

'Would it be any help if I was here?' he asked diffidently. 'I feel – helpless.'

Alex turned to him and gave a quick smile. 'No, it's fine.' He liked this worried, modest little man. 'I've got a couple of ideas, but it's early yet.'

'We go to lunch in the pub in town sometimes,' said Sayeed. 'There's a canteen, but it's good to get off the estate. Join us?'

All that day, and most of the next, Alex worked through Clobbercom's record of breakdowns and freezes, and looked beyond them at the day-to-day working of the company. It was the usual hybrid of old-fashioned mail order and e-commerce: well-designed, upmarket sweaters, T-shirts, sweatpants, drawstring trousers, lightweight chinos, loafers. They were advertised in a catalogue and a website, bought by credit card, and dispatched from a warehouse in distant Cumbernauld. The few paper orders were processed in the office, while the online and telephone trade was done from terminals in three dozen front rooms, which all seemed to be scattered around the immediate area.

'You don't have any really distant workers?' he asked in the pub on the second day.

'No,' said Sayeed. 'We like to be able to get Maintenance out to them in around an hour. They're in suburban houses round Brentwood, and a few cottages and farmhouses in the sticks. There's a couple which are a bit inaccessible, we get trouble in winter with phone lines coming down in the storms. But mainly they're quite handy.'

The mention of farmhouses made Alex blink: absorbed in the familiar job, he had almost forgotten that he was in a strange land.

'Is it nice country round here?' he asked wistfully. 'I've hardly seen it.'

'Nicer than people think,' said Eric from Sales. 'Lots of marshland and water meadows and cows and rivers. A bit to the north, it's lovely.'

'I must have a drive round. When I'm finished,' said Alex.

'I like North Essex a lot,' said Sayeed. 'Before I got this job I used to love driving round to see the girls and check the terminals.'

Some ribaldry followed, in which the women from the company enthusiastically joined; Alex, accustomed to the careful inter-gender relationships of Boston, blinked in surprise. He'd supposed that women talked this way among themselves, but not in front of men.

'He's *adorable*,' said Suzy McHugh from Marketing as they touched up their faces in the Ladies' before heading back at two o'clock. 'Like a lost little boy.'

'Cradlesnatcher,' said Leanne Morris, outlining a thin, ageing mouth with pink. 'Geeksnatcher.'

'Martin thinks he's good at his job, too.'

'Martin is desperate. Mr Dorman told him his own job's on the line.'

'Well, anyway, I could fancy giving Mr van Hyden a jump. So there.'

'Dirty bitch.'

On the fourth day, when Alex's inspection of the entire system was nearly complete, and after two more unexpected crashes which brought the worried little office to a halt for hours, Miss McHugh made her move.

'Hi-yee!' she said, sidling in with an unsolicited cup of tea and some chocolate biscuits.

'Hey,' said Alex absently, pecking at the keyboard.

'You're so-oh brilliant, like. Getting into all those codes and things. I'm, like, whoo! Just click on the little pictures.'

'Icons,' said Alex automatically. 'They're called icons.'

'Yeah. Anyway, Mandy and me wondered if you'd like to come to a party. Like, you must be bored in that hotel every night?'

'Where's the party?'

'Meet me outside at half-five?'

'Half after five?'

'Yeah. I can give you a lift.'

'Do I need to dress?'

'Nooooo . . .' said Suzy McHugh. 'Not a bit.' She winked, and Alex returned to his task, pushing the insipid milky tea as far away from him as possible. The smell of it nauseated him, and he never ceased to wonder at Martin Sayeed's intake of this mystifying brew, and of weak unpleasant coffee. The hotel food was beginning to pall on him, too: it was on the surface of things an international menu, but in fact always seemed to rely very heavily on grease and stodge. A plateful of alleged '*tapas*', including vast peppery potato wedges, had seriously depressed his spirits the night before, and made him ring Johnny for moral support.

'You'll get used to it,' said his boss, voice thin and crackling over the airwaves. 'You need some Brit home cooking. How're the girls?'

'None in sight.'

'You're just not looking.' Johnny had laughed, and signed off with a brisk: 'Do yourself a favour. Get laid.'

Suzy McHugh had the same idea. When Alex was strapped into the passenger seat of her dusty purple Mini Metro she threw him a sidelong glance and said: 'This party . . . I didn't tell you everything.' She was wearing a tight, low-cut top and a

71

very short skirt; her cascade of blonde hair lay temptingly over an expanse of tanned bosom, and she smelt of expensive musk.

'Shoot,' said Alex, amused. 'Is it an orgy, then?'

'For two,' she said. 'I just thought we should get together.'

'Oh,' said the young man inadequately. 'I dunno – I mean, I think you're really cute—'

Suzy looked at him with faint pity.

'You got a girlfriend?' she said.

'N-no,' admitted Alex.

'You one of those Born Again Christians? Mandy thinks you are.'

'No, I'm not,' said Alex, nettled. 'I guess I'm kinda Christian – my folks were – it was how I was brought up.' That hymn floated absurdly through his head: *Have thine own way, Lord, have thine own way* . . . Suzy certainly intended to.

'But not the kind of Christian,' she was insisting, 'that turns down a nice shag for no frigging reason?'

She was driving, fast and expertly, weaving through the traffic on the town's outskirts. He could see the pale slab shape of his hotel slip by, and wondered where they were going. He was shocked by her frankness but could not dislike her. She was blonde, pretty, good-humoured, straightforward and very much available. He was twenty-seven and lonely.

'I don't usually – on the first date – I mean, it's always been like a long-term thing for me.' He was flustered. Suzy was not.

'I'm not wanting to *marry* you, stupid,' she said. 'I got a boyfriend. He's on the rigs. Oil rigs, you know. We got a deal. He does what he wants in Aberdeen on his day leaves, and comes back for his long ones. So I do what I frigging well want. We're getting engaged this Christmas, and after that we'll prob'ly stop fooling around. You up for it, or not?'

Rather to his surprise, Alex found that he was up for it. *Thou hast committed fornication*, he quoted to himself. *But that was in another country* . . . At her cluttered little flat Suzy had a big stereo, a big – and not entirely fresh – bed, and a drawerful of sex toys ('off the telly') which Alex with some difficulty dissuaded her from demonstrating. Afterwards she drove him to his hotel, where he showered and slept more deeply than at any time since Grandma died.

'Guess who I shagged?' said Suzy blithely the next morning, dropping her heavy faux-fur bag and flicking her terminal on.

'The Yank?' said Mandy. 'Any good?'

'Mmm. Nice boy,' said Suzy smugly.

'You seeing him again?'

'Dunno. Might. Dean's coming home Tuesday for a week. Depends how long Alex takes to sort out the computers.'

'I might have a go,' said her friend enviously. 'Joe's like, useless these days.'

'I wish,' said Martin Sayeed to Eric later, 'that the girls would bloody well leave van Hyden alone! I've had to rout Mandy Harper out of my department twice, with her skirt up to her crotch.'

Alex, however, was disinclined for any further adventures. On the few occasions when he had been drawn into genuinely casual sex, he'd always fallen into melancholy self-dislike for days afterwards, and this was no exception. Suzy still greeted him with a blithe, grubby smile, still flirted her breasts at him in the corridors, and showed not the slightest sign of proprietorial feelings or of umbrage. He saw how little he had meant to her, and writhed inwardly with embarrassment. (Like I was a ruined maiden, he thought drily.) Nor had he any intention of noticing the determined advances of the dark and buxom

Mandy. He could not help feeling a pang of liking for these slutty, cheerful, generous, wholly unexpected English girls, but now he wanted to be clear of the Clobber.com office sooner rather than later. He worked on with passionate care.

In the evenings he avoided the girls and read the British newspapers in his hotel room, trying to work his way into the preoccupations of this foreign land. He read, with faint dismay, a series of scornful attacks on his President ('Goddamn!' he said on the phone to Johnny. 'I don't rate Dubya much myself, but over here, he's the polluting Satan-spawn from Hell.') He read profiles of political advisers and actors, of a ubiquitous football couple called Beckham, and a haughty, super-rich City fund manager called Lottie Vernon whose 'perfect lifestyle' with three neat children, a titled husband and a country mansion was alternately praised and excoriated by sour-mouthed female journalists.

He puzzled, feeling naive and adrift, over a scandal involving a reporter dressed as a sheikh duping the Queen's daughter-in-law into saying that the Prime Minister's wife was 'horrid'. He read six articles on the demise of Christianity in Britain, and five on some new kind of Lords, about whom nobody appeared to be happy. He followed the controversy over the election date. And, day after day on the television and the front pages, he saw heaps of sheep and cattle ablaze, blackened legs silhouetted against hellish flames. He began to take sides: decided that he was against the slaughter but admiring of the army, rather sympathetic towards the duped royal wife, suspicious of the perfectly groomed fund manager, and plain baffled by the Lords business.

He discovered a few favourite writers and began to seek out the newspapers they wrote in: by American standards the commentators were brief, epigrammatic and extraordinarily bad-tempered. He tried to answer the questions in TV quizzes, and decided he preferred a grey-blond man who smiled and cocked his head a lot to an elderly red-haired woman who scowled and pronounced words strangely. He read his first Harry Potter book, and despite a general aversion to witches and wizards, rather enjoyed it.

On Monday evening he said to Sayeed: 'I think I've got it. It was tricky, though. I'm not surprised you didn't get it, without Marty Lane's diagnostic program. It's not the firewall, not the security site. It's just an operator.'

'Really? A fault or a fraud?'

He hesitated.

'I would say fault. Might even be something she doesn't know about.'

'It's one of the women, then?'

'Yup. Think so. XO45.'

Martin Sayeed went over to a ledger on a shelf, and flicked through the pages.

'Doreen Clark. Sandy Lane Farm, Hennisham.' He closed it. 'She's a fairly new installation. One of our new-generation machines. Do you want to look at her terminal?'

It was on the tip of Alex's tongue to say that there was no need; he had tracked down precisely the sequence of key-strokes which, on twenty-seven occasions, had caused Mrs Clark's terminal to lay trails of cyberdynamite disruptive enough to crash her employer's entire commercial operation and endanger a hundred jobs. But he was suddenly curious about Sandy Lane Farm, and impulsively said: 'Yeah. I need to see it. We'd better make an appointment.'

'Bugger that!' said Sayeed, explosively. He tapped a query into his own machine. 'She's on shift tonight, six till nine. Let's get over there.'

It was still light as Martin Sayeed drove Alex through winding lanes, damp and flecked with tractor mud in the dappled evening sunlight. The wind and rain had eased over the weekend, and there had been real warmth in the sun for days. Looking out at pale new leaves and clumps of cowslip and primrose, Alex felt a stirring of long-awaited enchantment: *Oh, to be in England* . . . The farmhouse lay at the end of a long bumpy drive, beyond a thick pad of damp straw reeking of disinfectant and numerous signs saying FOOT AND MOUTH PRECAUTIONS. NO UNNECESSARY VISITORS. A gaunt young man stepped into their path as the car slowed. He had a gun on his arm, a grimy jacket and an expression of stony anger.

'What'cha want?'

'We're from Mrs Clark's company,' said Sayeed. 'We need to check her terminal. She's working a shift right now.' It was just after six.

'Have you been on any other farms? Either of you?'

'No. I'm sorry,' said Sayeed politely. 'I forgot about the foot-and-mouth, or I'd have rung ahead.'

The farmer's mouth twisted; it was clear that he had no esteem whatever for those so cushioned from horrid rural realities that they could forget, even for a minute, about the pyres and the slaughter and the daily terror of his trade.

'Do your feet on the straw. Properly. Make sure they're wet with the disinfectant. Then go straight into the house. Doreen's in the front room.' Alex guessed, with a pang of pity, that the young farmer would have very much liked to throw them off his land, but dare not because his wife's income was the only thing keeping his precarious operation going.

A small boy, limping in a calliper, met them at the door. 'You want my mum,' he piped. 'She's working. She's busy.'

'We're from her work,' said Martin, gently. 'Are you' – he glanced covertly at the note from Personnel in his hand – 'James?'

'Yes,' said the boy. 'How did you know I wasn't Adam? You knew because of my leg, didn't you?'

Martin Sayeed was silent. The boy barred his way.

'Didn't you? You knew I was the *cripple*. The *special needs*.' The two men were shaken by the child's rage and self-disgust.

'I knew you were the eldest one,' said Martin with admirable calm. He was three times a father himself. 'I knew who you were because I could see you weren't *six years old!*' In truth, the child looked barely more, but he was mollified.

'I'm eleven,' he said. 'Adam is, in fact, a big baby.'

'So can we see your mother?'

'James!' came a cry from the room beyond. 'Let the men in. Stop going on at them.' The door was flung open, and a distracted-looking woman with tousled red curls and freckles glared at the scene before her. 'I'm sorry, I'm sorry – Jamie, go and do your geography reading. I'll be testing you before bed.'

'Cripple reading,' said the child contemptuously to the men as he departed. 'For poor ickle Jamie Wamie with his bent leg.'

'Sorry,' said Mrs Clark again. 'He gets stroppy, not being at school this term. He's clever, but they won't take him at the High School because of fire regulations. Bastards, I say. They want him to go to the special school, just because he limps. He was fine at primary, but they just go on and on making excuses about the stairs. But that's our problem. Come in, for God's sake, before he starts on at you again.'

With cursory introductions, the two men went into the little room, where under dark low beams a sofa leaked its stuffing and a shabby, scarred old schoolroom table bore the slim monitor and keyboard supplied by Clobber.com. It had reverted to its screen saver, and the company's logo revolved with languid elegance in three dimensions on a deep blue background. Alex's sharp eye, however, spotted, half-covered by a faded Indian cotton throw, an ancient and dusty Amstrad PC on a rickety bamboo table. His mouth tightened in a dry half-smile. Sayeed, who had not noticed anything beyond his own terminal, bent over it and tapped in a code. Over his shoulder he said, 'Have you had any trouble with this, lately?'

'None at all,' said the redhead, cautiously. 'I've been doing a lot of extra hours, as you probably know. With the foot-and-mouth we can't sell any stock off the farm. It's been tough.'

'Yes, good . . .' said Sayeed absently. The woman was tense now: as the IT manager worked, Alex stood silent and watched her sturdy body take on the stillness of a listening animal. Sayeed continued tapping, but then after a time turned and said exasperatedly: 'I can't find it – Alex, are you sure this was the one?'

Now Doreen Clark's watchful tension was directed towards Alex.

'Could I try?' he said. After he had sat down he added, as if it had suddenly occurred to him, 'Hey, Martin – I'll tell you what'd find it. My laptop's in your car with Marty's diagnostic program on it. That might do it. It's under the coats in the boot, I reckon – and there's a grey box with some Zips in it that I need.'

Sayeed left the room, and a moment later they heard the house door open and shut. Alex swung round and said urgently, 'You've been using the terminal for surfing, right? Tell me! Quick! And I'll try to keep you out of schtuck.'

9

———◆◆◆———

Doreen paused for barely a moment before giving him her trust. 'Yes,' she said. 'The Amstrad got a lightning-strike. Blew up the modem. We've no money to fix anything. I do some private research jobs on the side. I want to pay for a school for Jamie.'

'So you used the company terminal and got on to the net through the server? How did you get round the EcomGuard program?'

She smiled, but then jumped guiltily at a sound in the hall. 'It's not him,' said Alex. 'There isn't any grey box of Zips, so he'll still be searching. Quick. How?'

'It's easy,' said Doreen. 'You can disable it. Jamie worked out a way. He isn't allowed to touch the terminal,' she added hurriedly, 'it's a strict rule. But he looked over my shoulder and told me how.' She pulled a piece of scribbled paper from her cardigan pocket. 'That's what he told me to do. I just had to customize the preference bar—'

'When did you start?' asked Alex, looking down and smiling at the elegant simplicity of Jamie's solution. In a few years, Marty would like to meet this kid. 'When was the first shift you worked after you'd done it?'

'The Amstrad blew up . . .' She frowned, and picked up a calendar lying on the desk and flicked back to February. 'On the big storm day. Lightning. I usually unplug the modem, but

79

we were in a panic about some lambs drowning out in the mud.' She shuddered. 'You see, we aren't allowed to move them, and they just die, it's horrible – so it was definitely that day. Look, here's the note I wrote of the computer shop number, I thought I could get a new modem. But no way. It would have cost an incredible amount. Apparently it's an obsolete model.'

Alex looked at the date. It was the day before the first crash.

The front door opened, then the room door, and Sayeed was back with them, worried about the non-appearance of the grey box. Alex swivelled the chair round and showed him a beaming face.

'No sweat,' he said. 'Sorted! It was the EcomGuard. It just kept kicking in and recognizing the company's own server as an intruder, so it froze everything. It's a failsafe, see. And like my colleague Marty Lane says, the one thing that failsafes always do is fail.'

'So we can cure it?'

'Just have done,' said Alex. 'By shutting down and logging this user ID right off. This terminal'll have to be reprogrammed. I reckon it first happened here because of a power surge in the big storm – Mrs Clark's just shown me what date it was on the calendar, and of course you're right at the end of the wire up here. Do you have surge protectors?'

'Not on the new-generation machines,' said Sayeed, with mingled exasperation and relief. 'Idiot engineers said they weren't needed! I should have stood my ground. Those guys work in Chelmsford and Colchester, and they don't know anything about the kind of power supply blips you get out on the farms. I'm sorry, Mrs Clark – it'll be a couple of days before we can get your terminal replaced, but we'll pay you a shift for tonight and tomorrow.'

'That's fine,' said Doreen Clark faintly, and a shudder made her red curls shake. 'That's very kind. You needn't . . .' Alex frowned at her warningly.

Sayeed crawled under the table, disconnected the company's equipment and cradled it in his arms. Alex opened the door, with a flourish, and closed it carefully as the IT manager left.

'I don't know what to say,' said the woman. She dropped her eyes, sniffed hard, and ran her sleeve across her face. 'Oh, God – if I'd lost my job—'

'It won't be long,' said Alex kindly, 'before that lippy kid of yours is pulling down a hundred thousand bucks a year. That was a neat little trick of his.'

'I shouldn't have done it,' said Doreen. 'But I got the research finished. Four hundred quid. You've no idea—'

'Shh!'

Sayeed came back, and Alex busied himself tidying up cables. Doreen recovered herself and asked lightly: 'Are you just over for this job, Mr van Hyden? What do you think of England?'

'I've hardly seen anything, past the hotel and the industrial park. I had a night in London, though. Saw Buckingham Palace by moonlight.'

'Have they put you in a nice hotel?'

'So-so. The food isn't so good.' She looked at him fixedly, eyebrows lifted, and he named the hotel.

With a slight nod, she saw the two men to the door and said again: 'Well, thanks, Mr Sayeed. For the shift money, I mean.'

'We look after our outworkers. You're our prime asset. Next to the designers,' he said magnanimously. It was dark now, and a thin east wind was beginning to whistle round the farmyard and across the chill muddy fields of bleating, in-

81

visible discontent. As they drove away Alex could see in the rear-view mirror the gaunt farmer trudging back to his door, young shoulders hunched against the cold and the despair of his calling. He saw Doreen Clark putting out an arm to draw him in, and thought suddenly of home, the old home, the rolling wheatlands and the strong kind simple-hearted people of the Midwest plain.

Here, in this intricate jigsaw of fields and lanes and telephone wires that swooped through branches, he had met his first British family. It was good that they were a farm family.

And I helped, he said to himself. *You're welcome, folks*. Then he felt ashamed, for his small easy deceit had been nothing, nothing at all, compared to the ways in which the beleaguered Clark family was having to help itself every day.

When Sayeed dropped him at the hotel, there was a message waiting with his key: 'Ring Mrs Clark.' He sat on the bed, kicked off his shoes, and did so.

'I didn't like to ask, with the boss there,' she said without preamble. 'But since you're a stranger here, and living in that awful concrete hotel, would it be very cheeky if I asked you to supper with us? Just for some proper food? Do you have time before you go?'

'That's very kind,' said Alex. 'Yes, I would really like that. I'm here for a couple more days, to talk through replacing EcomGuard.'

'Oh, no!' said Doreen with sudden remorse in her voice. 'But there's nothing wrong with EcomGuard.'

'Yes, there is,' said Alex. 'I hated it anyway, there are better systems, and we must be able to come up with something your Jamie can't crack. And all the other Jamies.'

'Well, OK. Tomorrow night? Have you got a car?'

'I walk in most mornings. It's close, so I don't have a hire car. I can get a cab.'

'No. Duncan'll pick you up from the hotel. He's got to see the bank manager in Brentwood. A bit of company on the way back might stop him from driving straight into the river afterwards.'

Alex went to bed early, and happy. From his pillow, just before sleeping, he rang Keith.

'I met some English folks. A family. Real nice people. I'm going to eat there.'

'Good for you. Makes a difference, huh? When I was in the war, in Holland, I remember there was a little girl who took a couple of us home, for her folks to see real American soldiers. They gave us some cheese, like rubber. I can still taste it.'

'They've got a disabled kid. It's a shame, he can't go to school because of the stairs and stuff, but he's really bright.'

'How old?'

'Ten, eleven? There's a baby brother too, I haven't seen him.'

The very banality of it soothed him inexpressibly. He was in England, and had friends on a farm, with kids. He might tell them he was half-English. Just to see their expressions. Alex said good night to his grandfather, rolled over and gave himself up to a dream of country lanes.

'You've never found out about your mother's family?' Doreen was incredulous, her tongue loosened by the wine he had brought and by a worrying concoction of her own, served before supper and identified as being made from elderflowers. They must, thought Alex as he choked on it, be among the most aggressive flowers known to botany.

'No. I didn't know much, beyond my birth certificate. It was only lately I found out that she was still alive when my dad took me to Iowa.' He was finding it easy to talk about his beginnings in this company: Duncan's aggressive intensity had given way, over food and wine, to a more benevolent air of friendly weariness, and Doreen was happily hospitable, presiding over her shepherd's pie with flushed, excitable charm. Alex guessed that there had not been much social life for her lately. They had talked of the foot-and-mouth disease for a while, at his instigation, but by the time Doreen served up the pudding ('Blackberry crumble, from our own hedges last autumn, thank God for freezers!') the family were firing questions at their guest.

'Didn't you have a mum then, when you were little?' asked Jamie, his mouth full. 'Wicked! So you could do anything you wanted?'

He slid his eyes sideways to his own mother, who made a face at him and said: 'He had a grandma, and trust me, they're tougher than us mothers.'

'They are,' said Alex. 'You wouldn't have lasted two rounds with my old grandma, kid. She breathed fire when I got outta line.'

'What, *really?*' Six-year-old Adam, who had got up from table and was roaming restlessly around the battered farmhouse kitchen, stopped dead and stared. 'She was a *dragon?*'

'Not a real dragon, poo-face,' said Jamie, kicking out at his brother with his calliper. 'There's no such thing.'

'There is!'

'Isn't! Ignorant poo-face!'

'Boys! Upstairs now,' said Doreen tranquilly, swigging her wine. Alex wished he had brought two bottles, not least since he feared that the elderflower drink would be brought out again shortly. 'No, seriously,' she continued. 'If you've got a birth certificate you've got your family history. It's the key. I could find out stuff for you. It's what I do.'

'Doreen's a historian,' said Duncan with some pride. 'She got a PhD. Family history and stuff. She doesn't just sell tracksuits online.'

'Duncan thinks Clobber.com is really naff,' said Doreen. 'He'd like me to be a professor by now.'

'Well, you could be,' said Duncan. 'If you hadn't married a stupid broke farmer.'

She blew him a kiss, and shook her curls flirtatiously. They shone in half a dozen shades of red beneath the dangling oil-lamp over the table.

'No, Alex, the point is that if you tell me your mother's full name and the details from the birth certificate, I'm quite likely to be able to find out some stuff. There'll be a death certificate, too, you see – and I can work out her age, and then get *her* birth certificate and start on the family history.'

'You haven't got a computer that works,' said Alex.

'Most of it's done by post, slowly. It's later on that the websites get useful. I'll have saved up by then,' said Doreen. And, lowering her voice: 'Duncan and I talked about the school thing. There's no way we can pay fees for Jamie anyway, so I might as well spend what I've saved on a computer that's less than ten years old.'

'Better idea,' said Alex. 'I can get any kind of discount, through the firm.' He was lying, but smoothly. 'So if you want to do my genealogy – and I know the birth certificate by heart, believe me – I can pay you by replacing your Amstrad with something that works.'

Doreen stared at him, entranced. 'Seriously?' she said. 'We're only talking about a day or so's work, and you've already saved my neck with Mr Sayeed—'

'Seriously. I'd like it,' said Alex. 'And it'd be better for Jamie to have an up-to-date machine in the house. They come with all kinds of educational software now, free.' He was getting very good at lying. 'So it'd be two birds with one stone.'

'It's too much,' said Duncan. 'You're too kind.' He spoke formally, but his eyes were on his wife's transported face. 'It would make a difference, though, I admit.'

'It'd latch me in to the twenty-first century,' said Doreen, recovering. 'And since we small farmers live mainly in the nineteenth, that is a greater advance than you can imagine.'

'I can imagine,' said Alex. On the way in, earlier, he and Duncan had made a detour to check on some lambing ewes; the experience was still with him and had caused him some difficulty with the shepherd's pie. 'I'd be glad to do it that way. Helps me, helps you, everyone's happy.'

'It'll be a while,' said Doreen. 'Probably after you've left the country, I'm afraid.'

'Fine,' said Alex. 'No hurry.' And then, as a comforting thought struck him, 'Can I bring the computer over, when I get it, so I can set it up and show Jamie a thing or two as well?'

'Oh, that would be . . .' Tears came easily to Doreen's eyes. 'Honestly, this is so great. We've been sort of – isolated – especially this winter. We have to be careful about visiting farming neighbours, anybody with stock anyhow – and what with Jamie stuck at home with no schoolfriends, it's been awful—'

Duncan threw a glance at Alex, embarrassed; Alex looked delicately away and said: 'Not tomorrow – the next day, OK? I wind up with the company tomorrow, then I was thinking of taking a trip up-country. With a hire car. See Scotland, maybe. I can get the computer, put it in the hire car, and come over here slowly, to test whether I'm fit to drive in this country. It's on the left, yeah?'

'Up our lane,' said Duncan, 'you'll find there is no right or left. Just the middle. Hope you're good at reversing for tractors.'

'I'm from Harvard. We never reverse for anyone,' said Alex; and Doreen had recovered her composure enough to laugh with them, and skip back to the sideboard for the elderflower wine.

———•◆•———

It rained, heavy water from a grey sky. The trees dripped, gutters ran, the roads were dark between the flowing dikes. Alex drove northward without much of a plan. He made his way to the bleak coastal marshes of Suffolk, and when the rain eased for a while he walked along a grey cold riverbank over which a castle brooded. It was his first castle, pleasingly empty and melancholy, and for all his isolation and the dampness of his jacket Alex took private and precious delight in it. It was just so effortlessly *old*. Passers-by who hurried to the village shop or parked their cars outside their crooked, pink-plastered cottages paid no attention to it at all: yet to Alex it was as if a living dinosaur had come to rest in its majesty among the green humps and hollows of the old fortification. He could not take his eyes off the grey castle, and when he approached it as a visitor he still half-expected to be repelled as unworthy. But there was nobody there, only a box for donations and a few curt signs about its age and construction. He took possession of it, running his hand over the old stone, trying to feel the hum of history.

At the top, leaning over the battlements in the mist, he had a moment of loneliness and remembered the day before, the jovial farewells to Martin Sayeed and his final visit to the Clark family with the new computer. The farmhouse was more threadbare, by daylight, than he had appreciated, and there were lines on Doreen's vivid face which he had not seen in the lamplight. Jamie had hovered beady-eyed behind the chair while he showed her the machine's desktop and the programs he had loaded. Impatient, the child interrupted his mother's questions.

'Mum, don't be spastic! It's obvious – look – there!'

'Darling, don't use that word.'

'Why not?'

'It's the name for a disability. A bad name. Using it as an insult is rude to people who – to people with –' She hesitated, trying to remember the medical term.

'To cripples?' jeered the boy. 'Like me, you mean?'

Alex flinched, but the mother was unperturbed. She had clearly suffered years of her little son's tongue.

'It's a different thing, weasel,' she said. 'Yours was a bone thing when you were little. You weren't born with it.'

'Well, if *I* don't mind people saying spastic –' said Jamie, banging his calliper on the floor. He had crept closer, and jabbed at the keyboard. 'Look!'

Alex smiled at the memory of the lame child's fierce temperament. Nobody would mess with that kid. Good. He thought of Doreen for a moment, and wondered whether she was old enough to be his mother. Not quite, he thought.

'You're the first real British woman I've known since I arrived,' he said as they drank a last cup of coffee. 'That means a lot, you know. To really like the first proper English woman that I meet in her own home'. He suddenly thought of Suzy, and blushed.

'Oh, dear,' said Doreen. 'Does it matter that I'm a quarter-Irish?'

'No, I can take a bit of a mix. I'm a bit Dutch myself.' He looked at her with such naked fondness that Doreen said carefully: 'You'd better know that I'm only one type. And there are lots of types. I might not be anything like your mother was. I'm a doctor's daughter from the south-east, but with a Geordie mother and an Irish granny, and I was at one of the last grammar schools in Britain, and at Leeds University, and I lived in London till I married Duncan and ended up here. That's me.'

'Fine,' said Alex, not quite seeing where she was leading.

'But the point is,' said Doreen patiently, 'that I could have been quite different and still counted as a perfectly ordinary British woman my age. I could have been a posh totty from Benenden brought up in the Pony Club, or a Scouse hard-girl, or a City trader with a weekend coke habit, or a jam-making churchwarden from the Women's Institute. Or I could have been Asian or West Indian or a militant Welsh speaker or a bag lady. I could have been any of those things, and still counted as bog-standard British. We're as different as – as Texans and New Yorkers and Eskimos.'

'What's a posh totty?' asked Alex, to delay having to think too hard about this.

'Upper-class girl. Not too bright, cooks in chalets. Duchess of York sort of thing.'

He knew what Doreen was telling him, but changed the subject. She wanted to warn him that his distant family, if he ever found them through her researches, might not be as near to his own taste as the family at Sandy Lane Farm. He allowed his thoughts to run speculatively over the others he had met at Brentwood: anxious Martin Sayeed, staid old Eric with his cough lozenges and his shiny suits, Suzy McHugh and Mandy . . . he shuddered, looking out into the mist.

He was ashamed of himself over Suzy, and the shame had begun to take a form of which he was even more ashamed. To be ashamed of his own shame was creepy. It was, to put it bluntly, snobbish. Alex was beginning to understand the social complexity of life in this small, odd, ancient, stratified society. Britain plainly was not quite modern, for all its changes and its brash new government: the shapes of old hierarchies moved just below the surface like monsters under ice. He saw this ever more clearly, as his Boston-trained social antennae gradually tuned in to the new patterns around him. Not for nothing had he been called 'Farmboy' for his first semester at Harvard; not for nothing had he heard his grandmother shouting at Grand-ad for watching *The Jerry Springer Show.*

For instance, it was now clear to him that Doreen was socially a cut above the tenant farmer she had married; and that by the same shabby-genteel alchemy this impoverished and precarious outworker was also a cut above her boss. There had been something about Sayeed's manner when he'd visited the house which made that obvious. It was equally clear, however, that Martin Sayeed looked down on the easy, sexy, noisy girls in the office; and that Suzy McHugh was aware that for all her expensive designer labels and chunky gold jewellery bought with oil-rig pay, quite a few people looked down on her. During their evening together he had noticed that the words 'snotty' and 'stuck-up' were her favourite terms of abuse.

Nor was it lost on him that Doreen – defining herself – went straight to the fact that her father was a doctor and her school a 'grammar', whatever that meant. And the women who cleaned the factory when he was working there late belonged to yet another group: the two British ones sniffed in disdain at the clanking, gilded Suzies and Mandies, and called Mr Sayeed 'darling' and him 'love'. He had a fancy that if they met Doreen, she would be 'Mrs Clark'. The careworn, beautiful

Asian cleaner, Nita, merely moved around the factory with a dreamy distant air, ignored all the nuances around her as she did her work in silence, and returned to whatever alien graceful culture awaited her at home.

Leaning into the mist, he realized that one of his puzzlements had grown had stronger during the past week rather than diminishing. Not only did he not know anything about his mother, but he had no idea to which class she belonged. It had never before occurred to him to wonder. Her being British – and English, so he thought – was enough to contemplate. Now his loneliness was aggravated by not knowing whether she had been a Doreen or a Mandy, a posh totty or a city chick or the offspring of a cosy jam-making family on a farm, or even a girl born to clean a factory floor.

Probably, he thought glumly, not the last. A cleaner would surely not have been able to afford enough drugs to kill her so very fast . . .

He got back into his tiny hire car and headed north again, hoping to find Norwich. The cathedral spire in a picture had inspired him: he thought of the night he had wandered round London, and how after finding his burger he had taken a wrong turning and found himself outside a grand building with flaming torches lit outside, real burning fire which in his disoriented state struck him as magical. Now, after the days in the industrial park, he longed for a cathedral. But he could not understand the map: in this watery corner of the country it seemed that the direct way could never work, and his route to Norwich was barred by rivers. Once the road came to a riverbank and a sign saying FERRY, but there was no ferry.

He wished he had a companion to read the map for him. After a while, having retraced his way from a dead-end, he came to a town which seemed to be a port, and suddenly the lights went red and the whole tarmac road reared up ahead of him as a ship came through. There were tall old Victorian hotels all along the front, and he decided to stay the night here with the sea before him.

But when he rang the bell of the nearest hotel – SEA VISTA – it was answered by a dark frightened woman in a headscarf, with a baby on her arm and a thin little girl cowering at her skirts. She gesticulated at him with a stream of incomprehensible pleading or abuse and held out papers, stained and greasy and many times folded, of which he could make no sense. As he retreated to alleviate her distress, a bent old man passing by said:

'Bed 'n' breakfast.'

'Yeah,' said Alex, turning to him hopefully. 'I'm looking for a bed and breakfast.'

'You a tourist?'

'Yep. Guess so.'

'These are bed and breakfast. Used to be tourist places, back in the sixties. Not now. Full of spongers now.'

'Spongers?'

The old man spat. 'Asylum seekers. Refugees. Afghans, Kosovons, gipsies, allsorts. They send 'em here. Give 'em vouchers. They don't bring money into the town, not them.'

'So they're welfare places?'

'Well, for some.' The old man shuffled away, cackling satirically. Alex went back to his car, which was surrounded by boys aimlessly kicking stones at its red paintwork and that of the few surrounding vehicles in the small car park by the sea. He drove on, out of the town, through tidy suburbs with swings and climbing frames in the gardens and vegetables growing in ludicrously tiny patches: a dozen leeks here, a square yard of potato-leaves there. To his relief he saw a sign:

NORWICH. At dusk, after some struggles with a one-way system, he checked into an efficient, impersonal hotel chosen mainly for having its own car park.

He lay on the bed, exhausted by the nervous effort of driving in a strange land, and after a while got up and wandered out into the streets. The cathedral was all he wanted: deep, silent, spacious. There was a reedy service being sung in one small part of its immensity, but he could walk around on his soft-soled shoes without feeling like an intruder. Then his mobile rang in his pocket and, overcome with shame, he raced some distance to the nearest door, jabbing at the button to silence it.

'Hiyee,' said Janis, far away. 'How're you doing?'

'OK. You just rang me in a cathedral. Like, six hundred years old. Medieval.'

'Cool.'

'Embarrassing, you mean. Is Johnny happy?'

'I'm ringing to tell you he's very happy. The British company rang up in delight. You're Candoo Solutions' top favourite international troubleshooter.'

'It was an easy one.'

'Marty also says to say, "Was she pretty?"'

'What? Was *who* pretty?'

'The outworker. Marty talked to the British guy. He says he reckons he knows what you were up to, but he didn't let on, and he hopes she was pretty. Don't ask me, I just pass on the messages.'

'Tell Marty she's very married and he's got a dirty mind.'

'It's not a mind, it's a hard disc.'

Cheered by this taste of home, Alex ate a good dinner with his copy of *David Copperfield* propped in front of him, and went back to his room. He plugged in the laptop, checked his emails and wondered how Doreen Clark would begin her researches. He supposed that it would be more methodical, official, and paper-bound than the Internet world he had lived in for so long. Clicking on his browser he called up his favourite search engine and idly typed in:

MOIRA GRAYSON
then
MOIRA CHARLOTTE GRAYSON

No answers match your search criteria, said the screen. Well, why should they? Moira was gone long before the Internet was born. He had typed the name in often, during the Isabelle period when he had only lately seen his birth certificate and conceived a fever to know more. He cut the name into its components and found, as usual, a raft of companies and book titles with Grayson in their name, one or two of them featuring a Moira or Maura, or something for sale in moiré silk.

He wiped the screen, yawned, and glanced around the impersonal hotel room for inspiration. Time to sleep, maybe. Then, turning back to the keyboard, he typed without thinking:

JULIA TAINTON MORROWACK

There was the usual pause, during which he stared at the words in front of him, unable to place them. Where had he heard the name? From Doreen? Or was it one of the Clobber.com outworkers on the lists Sayeed had scrolled through?

The screen blinked, then brought up the list of potential answers. The first one, with a '100%' sign, read:

JULIA TAINTON MORROWACK Herbal therapies,
Iver . . .

He clicked on it, and stared bemusedly at the website's
opening page. There was a picture of a thin, severe woman
with dark hair and eyes, a single spray of some herb in the
corner, and in restrained copperplate the legend:

JULIA TAINTON MORROWACK
Herbal Therapy Centre, nr Iver, Bucks
Residential courses, relaxation and herbotherapy treatments
tailored to individual requirements.
www.juliataintonmorrowack.com
email: info@juliataintonmorrowack.com
Enter here

He clicked on the last line, and found himself looking at a
picture of an old brick house, shot from a low angle suggesting
that the photographer was actually lying in the herb garden.
Links offered articles: 'Valerian anxiety therapies', 'Echinacea
for achievers', and 'Can St John's Wort be effective in a
massage context?' A leaf in the corner offered a link to
Bookings and a telephone number. A fancy health farm: that
was all. He must have seen an advertisement somewhere
during his combing of the newspapers. The name would have
been quoted in a lifestyle supplement. Like the New York
press, the London papers were always touting cures and
therapies for discontented women. The lofty-sounding British
name had a ring to it: it must have stuck in his head. Perhaps it
was his brain's way of telling him he needed a herbal cure.

His hand hovered over the mouse, ready to wipe the page
aside and close down the computer.

No. It was not that. It was something else, something connected with the idle futility of his last search. The two were fuzzily linked together in his mind. He had not done the mother-search for a couple of years, so clearly something had kicked in since, adding this name.

He frowned, then jumped up abruptly and went to his laptop bag. Unzipping the side pocket he pulled out his father's diary, and found what he wanted.

We got a hearing! Amazing: Pocahontas (NB: Julia Tainton Morrowack, 763 4988) is giving evidence. For us! Can't believe it . . .

14 April – I am the legal custodial parent of Alexander Grayson, shortly to be known as Alexander van Hyden. His mother is now officially an 'unfit parent'. You can say that again.

Alex turned the page. The name appeared once more:

17 May – On the plane. He's asleep, thank Christ. Tried to ring Morrowack to say thanks properly, but phone just rang and rang. Probably better. She must feel like shit anyway, saying what she did.

He flipped the rest of the pages, avoided looking at the photograph of his mother, and closed the little book. In front of him on the laptop screen shimmered the website of Julia Tainton Morrowack, herbalist and therapist. He clicked back to the first page, and tried to imagine that dark face with longer black hair around it. Pocahontas? Oh, yes. He remembered his grandfather saying: 'He made a call to England. To someone he told me looked like Pocahontas. A girl who'd helped him get care of you. It was her who told him your poor mom was dead.'

It had to be the same woman. Well, or her daughter. He could not tell the age of this still, austere face on the screen. But such a name could not be common: not all three names together, surely? And a hippie from the seventies, a drug user like this Pocahontas-Julia person, who had once been deep into what his father had called 'feminist crap' and lived with junkies, would quite likely be a herbalist by now. Alternative therapies. It fitted. During his time in Vancouver, he remembered, all the most health-obsessed alternative types out on the islands had been former druggies. It had to be her.

A great shudder took him. The dark unsmiling woman on the screen would know everything about his beginnings. She had seen him as a baby, spoken for his safety in court, effectively handed him to his father and so shaped his whole life. She had broken the news of Moira Grayson's death. She had all the answers.

Where the hell was Iver, Bucks?

Leaving the laptop open and glowing, he tore downstairs to his hire car and grabbed the ring-bound road atlas he had bought in Brentwood. Back in the room he riffled anxiously through the pages: Iver. Yes! He could get there. He had been planning to drive to Cambridge next, to find his father's old college, but the hell with that! He could get to Iver in a couple of hours, maybe three. By tomorrow night he would know –

Everything. A shiver ran through him.

II

In winter, when she had finished her meditation, Julia Morrowack always went straight to the greenhouses. Mienke and Dave were in charge of checking the watering equipment, and should have done it by seven each morning, but she was not by temperament or experience very trusting of the young.

When she had finished her tour of inspection in the fragrant glass caves, nipping a leaf here and stooping to check a plant there, she went into the desert heat of the long drying-shed and looked at the thermometers and humidity gauge. Sometimes she lifted the flat frames and shook the drying leaves on their cheesecloth stretchers, or fastidiously pushed in a loose tin-tack, lest the crumbling leaves fall through the corners into the tray below. Then she went down the outside cellar steps and unlocked the cool, dark store below, merely to glance around and reassure herself that all was well and that the rats had not muscled aside the latest concrete plug in the cracking old walls. Then, and only then, did the mistress of the house return to the great kitchen for her breakfast.

Mienke was serving today, and the garden trainee Dave, his ponytail trailing down his back, sat at the long rough table talking to a stout man in a striped towelling robe. Julia sighed. It was always the same: the one guest you would rather not see at breakfast was the only one who came down.

'Is Lady Vernon having her breakfast in her room? And Mr Lucas?' she asked, unnecessarily.

'*Ja*,' said Mienke, laying a green-speckled herb omelette down in front of the fat man. 'And Mr Lucas is leaving, he says.'

'But he's booked till the weekend!' Julia sat down, elbows on the table, spreading her hands upwards in a theatrical gesture of exasperation.

'He says he has a headache. He says the treatments are giving him headaches and rashes and he is not happy.'

'No refund. He knows that?'

'He knows this. Still he is going.' The Dutch girl poured a steaming pale green liquid into the fat man's cup. 'Zere you go, Alan.'

'Ghastly piss,' said the man morosely. 'Can't I have coffee?'

'Tomorrow. After lunch only, if you must.'

'Go on, Dave, you take my side. These women are so damn' bossy.'

'More than my job's worth, squire,' said Dave, in languid public-school tones. 'Besides, you're one of Julia's success stories. Everybody knows you ought to be dead by now, the way you live for the other fifty weeks a year. We're not risking that just because you're a caffeine addict.'

'There's more to life than low cholesterol.' The man drank his green tea with an expression of concentrated loathing. 'At least I can have the *FT*, can't I?'

'Lottie's got one. You can have it after her.'

'Pray God she makes some pencil marks on it. I could be a millionaire yet.'

'She won't,' said Dave serenely. 'I asked her for a tip the other day, to invest my twenty-first birthday money, and she bit my head off.'

Julia sat down at the head of the table, in a majestic chair with arms, and signalled to Mienke to pour her some of the tea. The group ate in silence for a while, and then: 'I'm actually quite glad Mr Lucas is leaving,' she said, reaching for the rough brown bread which lay on a wooden platter between them and beginning to spread it with honey. 'He doesn't believe in what we're doing. He quite upset Phoebe yesterday, sneering.'

'But you always say that it isn't about belief,' said the fat man, whose name was Alan. 'You always insist it isn't faith healing, it's a neglected branch of science.'

'It is.' She bit into her bread. 'It's forgotten pharmacology.'

'So, why does it matter if Lucas doesn't believe? You don't throw patients out of hospital because they lack faith in Interferon-B.'

'I just prefer it if people take this place seriously, and not as some sort of holiday camp.'

'Bloody rough old holiday camp, if you ask me. You know why I came here, anyway.'

'Because I cured your horse.'

'*Did* she? Honestly?' Dave was entranced. 'What horse?'

'Racehorse. Bentham's Bidding. Went on and won the Oaks,' said Alan. 'I thought, hell, if it works on horses it can't be horseshit, pardon my French. Horses aren't gullible.' He got up from the table and put his plate and cup into the sink. 'Look! Well-trained client!'

'More impressive if you actually washed them,' said Dave.

'The point about Mr Lucas,' said Julia Morrowack, finishing her small piece of bread and honey, 'is that he is obstructive and grumbles a lot. And upsets my daughter, hence my grandson. So I'm glad he's going. End of story.'

Mienke sat down to her own breakfast. 'Me too,' she said

meaningfully. 'Or I would be looking up some good herb to calm down his libido.'

'Camomile,' said Dave promptly. 'Big dose.'

'Monk's pepper. Vitex Agnus Castus. Regulates the sex drive and promotes chastity,' said Julia. She stood up. 'I'm going to see if Phoebe and Josh are planning on having breakfast this side of lunch.'

'How about senna pods?' said Alan facetiously from the door. 'Tie him down to the bog full-time and even you would be safe, Minxie.' He walked out, with a surprisingly light step for a stout man, chortling.

The Dutch girl rolled her eyes humorously, and began to eat her own breakfast, a thin cracker and some pale-green spread with flecks in it. The sharp trill of the telephone made her move as if to get up, but her employer was already on her feet, and gestured her to stay. Julia took the kitchen phone off its wall-hook by the noticeboard and said:

'Julia Tainton Morrowack Herbal. Good morning.' And, after a moment, 'Well – we don't usually work like that. It isn't a hotel. We only have three guest rooms at any one time.'

Then, after a moment's silence while the phone quacked anxiously, 'Oh, I see. Well, as it happens there is a room coming vacant today, quite unexpectedly.'

She grimaced at her staff of two. Mienke nodded. Julia was continuing: 'But I should make it clear, we have to warn all clients at the moment, it isn't going to be possible to take walks from the house. The footpaths are still shut. The foot-and-mouth disease precautions. It's road walking only, I'm afraid, or our little multigym.' More quacking, and after a few moments more she said, 'Yes. Well, thank you. We'll expect you around five-thirty. The meal is at six: we all eat together, and I should warn you we eat rather lightly in the evenings. Yes. Thank you. Safe journey.'

Julia put the phone down and said, 'An American. Sounds quite young. Very polite. Wants two days' detox, and to look around the place. Says he's interested in learning about herb science. Asked if he might help in the garden.'

'Good,' said Dave. 'We're up to strength again, then. Goodbye, Lucas. Hello, Mr Helpful.'

'Could have done without it, really,' said Julia. 'Especially with Phoebe taking Josh out of school for no reason, and poor Lottie trying to get some peace and quiet. But he's obviously not a journalist, and two days' board will come in handy. And you could do with some help, Dave, planting out the basil and anise and moving those heavy pots.'

'He could give *me* a help-hand, changing round the drying-trays,' said Mienke.

'And he'll be paying *us* to work his socks off,' said Dave. 'Good old Yanks.'

Many miles away, Alex put down the phone in his hotel room with a hand that shook violently. A long night of dreaming and waking and wondering had convinced him that his best hope lay in making a relationship with the Morrowack woman by staying in her spa, or whatever it was. At first light he had called up the website again, and tried to deduce what line of approach might work best. There were references to training placements, to clients in treatment working 'therapeutically' among the herbs, and to the possibility of short relaxation breaks. After an hour of waiting and calculating the routine of an imaginary institution, he at last judged it safe to call. Now at last – so he thought, and hoped – he had heard the clear clipped upper-class tones of Julia Tainton Morrowack herself.

Pocahontas, who had been his mother's friend and briefly his father's ally.

She had made it plain that she did not want him turning up much before supper. So he could, after all, go to Cambridge and look at his father's college. He picked up the mobile again with the intention of ringing Boston, but remembered that it was still night there. It seemed a remote life, long ago and unreal.

Before he collected his car, he walked down the road to a bookshop and bought a little book on medicinal herbs. He must win her trust. He must take it slow! Middle-aged folks didn't always like you to plunge straight into the murkier moments of their past. And every American knew that British people didn't really like you going into their homes. Even, he supposed, if you were paying.

He drove westward across the flat fenland, thinking about what he would say and do when he had made the acquaintance of Ms Morrowack. After parking with some difficulty he wandered round in search of his father's past. When he'd explained to her about visiting Cambridge, Doreen Clark had told him what to expect.

'There'll be a porter's lodge,' she said. 'Behind a little square window there will be a very old man with a face like a tortoise. He will remember everything, back to 1939 when he was taken on as a fourteen-year-old garden boy while the men went off to the army.'

Alex realized that he had probably pinned too much hope on this romantic description ('Ah-ha, oi well remember young Mr van Hyden, and that baby of his too – he was a fine young man, the image of yourself', etc). When he eventually found the right college the lodge was manned by a man of barely forty, with a brisk efficient manner and no inclination whatever to maunder about the past. 'We're not open to the public at the moment,' he said sternly, but relented when Alex said that his father had been there.

'Oh, right, sir. Suppose you walk round the front quad, get the look of the place.' Under the porter's studiedly casual eye, Alex walked once round, looking at the arched entrances to staircases and the archaic wooden name-boards; but no ghosts found him, only a detached pity for the father who had achieved the rare and extraordinary distinction of living in such a place, and then been undone by love and left it.

It was strange, he thought, to be older than your own father had ever been, and to pity him as a kind of younger brother. The reflection brought tears to his eyes, and he left hurriedly and drove on through the flat landscape, pausing from time to time on the hard shoulder to study the road map. When he got closer, and his surroundings were beginning to roll themselves into a new landscape, he opened the laptop on the seat beside him. In the thin spring evening light, he consulted the shimmering diagram he had found on the website, displaying the B-roads and lanes that led to his destination.

12

———•◆•———

The Centre, when he at last found it, was a surprise. It was smaller than its picture made it appear, and far prettier in the spring sunshine, with three or four acres of gardens, glasshouses and tile-roofed sheds scattered around it. The house was of warm red brick, with small wings and an ornately leaded semicircle of glass over the front door. At one end a lesser door, painted bright blue, stood open to a kitchen-garden where a young blonde woman was gathering plants of some kind – vegetables, he thought by their bulk. There was a gravel parking bay for cars, with one glossy blue BMW convertible, a Bentley, and a couple of older, very much dustier cars.

Alex hesitated, bag in hand, not knowing whether to ring the main bell or walk up to the kitchen garden and speak to the woman with the vegetables. In the end he chose formality, rang, and stood on the doorstep for several minutes before a rattle of footsteps on parquet floor preceded the flinging open of the door to reveal a large, faded hallway. There were stairs with varnished, slightly peeling banisters and a fine parquet floor in dire need of a polish, adorned with good but very frayed Persian rugs. The house smelt of candle-wax and sharp, peppery cooking.

The blonde woman was smiling at him: she was even younger than he had thought, with a small piquant face and bright blue eyes. Her hair, twisted carelessly into a knot on top of her head and wisps around it, was almost white-blonde. 'Hi!' she said, in an accent he could not place. 'I am Mienke. I keep the house. You want to see your room?' She seized his bag before he could stop her, and led the way up the stairs at a pace which made Alex reflect that she, at least, was a good advertisement for a herb-rich diet. On the landing they passed a thin, chic woman with short hennaed hair and slightly protuberant eyes, who neither smiled nor greeted them when the girl Mienke said casually, 'OK, Lottie? This is Alexander.' As she pushed a scuffed white-painted door open for him, she turned and said, 'That's one of our other clients, she's a regular. There is also Alan who comes here often. You'll meet them tonight, OK?'

'OK,' said Alex. 'And Miz Morrowack? Is she here?'

'*Ja*. She will talk to you about your detox.'

Alex looked round the room. It was like nowhere he had ever been, high-ceilinged and austerely grand, with heavy, faded petit-point curtains and an ancient washbasin boasting tarnished brass taps. The bed, a vast sagging thing, was covered in a patchwork quilt with several of the patches missing, showing a blue cotton lining of considerable age. There was an equally saggy armchair, bearing two cushions, one of them with a Peter Rabbit motif and the other covered in yellowing lace.

'The bathroom is next door,' said the Dutch girl – he had, by now, decided from the name and the accent that she must be Dutch. Backing into the corridor, she sidestepped and threw open another panelled door, revealing a huge bath with curved feet shaped like the paws of a lion. 'No shower, I'm afraid. We just have one room with a shower and milady has this always.' She grinned. 'So, welcome. Supper is at six o'clock, twenty minutes, OK?'

'Is there a key?' asked Alex. The girl looked at him, surprised.

'No,' she said. 'Not here. It's not a hotel.'

'Don't people worry about leaving stuff in the rooms?'

'Dey don't bring that kind of stuff,' said Mienke grandly, then rather spoiled the effect by saying, 'Or leave it in their cars, I guess.'

Alex combed his hair and looked for a while into the spotted mirror, trying to compose his face into that of an earnest student of herbology. He flipped through his book, and prepared a couple of questions about linden flowers and whether thyme was better for catarrh if you used it fresh or in a dried infusion. He was nervous now. This household was too self-assured for him: it wore its shabbiness with an aristocratic panache for which he had no challenge or equivalent. The Dutch girl was friendly enough, but the henna-haired woman on the landing looked intimidating in what he thought of as a very English way. She had barely looked at him, a male stranger, and only nodded to the blonde housekeeper. He wondered about the others. At a minute before six by his watch, he went cautiously downstairs, treading as lightly as he could on the creaking steps, and paused, listening to see what door might lead to the dining room.

At the end of the hall, where the parquet turned to black-and-white flagstones in the arch of an empty doorway, he heard a clinking sound and low conversation. He moved towards it, and as he did the farthest door opened and a tall, dark, crop-haired woman appeared silhouetted against a brighter light.

'Mr van Hyden. Forgive me for not greeting you, I was making soup,' she said, advancing towards him. 'Is your room all right? We had a client called away unexpectedly this morning, but my daughter Phoebe tells me she changed the bed and towels.'

'Yes – fine,' said Alex. 'You are Miz Morrowack?'

'Julia Tainton Morrowack. Yes, indeed. I am she.' In the dim light of the hallway he saw her chiselled, dark features and the sleek cap of her hair. She must be in her forties, but there was not a trace of grey, nor the dead look of dye. Her short hair glistened blue-black like the wing of a raven. His imagination lengthened it, hung it round her narrow face and saw, he was sure, the angry Pocahontas that his father had confronted in that sordid house in 1974. He wanted to say it straight away: 'Did you know Moira Grayson, back in the seventies? She was my mother.' Ridiculous, stupid, lethal. He fought the urge and said instead: 'I'm real pleased you had space for me. I admire the concept of natural medicines and the idea that you, like, grow everything and dry it and all.'

'It matters,' said the woman crisply. 'Commercial processes can lose a lot of the properties. Some of the stuff you get in jars is just dead dust.'

'Can I maybe help a little, this couple of days?'

'Yes. Dave, who does the heavy work, will give you some jobs tomorrow. And Mienke will show you how the drying is done. You said you wanted a detox?'

'Yeah, but – I'm quite a hungry guy,' said Alex apologetically. The peppery smell from the kitchen was making this clear to him, and he rather wished he had stopped on the freeway for a burger.

'It isn't the quantity, it's the quality,' said Julia. 'You can eat as much as you want. Tonight's soup is a calming specific. Our two other guests and my daughter particularly need that, and one is a vegetarian, which I am not. So we have a parsnip and beet soup with a tincture of Valerian, but that shouldn't taste because of the pepper.'

'Are they your own recipes?' asked Alex faintly.

'Yes,' said Julia simply.

At the table, he now saw, a group of people was already gathered, faces turned towards him in cool, polite enquiry. Mienke stood behind them by a vast blue stove, her pretty face framed in bunches of herbs and small, tight onions. She smiled, but the group at the table hardly twitched a muscle as he said: 'Hi. I'm Alex.'

'Dave,' said a young, long-haired boy in an accent so redolent of a smart public school that Alex wondered how on earth he had grown his hair so long in the short interval since escaping it.

'Alan Mackinnon,' said a fat, middle-aged man with pale eyes and an indefinable air of meaning mischief.

'I'm Phoebe, right, and this is Josh,' muttered a waif-like creature with Julia's bone structure but her hair in bleached spikes. A thin boy of about six or seven sat close to her, unblinking, his big eyes on the newcomer.

The chic, hennaed woman spoke last, as if reluctantly.

'Lottie. How d'you do?' Her eyes slid away, bored. Alex divined that communal meals were not the woman's usual style.

He was right. She had, in fact, been remonstrating with Julia just before he arrived.

'For fuck's sake, Jule' she had complained, 'why can't I take my soup upstairs?'

'Because it's part of your treatment,' replied Ms Morrowack unsympathetically. 'You dig the garden, you eat the food, you have the baths, you submit yourself to the community life.'

'Lucas didn't.'

'Lucas has gone. And I didn't like him, as well you know. Anyway, it's only us and Alan.'

'And some earnest bloody Yank.'

'Half an hour. You know it does you good not to be in control all the time. Shh, here he comes creeping down the stairs.'

Lottie had shrugged her slim shoulders, drawn a pale green pashmina more tightly round them, and acquiesced.

Now, as Alex stammered a greeting, the light-eyed Alan added to his embarrassment by saying in a cool drawling voice: 'She's a *lady*, you know. A real English title.' Lottie raked him with a cold, angry stare, more or less ignoring the young American.

'Shut up, Alan,' said Julia, moving to ladle out the reddish-orange soup. 'Lottie rarely uses the title. It's her husband's.'

'Ought to use it. I would, if I had one,' said Alan. 'Impresses people. You're impressed, aren't you, mah fellow American?'

'Don't pay any attention,' said Julia. 'He thinks he's in a Noël Coward play but really he's a rather bad soap character. Not even P.G. Wodehouse.' She put down the fat man's plate of soup, rather hard, and deliberately moved the bread out of his reach. 'Now, I should explain. You'll find that at meal-times, while we eat, we don't talk because it slows digestion. Until we're all finished, someone reads aloud. Dave, I think it's your turn.'

She put his plate of soup on the stove to keep warm, and motioned the younger Englishman to a lectern which Alex had not previously noticed. Jeez, he thought, like in a medieval monastery! The boy began to read, without much expression.

'"*The juice of the sow-thistle, Culpeper tells us, is cooling and somewhat binding, and very fit to cool a hot stomach and ease the pain thereof. The milk, that is taken from the stalks when they are broken, given in drink, is very beneficial to those that are short-winded and have a wheezing . . ." '*

Alex stole a glance at the fat man Alan, to see whether he was giggling, but Alan remained unreadable. Lady Vernon looked bored, Julia and Mienke serene, and Phoebe had the air of being somewhere else entirely. The child merely ate, his big eyes on the reader.

' ". . . *Pliny informs us that they are efficacious against gravel, and that a decoction of the leaves and stalks is good for nursing mothers; that the juice or distilled water is good for all inflammation, wheals and eruptions, also for haemhorroids." '*

This young Dave was, thought Alex wonderingly, quite immune to comic impulses. Johnny or Marty would by now have been hooting aloud. He rather honoured the cool young man for his control, or possibly lack of humour, and wondered with vague dread whether if he stayed long enough, his own turn might come to confront this reading task.

' "*The juice is also useful in deafness either from accidental stoppage, gout or old age. Four spoonsful of the juice of the leaves, two of salad oil, and one teaspoonful of salt, shake the whole well together and put some on cotton dipped in this composition into the ears and you may reasonably expect a good degree of recovery . . ." '*

Dave turned the page and paused. Alex had finished his soup, which was not too unpleasant, and laid the spoon down with the smallest clatter he could manage. The others were still eating, slowly and deliberately. The hennaed woman, Lottie, was sniffing at her spoon with each mouthful, as if to inhale some virtue from the dish. Alan reached for the heavy brown bread on the platter, and dipped some in his soup. The reader continued.

' ". . . *The juice boiled or thoroughly heated in a little oil of bitter almonds in the peel of a pomegranate and dropped into the ears is a sure remedy for deafness. Also it is wonderfully efficacious for women to wash their faces with to clear the skin and give it lustre. The leaves should be used fresh gathered always, a strong infusion of them working by urine and opening obstructions. Some eat them in salads, but the infusion has more power. The leaves are also,*" ' he concluded, ' "*said to cure hares of madness.*" '

Glancing at the hostess, who nodded slightly, Dave laid the book down, fetched his own soup, and began to eat it. The others finished theirs and sat watching him. A few desultory remarks were exchanged, though the chic woman Lottie said nothing.

After a while Julia tapped the table and said: 'Right. Now, jobs for tomorrow.' She began allocating tasks, sending Alex to the garden with Dave to move growing pots out of their winter shelter, Alan to tidy the drying-racks with Mienke, and Phoebe to 'cook the lunch with me, please'. There was something passionless and heavily controlled about her manner: Alex could not place it, but wondered whether it had its origin in a religious or therapeutic style of behaviour. Certainly the guests, or clients, and the two employees of the house seemed perfectly at home with it. Perhaps it was just another kind of Englishness. If so, he thought, he preferred the breathy friendliness of Doreen Clark and the kind, solemn reserve of her husband. Those he could relate to. This was weird, like California but without the insistence that everybody have a nice day. He ate some of the bread, which was heavy and turned to a kind of damp nutty dough in his mouth as he chewed it. It did not taste bad, and it made the aftertaste of the soup less acrid. Soon he found he was no longer hungry, and also to his surprise that he was no longer tense. Shit, perhaps this herb stuff actually worked.

'Can I help clear up?' he asked as the group began to disperse.

'It isn't your turn,' said Julia. 'Dave and Alan tonight. The rest of us generally go and sit in the common-room, and read or talk.'

'I'm going in to Aylesbury,' said Phoebe abruptly. It was almost the first thing she had said all evening. 'D'you mind if I leave Josh?'

'Fine,' said her mother. Then watchfully, 'You'll be back early?'

'I am *not* going to score,' snapped Phoebe, apparently not caring who was listening. 'I am just going to the *cinema*, to get away from here for a couple of hours. You have to *trust* me.'

'I was thinking of going to the cinema,' said the woman called Lottie, smoothly. 'I could drive you. Save your petrol.'

Julia shot her a grateful glance. 'What a good idea,' she said with a forced brightness which Alex thought was not much like her normal manner, but strikingly like any worried mother in any culture. Like Grandma, when he used to go bowling in Des Moines when he was fifteen.

'But you'll watch Josh?' The girl Phoebe was impatient.

'Yes, Josh can play chess with me.'

'Or me,' said Alex with sudden bravery. The kid, at least, looked more or less normal. 'Hey, I like chess. Will you give me a game?'

The child regarded him with big, cool eyes.

'OK,' he said. 'I play white. It helps me think. You play black.'

They played two games: Alex lost the first one to the child on purpose, and the second one by accident. He was distracted by the subtly horrible taste of the evening drink which had been brought to him by Mienke with the single word, 'Vervain.'

117

'You're not very good, are you?' said Josh. 'My grandma isn't very good either and my mum can't remember the moves. Where do you live? Where's your house?'

'I don't have a house. I have an apartment. What you call a flat, I think. It's right at the top of a building in Boston, Massachussetts.'

'That's where Americans threw tea in the harbour.'

'S'right.'

Julia, who was sewing something in the corner, said, 'Bedtime, Joshie,' and the child grimaced and stood up with surprising obedience.

'Can I move pots with Alex in the morning?'

'Yes. Now, bed.'

The boy left the room, and Alex said to his hostess: 'He sure is a bright kid.'

'He's fine. He does all right.'

There was a silence in which Alex glanced over at the only other occupant of the room, Alan Mackinnon. He could not broach the topic of his past with an onlooker there. In any case, after a moment or two Julia shook out her sewing, folded it, put it into a lidded table with a mother-of-pearl inlay, and said: 'I'll go and see to Josh. Goodnight. I get up at five, so I sleep early.'

When she was gone, Alan put down the book he had been reading and said: 'You must think this is rum setup, Mr van Hyden.'

'It's – ah – unusual. For me. But this is my first time in England,' said the American diplomatically.

'Even for England it's rum. Trust me. Christ, if you're going back to Boston to tell them we're all living in setups like Julia Morrowack's, that'll be the end of the Special Relationship. This, my boy, is unique.'

'I kinda thought so,' said Alex. 'It's, like, a cure, right?'

'Tailor-made,' said the fat man. 'Topflight. For me, it's the liver. Maltreated for years, despaired of by the medical profession, now rescued by decoctions of lichwort and stinking dog-fennel, or somesuch witches' brew. I refuse to know the disgusting names of these weeds.'

'But she's good?'

'She's absolutely the best. Medically. One puts up with the compulsory gardening and the dreary mealtime readings about Pliny's urinary thistle cures, because it's that or a bloody liver transplant. And nobody will give me their liver willingly because I drink and smoke too much.'

'So everyone's on a different sort of program?' Alex thought that he could, at least, gather information about Julia's present before he plunged into her past.

'Yup. Usually detox, relaxation, candle meditation – she does that in the mornings. Oh, my, you have a treat in store! I've been let off. Probably my breath would cause an explosion if put near the candle. And you do get *near*, dear boy. People's noses have singe-marks, haven't you noticed?' Alan had pulled a flat, curved flask from his pocket and emptied its golden contents into the glass which had held his prescribed drink. 'But there are some specialities. Livers like mine are one of them. And the daughter's being weaned off crack, as you may have noticed from that little scene just now.'

'Oh.' Alex felt uncomfortable at this frankness, but equally desperate for more of it. 'So does Julia – Miz Morrowack, I mean – know a lot about drug addiction?'

'They say,' drawled Alan happily, 'that she knows it *very* first-hand, but it isn't discussed. Oh, no. Julia is not one to capitalize on her seedy past in *Hello!* magazine. Far too grand. And her royal connections wouldn't like it either. Very classy joint this, though you wouldn't think it. You know little

Mienke? She's a huge, huge heiress back home in Holland – one of the Haarlandts, you know.'

Alex made an assenting sound, fascinated.

'Diamonds,' said the fat man happily. 'But she's working here for twenty quid a week plus board, just to sit at Julia's feet and learn the inner meaning of oregano leaves and why it is a capital offence to dry moose-berries in the microwave. And then' – he was getting into his stride now – 'there's Milady Vernon, the only regular who's more regular than me. And the only one, did you notice, who doesn't have to pretend to do little jobs around the place. You know who she is, I suppose?'

'No, not really.'

'Only *Lottie Vernon!* Queen of the City, star fund manager, self-raised millionairess, have-it-all superwoman . . . bloody hell, I suppose her fame hasn't spread to the States yet. Can't open a paper here without profiles of her looking smug. Hang on, there was a magazine last Sunday, perhaps it's here . . .' He began to rummage in the magazine rack beside his deep chair.

'I suppose the financial community at home would probably know her. Wall Street. I'm not really in that area,' said Alex. 'I think I saw a story about her last week.'

'Yee-ees – she's made some big killing, got one of the railway franchise companies eating out of her lilywhite hand and forced another one into receivership. Wouldn't want to meet *her* down a dark alley.'

Alex was silent, shocked. The party had seemed so united at dinner: easy with one another. But perhaps that was only his perception because he felt so much the outsider. Alan, impervious to his shock, waved the magazine page at him and continued blithely: 'Frigid, I'd say. Doubt that Admiral Sir Peter Vernon gets much fun there. Now Julia – whoo! Watch yourself there, boy. Hot little mare.' Alan Mackinnon swigged his drink noisily.

'She's old enough . . .' protested Alex, then fell silent. Old enough to be his mother; well, yes. She had *known* his mother.

He felt oppressed; he did not want to be in this faded old room, drinking foul tepid brews with this malicious little man. He had to speak to Julia, and go. This expensive, troublesome place would get him down pretty soon. One more night would be more than enough. He would ask her in the morning. In the garden, maybe.

13

———◦◆◦———

Phoebe and Lady Vernon got back at around ten-thirty to a dark and silent house.

'Everyone's in bed,' said Lottie with a rather forced brightness, as the car pulled up. It had been a monosyllabic outing, the mindless interlude in the cinema a relief. An evening in Phoebe's company was not something she would have sought. Nor was she much used to the company of the young – except her own biddable children and her even more biddable young subordinates at DGB Investments. But one came to Julia's to change one's perspective; and besides, there was a debt of friendship due. Lottie had heard enough about the difficulties that flickered between mother and daughter to consider it her job to assist. Having a devoted and domestic husband of her own, she was filled with horror and pity when she thought of Julia bringing up this surly creature alone. So as she turned off the car's engine and glanced up at the dim windows, she was seeking to prolong the moment. 'Early nights you have here.'

'*Tell* me about it,' said Phoebe. 'Does my head in.' Then, with a rush of confidence, she added, 'The thing is, I mean, what they don't tell you in detox is—'

She halted. Lottie turned her head cautiously, careful not to look too interested. They sat in the cocooned warmth of the car, putting off the moment of opening the door and letting in the chilly night air. The intimacy of it appeared to have thawed the gaunt, angry girl. She had not mentioned her treatment all evening. After a moment the older woman gave an interrogative, 'Mmm?'

'What they don't tell you about detox, like, is how bloody boring real life is. I mean, without the drugs. How it just goes on, day after day, with no highs and lows and nothing exciting – shit, I could just do with some rocket fuel! You know? Only I mustn't, because of Josh.'

'I know,' said Lottie quietly. 'It's like Julia always says. It's not the pain, it's not the loss of a pleasure. It's not even like going on a diet. It's putting up with the sheer bloody dullness of not shooting up, or smoking, or whatever. But after a bit, you know, life seems less dull.'

'So *she* says,' muttered Phoebe. 'She loves her work, though. I remember when she started the pharmacology degree, then got seriously into the herbal qualifications – I was about five, and she just changed so much . . . like a fire being lit. Studying just made her so *happy*. I could never get over that, hating school like I did.'

'Do you think she was dull and flat before that?'

'Not when she was with Dad, p'raps. She talks about him sometimes as if that was an OK time. But after he went, so she had no Dad and no drugs . . .'

'Mmm. But she had you.'

'Like I've got Josh,' said the girl crossly. 'What you're saying is, like, he ought to be enough? That with a kid you shouldn't even want any fun?'

'Could be.' Lottie shifted in her seat, staring out into the misty darkness and feeling her shoulders stiffening. 'Ouch! Cramp.'

'D'you think it's your new programme?' Phoebe had been the daughter of a herbalist for most of her life; it was easy to divert her with talk of a physical symptom.

124

'No,' said Lottie, who had counted on precisely that. 'Only the kava-kava is new, and I'm not taking much of that. Julia isn't sure about it. No, the cramp is just stiff shoulders from work stress, more like. I'd go crazy, you know, if I didn't come here for these three nights a month.'

'I've often wondered why. You've been coming for years, haven't you? Before I left home, even?'

'Yes. It was a wonderful discovery for me. Working mothers, you know. We need time out of everything.'

'You could go to a health farm and be a bloody sight more comfortable.' Phoebe opened the car door, shivering as the east wind hit her.

'Wouldn't do so much good. And Julia does let me off the housework and gardening these days, I always hated that.'

'She lets you have your *laptop* with you, which is even more amazing. You break every house rule there is.'

'She knows I only do the bare minimum while I'm here. Just to keep in touch with the markets. I couldn't actually have this luxury otherwise. In my job, if you miss a day you're dead meat.'

They were talking lightly now, but Lottie felt that they had somehow reached a slightly higher level of mutual understanding. Pulling her fur jacket close around her as they walked to the kitchen door, she reflected that she must tell Julia how well it had gone. Phoebe had admitted her ennui, her boredom and discontent, her temptation. It was a step forward. Naming a feeling made you safe from it.

Phoebe, who had lingered for a moment looking at the cold moon, caught up and said: 'What d'you make of the Yank?'

'Better than Mr Lucas. God, I don't know how Julia ends up with people like that creep! Normally she's so meticulous about screening people.'

'I think the Alex guy is quite dishy. In a healthy sort of way. Don't Americans have amazing teeth?'

Lottie smiled. 'He been grinning at you?'

'Yeah, and check out the big shoulders. You sort of feel you ought to be walking out ahead of him with two fluffy pom-poms, shouting out initials and going, "Rah, rah!" '

Lottie laughed, genuinely amused. 'You want to be his cheerleader?'

'Well, I dunno.' Phoebe relapsed into her habitual air of brooding gloom. 'I generally go for skinny guys who do drugs. It was just that when I saw him, I had this little feeling – like, nothing very strong, I don't desperately fancy him or anything – but he looked sort of like he could show you another way to *be*. Know what I mean?'

Her voice rose at the end of sentences always, but this was, Lottie decided, a genuine query. She stepped into the kitchen, wriggled out of her coat and hung it behind the door, the costly fur dangling casually beside Dave's waxed gardening jacket and Mienke's puffy anorak.

'Yes,' she said. 'I know exactly what you mean. Sort of wide-eyed, optimistic, nothing very complicated . . . it has its appeal.'

'Right,' said Phoebe. 'Like you sometimes feel cats must think about dogs. Sort of, yeah! Whooh! How great would it be, to be like that? Wagging your tail. Always pleased. Nothing complicated. That fur coat,' she added inconsequentially, perhaps reminded of it by her last simile, 'Ma really hates it, you know? She's against fur.'

'Well, I'm not,' said Lady Vernon with some hauteur. 'And even if she is a friend, I do *pay* her. And I only take orders over treatments, not over what I wear. So she can lump it.'

'Cool,' said Phoebe. 'Josh likes it, anyway. He was being a bear in it when you were here last month.'

'You're only saying that,' said Lottie, 'to stop me hanging my mink jacket on the kitchen door where he can get at it.'

'You think he can't get into your room?'

Both women went upstairs laughing. In the little room over the porch Julia woke and heard her daughter's giggles, and the nightmare which had been troubling her began to recede into harmlessness.

When Alex appeared at breakfast he found it less silent and harmonious than dinner had been. Mienke was at the sink with Dave alongside her drying a plate, and Alan Mackinnon was eating what looked like a green fishcake with an air of distaste, and drinking a mugful of steaming dark-brown liquid with pieces of bark in it. Sometimes a sliver of bark caught in the hairs of his nose and caused him to splutter. Phoebe could be glimpsed outside, calling to her son in a querulous voice.

The other two at the far end of the table, however, were having some kind of argument in low, intense voices.

'You weren't leaving till tomorrow,' said Julia, her nostrils pinched. 'You need the three days.'

'I have to go today. I can take the infusions with me,' said Lottie Vernon, who was dressed in a business suit with an immaculate, if rather masculine, pale-blue shirt. 'I've no option. I need to get to the office. New York was really bad last night, and Murray and Adeline are going to screw up big-time if I don't take the reins back. Jules, it's a falling market. I don't have the choice.'

Dave, looking embarrassed, put down his tea-cloth and slipped out into the garden.

'You've never broken your treatment before,' complained Julia. 'And it's only a matter of twenty-four hours. You know the risks that stress . . .'

She broke off, glancing at Alex in the doorway and at Alan Mackinnon's interested, malicious face, which by now had an uncomely brown stain on the upper lip like a faint moustache. 'Come outside.'

The two women stood up sharply and stepped through the garden door. A moment later Josh raced in, grabbed a piece of bread, spooned honey on it and crammed it into his mouth. His mother was behind him, clad despite the chilly morning in low-slung jeans and a blue cotton crop-top which left her navel bare.

'There,' said the boy through his mouthful. 'So, I've had breakfast. So, now leave me alone, I want to help Dave with the pots.'

'Sit down. Drink your tea,' snapped Phoebe.

'It's not real tea. It's pooey old grass clippings.'

'Good lad,' said Alan. 'You haven't got a duff liver yet, so why bother with pooey old grass clippings, like me?'

'Shut up!' said Phoebe angrily. Alan gazed at her bare midriff with approval. 'Don't encourage him!'

Alan continued gazing in a manner which the American could only describe to himself as fresh. No, worse than fresh: insulting. Phoebe turned away, leaving only the nubbles of her spine showing, vulnerable and pale. Alex sat down, uncertain what to do, and reflecting that he had never before paid a hundred and fifty dollars a night for accommodation where the management were so bizarrely unconcerned about his comfort. The bed had been sagging, the room in the morning bitterly cold. In the night he had woken, and unable to get back to sleep had leafed through the Sunday magazine Alan had given him; lifestyle advice, make-up tips, excited reviews of movies he had seen six months earlier in Boston, and the long, catty profile of his fellow-guest, Lady Vernon.

'*For her children — Eden, Damien and Jocasta — the luxurious surroundings of their London and country homes and the cachet of top public schools must go some way towards compensating for their mother's adherence to the long-hours culture of a top fund manager in an edgy City.*' In other words, he thought sleepily, the journalist meant to imply that she neglected her kids for her career. What bitches they were, these British journalists. He had read too much of this stuff lately; it began to make him queasy.

He'd tried to read on: '*Her court is, in its way, as formal as Elizabeth I's — with Admiral Sir Peter as her Raleigh, and a discreet côterie of the rich and influential holding never-leaked conversations at her dinner-table . . .*'

He'd skimmed down, feeling impatient: '*Rumours abound that Lottie Vernon has an interest in alternative health therapies, but unlike her compeers in the royal family, or indeed the Prime Minister's wife Cherie Blair, none of her gurus or healers has ever spoken publicly about it. So, blue plastic pyramids, inflatable trousers or t'ai chi? We may never know . . .*'

Well, he knew. She came here to be pushed around and fed green-and-brown herbal crap like the rest of them. Now Mienke, with a melting smile, put down a sinister speckled omelette in front of Alex and ladled a thick khaki drink into a mug from the copper on the stove.

'What's this?' he asked weakly.

'Your programme,' said Mienke. She glanced at a sheet pinned to the kitchen wall. 'That's right. Detox with protein. You have to have the eggs because you are doing physical work today.'

'Oh. Right.' He began to eat it, then looked around the table.

'You're after salt,' said Mackinnon. 'Dream on, mate. Sodium kills. Mind you, this morning I'd gladly impale myself on a nice salty plateful of bacon and eggs.'

Alex was disinclined to be drawn into more conversation with this man, but the only alternative was Phoebe, who was gnawing at a raw carrot and throwing him occasional languishing glances, or Mienke, who was vigorously brushing down wooden trays by the sink. The fat man was talking to him again.

'D'you want a tip?' he asked. 'The one pleasure of the wicked world which one is not denied here is a flutter. Two-thirty, Kempton Park. Something of the Night. He's half mine, and I know a thing or two the bookies don't. He's a cert. Long outsider, forty to one, you'll make a mint. Shall I put a pony on for you?'

'OK,' said Alex absently. He was looking at the Dutch girl. He liked her face, mild and open even as she gave her task a childlike concentration.

'Money upfront,' said Alan Mackinnon briskly. He pulled out his wallet and looked expectantly at the American.

'Aw – I should've asked what a pony is,' said the unwilling gambler, hauling his attention back to the wheedling little man.

'Twenty-five quid. Twenty-five pounds.'

'I don't usually bet on horses,' said Alex. 'But as I'm only here for a couple of weeks, perhaps I ought to bet on an English horse. For luck.' He took out his own wallet and peeled off a twenty and a five, handing them over with a flourish.

'Good man.' Alan rose from the table and said, 'I'll call now. Before the lines get busy. I'm putting a hundred on myself. Good little horse.'

Mienke clattered off to the shed with her armful of wooden trays, saying, 'Five minutes, Julia? Is that OK?' Phoebe followed Josh into the sunlit garden, and Alex realized that he was alone. Better still, Julia Morrowack was heading back to the kitchen door, without Lady Vernon. This was the moment. He would ask, and once he knew he could go.

She came in, a tall spare forbidding figure, washed her hands and dried them on the grimy roller-towel behind the door. Turning, she said to him: 'OK? In ten minutes or so it's the morning meditation. I take it you'll join me and Mienke? David has his own programme.'

'Can I ask you something first?'

'It's yogic meditation,' she said with a touch of impatience. 'Nothing physical. A dim room, a candle, and an opportunity to focus.'

'No, not about that. Of course, I mean, I'll do it. But I want to ask something else.'

'Do so.'

He took a deep breath and said, with quavering formality: 'I have reason to think that you met my father Christian in 1974, around the time he was getting custody of me from my natural mother Moira Grayson.'

14

<hr />

Julia froze. There was, thought Alex, no other way to describe the sudden hostile stillness that made her pale face whiter and left the angular lines of her body as rigid and tense as a cornered animal. When the first fleeting shock passed, her initial movement was to turn and glance at the garden door as if fearful that somebody had heard. Then she moved to close it, and next walked swiftly across the flagstones and closed the other door. They were alone in her cave of a kitchen, facing one another under bunches of leaves and onions.

The shock and stillness of the change took Alex aback. It was as if he had pushed a button and returned the world to an Ice Age. Even the square of sunlight in the window seemed to have grown cold.

'What do you want?' asked Julia Morrowack harshly. 'What have you come here for?'

'Because I don't know anything *about* it all,' said Alex feebly. His voice sounded to him like a whine. Unnerved and weakened by the violence of her response, he could only plough desperately on. It was clear that this would be his only chance: by the look on her face he would be chased out of this house within minutes. 'I just need to know a bit about when I was born. Sort of my roots.'

'You could ask your *father*,' she said. Her voice was cold now, self-possession creeping back. 'He was there.'

Alex was silent as she continued, almost petulantly, 'You shouldn't burst in on people, after all these years, raking up the past. It's not fair.'

'I've got some right to know. I know my mother died,' he said, plaintive now. 'But I might have relatives living here.'

In the silence, a car started outside on the drive, revved sharply into reverse and accelerated away. Julia pressed her lips together, and for the first time he thought that a look of calculation flitted across her face. The sound of the car died away, then: 'You haven't,' she said baldly. 'None.'

'My mother's family? Parents, brothers? She had a brother. I was named after him.' Julia jumped and stared.

'You know *that*?'

'Yes, but only from one line in Dad's diary.'

She relaxed a little. 'Well, I'm afraid you haven't got relatives. Not that I know of. Sh—her parents died long ago. Her brother Alexander was killed in a car crash when she was fifteen. That was when – ' she stopped, and another silence fell between them.

'But you gotta see that even knowing that fact is like gold to me,' said Alex slowly. 'It means I know something about my mother. Even if it's a sad thing.'

Julia's face, still white, stayed impassive but for a touch of something which might have been irritation, but might equally have been fear.

'Look,' she said, 'I told you, it's none of my business. Ask Bud or whatever his name was. Ask your father.'

'I can't,' said Alex flatly. Now he was pale too, and his breath came with difficulty, forced from him by a new aggression. Fuck this woman! Fuck her haughty British up-yours attitude! In a rush he said:

'I *can't* ask him. He's been dead for twenty-five years. When

134

I was two years old my Uncle Al shot him, and then himself. He came home nuts after Vietnam. Just another little old American story. OK?'

He was trembling. He had never told a woman this; nor anybody outside his hometown, not even Johnny or Marty. He had broken with his first love Mary-Jo Hoogstraaten because – fancying herself as a counsellor and knowing the tale from neighbourhood gossip – she had wanted him to share his feelings about it. Now his words hung dreadful on the air, like a filthy spell he could not recant.

Yet with dawning amazement he realized that the spell, the sacrifice of his secret, had worked. Julia dropped her eyes, head bent so that he saw streaks of grey at her crown. She stared at the flagstones for a moment and then said, in a different tone: 'I'm sorry.'

He was silent. He divined that it had made a difference. Perhaps now, knowing that he had no link at all with his babyhood, she might agree to tell him a little more about the long-ago love affair of Moira Grayson and Christian van Hyden.

Something warned him that the less he said, the better it would go. But the silence stretched on for so long that eventually he said very softly, almost apologetically: 'You've got a daughter. You've got a grandson. You'd want them to know, if there wasn't anyone left. To know the history.'

Her head came upright again, the angular shoulders went back, and she stood as tall as he.

'All right,' said Julia, mistress of herself and her house once more. 'But not now. I'll tell you about Moira tonight. I keep a little office, for the paperwork, at the back of the hall. Nobody disturbs me there. Come after supper.'

'Thank you,' said Alex. And then gently: 'I won't come and

spoil your meditation time now. I'll go and help Dave with those pots, shall I?'

For the first hour Alex worked in a daze, carrying the heavy pots under Dave's direction. He was afflicted by the hollow, shivering sense of shame which had always haunted him when his father's death was spoken of. It was why he had dumped Mary-Jo, why he had worked all hours to get a scholarship to distant Harvard, why he avoided the neighbours as much as possible when he went to see his grandparents. People still whispered and murmured in pity, or at least he was convinced that they did. Hell, he would have. To lose one parent to criminal lunacy might be accorded a misfortune, to lose both . . . shit! His English class had done *The Importance* under an enlightened Anglophile professor at High School, and Mary-Jo had shot him significant, sympathetic glances every time Lady Bracknell loosed off the famous line.

Now he had impulsively released the awful information in this new country, where nobody knew him at all. Only the thought of Julia's unsmiling, guarded discretion comforted him. He should throw himself on her mercy tonight, and make her promise never to tell another living soul.

The watery morning sunshine grew stronger, and with the warmth on his back his spirits returned. After all, he was close to his objective, and soon would know enough about his beginnings to put light and shade and colour and flesh on to the mystery of his mother. Then he could pass onward into the rest of his life. Digging his fingers into the soft compost of the big pots, he thought of graves and farewells, and decided that once he had assimilated his unknown mother's story, he could bid her ghost a decent filial goodbye and return to his old life.

Besides, he was acquiring some solid knowledge of her country. Already the romantic absurdity of his old dreams about England made him smile. He was learning its reality: he had solved one of its small computer problems, been thanked by one of its companies, visited one of its farms and made a good friend in Doreen. He had driven its awful roads, been seduced against his judgement by one of its women, and fed terrible soup by another. He had even placed a bet on one of its racehorses, and now he was digging in England's soil to make the healing green plants grow. Not bad for ten days: not a bad *Return of the Native*.

Dave stopped every two hours, to go through a series of stretching and bowing motions. At noon, Alex watched him and afterwards said: 'Is that Yoga?''

'Yes,' said the young man. 'It's a refinement of classic Hatha Yoga, designed to be done in six short sessions during the working day. I prefer it to the two hours each evening which I used to do.'

'Bit tiring, huh?'

'No, invigorating,' said Dave rather sententiously. 'That was the problem. I was so full of life force that I could never sleep. But I need energy for physical work, so now I prefer to access it all through the day.'

'It was impressive when you were standing on your head just now,' said Alex respectfully. He was sitting on an upturned empty pot, while Dave folded and unfolded his long brown arms in what was by now recognizable as the last and least intense movement of his sequence.

'I used to stand on my head for forty-five minutes each night,' said Dave. Suddenly, rather sweetly, he had discarded his guru's solemnity and betrayed his youth in the boast. Alex smiled and gave him the applause he needed.

'Jeez! I'd never keep my balance!'

'Do you do yogic exercise?'

'I go to the gym,' said Alex. 'To be honest, I was rather missing it before today. It's been good to get some exercise.' He stood up. 'Back to work.'

'You are tense,' said Dave, returning to his guru's manner. 'It's compromising your strength, I can see it. Try this.' To Alex's surprise, the ponytailed young man swiftly put his hands on his shoulders and forced him to his knees, then to a sitting position on the grass. He sat opposite and began to demonstrate some simple stretches and poses. Alex mirrored him, and after a moment or two looked to one side and saw that Mienke and Phoebe had emerged from the shed and kitchen and were seated alongside him, copying Dave's movements.

'Hey, it's a masterclass,' he said.

'Quiet,' said Dave. 'Concentrate. The arm higher, like a tulip petal, high and brave.'

'I know about tulips,' said Mienke with an unexpected grin. 'I am Dutch.' She raised a smooth, beautiful pale brown arm.

'Shh!' said Dave. 'Now . . . calmly . . . pull strength from the spine.'

Alex, although the stretching was doing his tense back good, entertained the brief mutinous thought that it was a bit much to have come thousands of miles eastward to the old world – to stuffy old imperial Britain – just to find himself walled up with a houseful of alternative kooks as weird as you would find on any West Coast campus. But obediently, in consort with the three others, he completed the movements, lay flat for a moment on the damp grass, and thanked Dave as he stood up.

Mienke got up too, and walked back towards the drying-sheds, but Phoebe showed an inclination to linger.

'So, how're you doing?' she said, looking up at him from the grass. She was sitting back at an angle, propped on her arms so that her small breasts jutted out. He could see her navel beneath the cropped vest. She was very, very thin, and her skin was whiter even than her mother's.

Alex put out a hand 'Fine. But you'll get cold lying on that grass. C'm on.'

'I never get colds,' said Phoebe, accepting his hand and swinging lightly to her feet. 'I'm a recovering addict and I drink too much and I had Josh when I was fifteen and didn't know who was the father. And I sleep with just about every-body. But I don't smoke or bitch and I never, ever get ill.'

'That must be down to your mother and her herbs,' said Alex lightly, embarrassed by the frankness – and the clear intention – of her personal manifesto. 'You'd have to be healthy.'

'Yeah, she got into herbalism when I was little,' said Phoebe. 'All I remember about being a kid was green speckly food. Green, green, green. Even my birthday cakes had special seeds and green bits in them.'

'She's very calm, isn't she?' He was fishing now. The more he knew about Julia, the better he could handle her tonight.

'Valerian and St John's Wort. She'd be a basket case otherwise. You know she was once an addict too? She only finally came off methadone when she got pregnant with me.'

Alex was silent. This skinny little girl was too free with her mouth, a loose cannon. But he might learn something useful. Phoebe went on: 'So, you see, it's hereditary. People like us. Addictive personalities. Whatever we get into, we go too far, OK? Drugs, drink, herbs, sex . . .' She shot him an inviting glance. 'And now for my ma it's the healing kick. Me, I'd love to be moderate but I never will be. Josh is moderate. Quite a cold little fish actually. When he gets older I s'pose he'll do drugs, everyone does really, but I don't think he'll be an addict.'

'I hope not. He's a nice kid,' said Alex politely. Then, 'I better get back to work.'

'I'm supposed to be making lunch,' said Phoebe with an expression of gloom. 'Couscous, I think.' She stretched, revealing even more stomach, and gave him another sidelong glance to see whether she was having an effect. Actually, she was. He did not find her particularly attractive, with her dishevelled hair, thin shoulders and high, affectedly cockney voice; but there was an air of headlong voracity about her which made him restless. He turned away, to see Josh in the distance beyond the garden hedge. The child was walking across a meadow, his red sweatshirt standing out sharply against the dull green.

'Hey, is he all right?'

'Yeah,' said Phoebe, yawning. 'He's fine.' She wandered off towards the kitchen with an air of disappointment. But Alex kept a troubled eye on the boy's wanderings for the next hour, glad of the openness of the country. Only twice did the small figure vanish behind trees or hedges, and each time the watcher stopped work and stood, eyes fixed on the obstruction, until the little red dot reappeared.

The day dragged on. Lunch was adequate and satisfying but cold, and to Alex's mind depressing. At three o'clock Alan Mackinnon, who had been helping in a desultory manner with some planting, sloped off indoors muttering some indeterminate excuse. At half-past three he emerged grinning, and interrupted Alex's task of aerating a deep-bed.

'Forty to one!' he said. 'Easiest grand you ever made!'

'What?' asked Alex, puzzled.

'Something of the Night. My horse. He won. You won.'

'Jeez! You mean, you really placed that bet?'

'Next step: reinvest,' said the little man briskly. 'Who needs Lottie Vernon and her city chums? You and I, we know how to make our fortunes without arsing around with investments. What say I put your grand on the four ten at Kempton? Another little tip of mine?'

'Um – I dunno – it's not something I do—'

'Good horse. Dutch Courage. Ten to one.'

Alex glanced towards the sheds where Mienke stood, one hand on her aching back, smiling down at the child Josh with wisps of golden hair falling in disarray around her face.

'OK,' he said, half to himself. 'Dutch Courage it is.'

'Ah-ha! Smitten, I see. Not the first!' Alan had vanished, laughing, before the American could deny it, and he dug on with embarrassed fury. He needed to get out of this place. Tonight, Julia: tomorrow, the open road.

———•◦•———

15

'I knew the Graysons from home,' began Julia. They were sitting in her small untidy office, she at the desk and he on a slightly sagging chair. She looked down at him: he decided that this was not by accident. 'We lived quite close, in Gloucestershire. Children's parties, Pony Club, that sort of thing.'

'So she had a rich family?'

Julia looked at him as if he had made a bad smell.

'No-oh,' she drawled. 'Not what you Americans think of as rich. Her father was our local MFH.' She saw his incomprehension and translated with exaggerated patience. 'Master of foxhounds. Hunting. But he was anything but rich. Army pension and family house. He was quite old when she was born. Her mother kept horses at livery. They sent Alexander and Moira to school, obviously. But they could never afford boarding, only day.'

Alex nodded, trying to be quiet. He guessed that he would get more information if he allowed Julia to tell it the way that came naturally. If her references were obscure, he could always check them out later. The important thing now was to listen and remember every word.

'I used to see her from time to time in the holidays, Pony Club Camp and all that.' She shuddered. 'It was a pretty unreconstructed social circle. The nineteen-fifties went on till nineteen-eighty, where we lived. But once we were into A-levels I didn't see her so much. My father was an academic.' Alex failed to understand the connection, but kept his pledge of silence. 'I did hear about Alexander being killed, of course.'

She stopped. Despite her hybrid arrogance, half-aristocratic and half-hip, she seemed vulnerable. To help her, Alex murmured: 'How did it happen?'

'Stolen car.' Julia pushed her hair back and stared away from him, at the dark square of the window. 'He was a bit wild. She was always the quiet one. But after that happened, she was really all over the place. I didn't know her so well then, but I remember that she was thrown out of school for cannabis, a month before A-levels, and her parents entered her privately for the exams at the FE College. And then she just amazed everyone, got three As and walked straight into a place at Cambridge. So I saw a bit more of her then, because my dad got a job at Churchill College and we moved.'

Alex gaped. 'My *mother* was a student at Cambridge as well as my father?'

'Uh-huh. For a bit. She was very bright. Mathematician.'

'What happened? I mean, why just for a year?'

'She met the Yank – your dad, I mean – because he came up early in the summer, just to look around. He had one of those American scholarship things.' Alex nodded. In his childhood his grandmother had told him time and time again about the pride, the brilliance and the glory of Christian's achievement.

'He was starting in October, like they all do, but he got a job in a restaurant for the summer term before. Just to get the measure of the place. A lot of the Yanks used to do that. And he met her.'

Alex waited.

'They were pretty thick all through that term. She was

terribly pretty, and very bright, and a hell of a good arguer. She and I saw a lot of each other by then, because I was retaking an A-level at the tutorial college.' Alex noted that as Julia remembered her youth she gradually discarded the witch-like dignity of her normal persona, and spoke more like the breathless county-bred girl she had once been. 'She never actually introduced me to her Yank, though. She just called him 'my Buddy'. Jokily, you know. I think she liked to blow off steam about him when he wasn't there. It wasn't a terribly harmonious partnership.' She glanced at Alex, who carefully showed no reaction. The silence stretched out between them.

'But she got pregnant?' he said eventually. 'With me?'

'I don't know when she knew. She didn't tell me about it till autumn. By that time things had changed a bit.'

'What?' He could not help himself, the silences defeated him: but he knew that every fresh question from him made her tenser and less forthcoming. He pressed his lips together and vowed again to say nothing else unless he was forced to. It was too late: he had made her wary again.

'Look, you don't need to know,' she said with an air of exasperation. 'You must know about drugs and stuff? How people change. It's not exactly unknown in America, is it? And it's not unlike alcoholism. It's a disease.' She was, he saw, struggling to regain her matriarchal and professional dignity, but her fingers wrestled with a pencil, pressing so hard that he saw them whiten.

'I'd heard it was heroin.' He cursed himself. *Say nothing*.

'Smack, yes.' She put down the pencil and gave him a hard look. For a terrible moment he thought she was going to finish there and dismiss him, but suddenly she came out with an entirely unexpected, exculpatory rush of explanation.

'Look, they had some kind of fight. He wouldn't leave her

alone, and she was pissed off with him going on and on at her to give up smoking weed, and marry him, and turn into some kind of GI bride in bloody Kentucky or somewhere. I mean, Jesus!' Alex got a clear glimpse of his father's scornful feminist Pocahontas. 'And he wanted her to stay on and do some kind of barmaid job or something. Live in his scabby bedsit. She'd told him she was pregnant by then. But Cambridge is just ghastly in the summer anyway, full of Japs and Yank tourists and conferences, so she told him where he got off, and went home to the country. She rang me once or twice, very fed up.'

Julia paused, head back, as if she was inwardly listening to the shrill complaint of her friend down the telephone.

'I think things were difficult. She always rang from the village phone box. Her mother was ill, her dad had a bit of a temper, she was bored. And she knew all the dealers in Stroud, from school. Obviously. So that's how the bad stuff started.'

Alex could not stop himself. 'You mean, she only got into the hard drugs just that summer? When she *knew* she was *pregnant?*'

Julia glared across her desk, matriarchal again. 'Look, I said I'd tell you what happened. I didn't say I'd listen while you sat in judgement over a girl of nineteen you never even met.'

Alex inclined his head, as if in apology, but a pulse of anger was rising within him. *A girl of nineteen you never even met.* Not *met* her? He was *inside* her, a foetus trapped at the mercy of this irresponsible smackhead, for God's sake. He was born a junkie, with the high thin agonized cry which had broken his young father's heart. *Sit in judgement*, indeed! Arrogant bitches!

At that moment his unknown mother became, in his mind, one with the cold, remote figure across the desk. They were in it together.

Julia resumed: 'So there's not much more to tell. She got very deep into the drugs, and she didn't come back to Cambridge in the autumn. I left home around then, and – well, I was pretty angry about a lot of things. I'd done badly in my re-sit exam and missed a place at the university.' She paused, almost as if expecting him to commiserate. He did not. A muscle in his cheek was jumping, and he put up a hand to steady it. After a moment she resumed.

'So we met up in London, and my boyfriend Neville was setting up a squat in Notting Hill. Some foreign bank owned it and it was always empty. We all did a lot of drugs. You just did, back then. Shark got into a bad place. But that's where you were born. I delivered you. In the house.'

There was no sign of softening in her face. Her eyes were dark and opaque, her brows knitted. 'And if you want the full picture, your father turned up on a bloody bad day and announced he was taking you. He just wrapped you in my shawl, and went. If it hadn't been a bad day, who knows?'

She frowned more deeply. 'I was scared. It was a responsibility, none of us knew anything about babies, and Nev was threatening to throw Shark out before she got us all into more trouble. She was bloody indiscreet about doing deals on the street. So the truth is that I helped your father get hold of the kid – of you, I mean. I gave evidence to the court about her being an unfit mother. I've been ashamed of that ever since.'

'Why?' Alex was really angry now. 'Why are you ashamed that you helped him – Christian – get his own baby out of a house like that?'

'Because he was such a pompous prick,' said Julia, and if he had not already tasted her contempt, he would have thought she had forgotten whose son she was talking to. 'Typical Yank.

147

Clean-living, shiny, grinning white teeth, invincible born-again righteousness . . . I couldn't stand him, if you must know.' His expression must have registered with her and she softened her words, though with an air of unwillingness. 'Look, we were all very young.'

He felt sick, and wanted more than anything to drive away from this house and this woman. But there was one more question and he had to ask it.

'Did she – did my mother feel at all . . .' He faltered, and for once Julia divined his trouble and helped him, though still with the same grudging manner.

'She thought you were cute. She called you Sunboy. She had good days. But then she'd sort of forget everything. You do that, when you're hooked. You focus on the next hit, you have to have it, nothing else matters. And she wasn't well. She had liver damage.'

'So would you say,' Alex asked, his voice slow and harsh, 'that losing me is what killed my mother? For some reason, I seem to need to know that. Then I'll go away.'

'No,' said Julia, and all the old scorn was back. 'If you think women die of things like that, you've got a pretty sentimental view of us.' She stood up. 'So now you know. She was my friend, she had troubles, she screwed up, shit happens. Like your uncle's thing with Vietnam. Lucky people get over bad starts. You're OK, you've come through, you're the winner, life goes on. End of story.'

Alex stood, too, to block her way to the study door.

'Will you tell me how she died?'

'What do you know?' she parried.

'My dad went to the hospital in the Fulham Road.' He had re-read the diary just before dinner. 'The nurse told him she was dying and he wasn't allowed to see her. He reckoned the nurse thought he was a dealer. Then, back in Iowa, he phoned you and you told him she was dead. My grandad knew that, but he doesn't know any details. So will you tell me about when she died?'

'No,' said Julia, her hand on the doorknob. 'It's bad to go over things like that.'

'Was it when she left hospital?'

'Look,' she said in the same flat tone, 'I'm not going to tell you anything else. There isn't much anyway. I told you, her liver was badly damaged. That happens sometimes. Apparently she'd had jaundice when she was a kid and that's really bad news for people who do smack later on. Just, for God's sake, move on!'

Her tone changed, becoming even brisker. 'Are you leaving tonight or in the morning?'

'Now,' said Alex, bitterly. 'Right now. I'd better settle up.'

'No,' said Julia. 'Be my guest.' She went back to the desk and pulled out of a clip the form he had filled in for Mienke with his name and address and card details, and tore it into small pieces which she thrust at him.

'Now go. Don't look back.'

She gave him a smile, but it was brief, and dry. He let the scraps of paper fall to the floor and turned away from her without a word.

His eyes misted with angry tears, Alex threw his things into a bag and drove away, breakneck down the narrow lanes, losing his way twice before he found the wide carriageway and his lights picked out the signs to distant towns. None of the names meant anything, none of the directions mattered. He drove until he was tired, then took a slip road and found himself in a high street lined with impressive stone buildings, their details picked out by streetlamps and their ground floors striped with brash illuminated corporate logos. One of these was McDonald's. Gratefully, he left the car on a meter and slipped in to seek the familiar food. After Julia's austere green soups the greasy, salty savour brought him back to himself, and he rang Johnny at home and told him that he had done with his British holiday, and would be home as soon as he could get a flight.

Two Big Macs later he walked into a hotel called the Crown, and was shown to a room which smelt of radiator dust and floor-polish, and whose sloping floorboards supported a four-poster bed sagging with weary antiquity but swagged with cheap, crackling synthetic curtains. He had no heart to explore the town but once in the bed, between itchy brushed-nylon sheets, his weariness vanished and he slept badly. At one stage during the night he thought that he woke up and found his limbs shrunken to baby size, his head too heavy to lift, his stomach stabbed by griping pain. He cried out, and the cry woke him properly; but he lay for a long while shivering, unable to shake off the terrible conviction that he had for a moment become a helpless infant again. Street lights filtered through the drably floral curtains and the ruffled net hangings of the bed, and until the small hours drunken shouts came up from the market square below. Once there was a long bout of angry female nagging: 'Shurrup! Shurrup! Just bloody shurrup and git on aht ev it!' A man, slurring obscenities, seemed to be getting the worst of the exchange.

In the morning, there was a chirruping message from Janis on his phone. There were no flights until the next day, she said, so, 'Do more touring! See more castles! Have a good day – we're fine here, waiting to hear the adventures!' He switched on the television: there were more pictures of animal pyres, blackened hoofs and bloated bellies silhouetted against flames while sad stoical wrinkled farmers looked on. He thought of Duncan Clark and the gay desperate bravery of the little family in the Essex farmhouse. At seven-thirty he went down to the empty restaurant, which smelt of stale beer, and piled his bowl with dusty muesli and pale tinned fruit from the sideboard. Another day of this life seemed suddenly intolerable.

'D'you want the full English?' asked the landlord glumly. 'Only, Mavis who makes it doesn't come in till eight. Not on a Sunday.'

'Oh,' said Alex, 'is it Sunday? Sorry. This'll be fine.' He ate without pleasure, paid up and went out in the drizzle to his car. A moment's study of the map showed him that the airport was handy for several historic-sounding towns, and with a certain gloomy determination he set off for a final day's tourism.

Nothing charmed him, nothing caught his fancy. The curse of foot-and-mouth disease lay over the green pastures; there was an empty, depressed air to the tourist sights and his heart was unreasonably chilled by the angry red-and-white skeins of plastic tape and official signs of interdiction which barred every trail from every car-park. The rain eased by lunchtime, but the sky remained a grey and lifeless dome.

Once, standing by a wide brown river with a palace and a castle on the skyline, Alex thought that this must be what it was like to be very old. Slow, cold, with no pleasure in anything any more. Sometimes he tried to shake himself into feeling, but whenever he tried to think about what Julia Morrowack had told him his mind failed to focus, fleeing into a numb greyness like the sky overhead. The host nation, as represented in the pay-booths and cafés, appeared not to notice the visitor's depression, with the single exception of a jolly West Indian lady in a tight red dress who called, 'Cheer up, my darlin!' to him when he absently cannoned into her in Windsor High Street.

At the end of the day he found another town and another market-square hotel with a king's head on its sign, which he calculated to be barely an hour away from the airport. Ascending some crooked, creaking stairs past hunting-prints to his room, he considered going straight to bed, or at least getting under the covers and surfing the net on his laptop. He glanced at his watch. Hell, it was seven o'clock! Admonishing himself, he took a quick unsatisfactory shower with the faded pink rubber tubing provided in the tiny bathroom, and went out into the square.

Opposite the hotel was a handsome, foursquare Market Hall, and for once there was a large and apparently happy crowd of people trooping into it. He advanced to investigate, and saw a sandwich-board propped up outside, proclaiming a brass band concert in aid of some Services charity. For almost the first time that day, Alex smiled. Yup, this would do. He had always been able to lose himself in music. A dim auditorium was what he needed.

There were, said the chatty lady at the desk, 'Just a few tickets left, you *are* lucky!' She smiled, and he smiled back, almost rejoicing in the contrast with the previous glumness of his day. The audience were mainly old, with many of the men in blazers with brass buttons, and the women a sea of bobbing grey and white permed heads. A few younger couples were among them, and one party of schoolchildren, giggling together under the eye of an amused young woman teacher who except for her dark hair reminded him strongly of Doreen Clark.

He had thought about the Clarks a few times during the day, trying to use them as a benchmark of friendly accessibility against which to measure the dourness of their countrymen in a blighted spring. Once, he had considered ringing up just to hear Doreen's matter-of-fact voice. But no: she might think he was hustling her for genealogical information in payment for the computer. He didn't need it now, but had not the heart to tell her so. He would email when he was safe back in the States.

Relaxing, as far as possible, in his hard wooden chair he closed his eyes and waited for the music. The programme on his lap, adorned with coats-of-arms and mottoes and appeals for Services charities, remained unopened. It was a habit he had: he rarely read concert bills until afterwards, preferring to let the music speak directly. In his days with Isabelle it had driven her crazy. 'That is so hippie,' she would say. 'You wouldn't read a book without knowing who wrote it and when.'

'I would,' said Alex. 'If it wasn't printed big on the cover. Certainly that's how you read a poem properly. Naked.'

'Lazy,' said Isabelle. She made notes in the margin of concert programmes, for her liberal arts course. Alex would smile and sit back, eyes closed, open to emotion.

In this case he was open to a blasting brass fanfare. He allowed it to take him along, hoping to feel a stirring of martial and ancient splendour, a state he had not achieved on the battlements or in the public rooms of any of the day's castles and palaces. The tactic had limited success. He opened his eyes and saw that many of the middle-aged and elderly audience were rapt, swaying very slightly with the beat. Well, hell: it was their army, after all.

He listened on, through an accomplished waltz-time number and another march. Gradually he found he was less angry but increasingly melancholy. It seemed to him now that despite Doreen and Clobber.com and his day of digging the Morrowack garden, he had entirely failed to engage with this stiff enigmatic mother-country of his. Apart from the Clark family, fading now into memory, the most approachable and direct person he had met was the little Dutch girl Mienke.

The rest of them at Iver had been – hell, spooky. The Addams family: arrogant Julia, wraithlike Phoebe, malicious fat little Alan, and that cold, chic Vernon woman. Morticia Addams, Cruella de Ville, Uncle Fester, and a visiting witch. Sadly, he realized that whenever he thought of England now it would not be in terms of a precious isle in a silver sea, a country lane or a castle rampart. It would be a memory of dust, hard pillows, Suzy McHugh's rapacity, newsreels full of burning cattle, Saturday drunks in market squares, Julia's cool stare, Alan's titter, loneliness and rebuff. The unbearable fact was that after all the years of silly romantic fantasy, in real life he didn't much like it here.

The band broke into his reverie with a sound that shot a thrill through him. Weary of its brisk marches and staid waltzes, it swung into an energetic rendering of 'Chattanooga Choo Choo' and then, with barely time to catch its breath, into 'Two O'Clock Jump'. When this cathartic change occurred Alex opened his eyes and looked down at the programme. '*American Moments*', it said, and in small print, '*For the boys in the band at Upper Heyford – we'll miss you!*'

He joined the applause and was pleased to see that this eminently respectable audience was not above stamping its feet. Suddenly the hall was awake, American, unchained from its nostalgic dreams. The finale of the sequence – 'Stars and Stripes Forever' – made him duck his head to hide the tears from his neighbours. Time to go home. Yes, high time. It was the interval, and he decided to leave and not come back.

But, 'Thanks, boys,' he muttered under his breath as the band trooped off the stage, pink-faced and perspiring. 'Thanks. We'll call it quits.'

16

Admiral Sir Peter Vernon padded across a beautiful rose-pink Persian carpet in his socks and shirtsleeves, a glass in either hand.

'Here goes, Lott,' he said to his wife, handing her the drink. 'Or are you still on the old Number One Punishment Diet?'

'I should be,' said his lady, accepting it with a little shiver of pleasure at the clink of ice and the sharp aroma of vermouth. 'I left a day early. Had to go in to DGB and sort out Murray and Adeline. Christ, we sail near the wind sometimes. I could have driven back up there for dinner and morning meditation, but I spent last night in the flat. Julia was furious.'

'Never known you do *that* before. Thought it was a religious observance,' said the Admiral, padding back to his own chair. 'My body is a temple, I lay aside the sordid world, a dedicated three days' resurrection . . . all that.'

'Well, it has been,' admitted Lottie. 'We were counting. It's nearly fifteen years now since she set the place up. Before that I used to go to a health farm. Before we got married. But Jules does me more good. And it seemed a good idea to set the routine in stone. That's the only way that breaks don't get nibbled away by work.'

'Whatever rings your bell,' said Peter absently. 'Anyway, Eden rang. Though I have to tell you he's decided he wants to be called just plain Den, as of now. As in Dirty Den. He wants fifty quid for new rugger boots.'

'Did you send it?'

'I will tomorrow. I rang the housemaster and it's all pukka. He does need the money for boots. Well, forty quid of it anyway.'

'God, you don't trust them an *inch*, do you?' The mother sounded irritated, and took a draught of her martini as if to quell the temptation to snap. 'What do you think he'd spend it on? Drink?'

'Or drugs,' said Peter levelly. 'These days you have to have some idea of where kids' money goes.'

His wife threw him a sharp look. 'Damien rung?'

'Not for days. I'm not sure what's going on. He was quite upset on Monday, something about French detention. I sometimes wonder whether he's old enough for boarding.'

''Course he is. Loves it,' said the mother, holding out her glass for a refill. 'Is Jocasta home tonight?'

'Yes. Astrid's fetching her. She slept over at Ally Johnson's.' Obediently, Peter rose and refilled his wife's glass.

'She having supper with us?'

'Says she'll have a pizza, 'cos Maria's doing liver-and-bacon. Get a bit of iron in you, girl, I thought. After Julia's holy meatlessness.' He gave her a fond look with the second drink, and she smiled a little, tilting her smooth glossy head back to look up at the lean patrician figure with its shock of white hair. Oh, yes, she had chosen well. As always. Peter was what she needed. She sipped.

'Sweet. Well, she can come and have pudding with us.'

'She will. It's cassata. Mine, not Maria's. I love that new Gelato machine.'

Peter liked being what his friends mockingly called a house-husband. Some of them, particularly those former naval colleagues who had spent most of their Service life steering desks, marvelled loudly at his willingness to throw off the excitements of command and control and live a largely domestic life, enlivened only by brief bouts of 'consultancy' to foreign buyers of seaborne armaments. This, they said to one another, was a man who had commanded four ships and fought in the Falklands War; who had risen to high responsibilities and been spoken of as a potential Second Sea Lord. Then he surprised them all by taking retirement on his fiftieth birthday to play second-fiddle to a powerful wife and look after his two small sons and baby daughter.

'Well,' he would say lightly at the time, 'someone's got to be around. Eden's only six and Damy's four, and Lottie was back at work kicking bankers' arses two days after the baby. It's standard strategy: spot the gap in the line, then bloody fill it.' That was eight years ago: he had shown no signs of changing his mind or pining for the dignities that accrue to a distinguished professional man in his fifties.

'I actually like the kids,' he would say breezily. 'Bloody sight more interesting than anyone in the Admiralty or Northwood, face it. And as it happens I am a hell of a good school-gate mum. Ask anyone. I made a Victoria sponge last week out of Delia Smith, because Damy said real mothers made their own cakes and the latest housekeeper only does gooey gâteaux.'

What he did not articulate was that in truth he had been bored, stunned, depressed and edgy for several years after the Falklands. To fight a naval war, however small, had been a kind of privilege. Coming out of a blue sky after years of peacekeeping and flag-waving, the chance to fire and risk fire in a sea-battle had reconnected a demoralized generation of sailors to the history of their hard trade and the sufferings of their ancestors. It was never going to be easy, after that, to return to a shrinking Navy and a series of interfering governments; to spend long afternoons debating tomfool motions about gay rights or how to administer humiliating financial curbs on fuel use.

He could have searched for another job, and there were a few jobs still in the Navy that might have tempted him; but when he looked dispassionately at the state of his home he saw what had to be done. Lottie was paid two million pounds that year, as she transferred to the new bank; it was tied up in a series of complex bonuses and share options he hardly understood. She was preoccupied with her fund management job, by day and (it seemed to him) also by night. It left her very little energy for the rest. A late-life husband, he adored Lottie without any illusions about her faults, and wanted to make her life easier and their children safer.

So it seemed to the Admiral – for such he was, newly promoted to yet another noisome desk job – the most natural thing in the world to renounce one Service for another and use whatever gifts he had to be a proper father and keep a rein on the various Marias and Astrids and Mollies and Fred-the-Gardeners who seemed necessary to the running of Lottie's homes.

He alone could both watch over his children and maintain domestic standards high enough not to provoke one of his wife's famous bouts of temper. If Lottie was calm and happy, so would the children be. If he was near them, he could pass on what he had learnt from his life, an idea which filled him with a deep satisfaction. He did not miss his colleagues, although recently certain convictions about education, garnered from the village primary school, had led him to correspond and lay charitable plans with kindred spirits about visits to ships, sail-training and the like. He liked to read historical biographies and correspond by email with their authors. He obediently joined Lottie in the Docklands flat when she had a dinner-party, but preferred to stay in their country house and do a little shooting and fishing with country neighbours.

The inevitable shift of power within the marriage bothered him very little either, except over the business of boarding-schools. Eden, a large extrovert fourteen-year-old, was happy enough at Rugby and would have been, the father conceded, dreadfully bored if he'd had to come home every evening of the year and sleep behind the high-security gates of Moarc Park. Damien, however, had loved the local village school and was unhappy to be removed by Lottie's edict to a prep boarding school at eight. He was not much happier at ten. His more thoughtful teachers spoke in termly reports of 'quietness' and 'isolation' and 'difficulty relating to his peers', while the more robust ones said that he 'must make an effort to socialize' and 'needs to contribute more to the school com-munity'. Peter's heart would turn over with pity and shame as he read these reports; he should have fought for his boy.

But Lottie was impatient. 'He needs the company,' she would say. 'And academically it's very good. Far better than scuffling around in the council school, it's so *disorganized*.' She had never had much patience with the smiling, unfashionably rumpled staff of the village school and regarded its end-of-year plays (when she could get there in time) as 'amateurish'. Jocasta was still there but Lottie, it sometimes seemed to her husband, was almost indecently anxious to get her filed away in a boarding school too.

'Well,' she would say when her husband challenged her, 'she ought to be in a feeder prep if she's going to settle into Benenden, and I concentrate better at work when I know they're in a proper system. And boarding's surely better than the tender mercies of all these foreign girls, and the groom, and Maria? Even if you're at home. I mean, they're here for weeks and weeks anyway, great long holidays. And at school they've got friends.'

Not Damien, thought Peter sadly. He and his middle child took long walks in the holidays and played draughts and halma through the evenings. Sometimes he thought – indeed feared – that he was in fact Damien's only confidant. Jocasta seemed happy enough anywhere, the secure baby of the family; he was less worried about her. Now he merely said: 'Well, anyway, Jocasta'll be thrilled you're back early.'

He went off to the kitchen to engage in some progress-chasing of the supper. Lottie sank into her chair and kicked off her London shoes. The drink, bitter and ice-cold, made her shudder and smile. Peter had curled the zest of an organic lemon for her, the way she liked it, and around her the house spread quiet, warm and orderly. Her style, as reported in countless magazine profiles, was New Country: minimal chintz, no frills or pleats, just acres of properly laid parquet floor, fine rugs, pale cream paint, vast wood fires and striking pieces of modern sculpture. She was wordlessly grateful to Peter for keeping it as well as he did: when the boys were small, in the first few years of their marriage, she had struggled in something near panic to keep her life under this kind of control.

For by the time Jocasta was born, her role at DGB International was expanding and advancing at an almost frightening rate, with bonuses and new responsibilities hurled at her weekly; suddenly her unique flair, developed over dull dutiful years in the Reports department at Neptunia, was being recognized and celebrated. But at home the little boys fought and whined, highly paid nannies emoted and made demands and walked out without notice, housekeepers served up indigestible rubbish, and garden staff asked questions about guttering and flowerbeds for which she had absolutely no time.

The job of managing the home was infinitely more arduous to her than the challenges of work, and at times she had almost loathed her children for making this sticky, emotional mess out of what should have been her place of refuge and repose. In those days, her monthly three days at Julia's was the only thing that kept her from – 'chaos' she said to herself, preferring not to specify even to herself precisely what she meant by that word. In some ways, indeed, she was more at home with Julia's sullen daughter than with her own small sons. But even so, her outbursts of rage at husband and children became a harsh, uneasy blight on their lives in a tall, gardenless house in Notting Hill.

So Peter had seen how it was, resigned from the Navy and taken the reins. His regime began by organizing a move to Moare Park and the replacement of Notting Hill by a large, neat, minimalist Docklands flat. Lottie was dumbly grateful for the calming of the domestic blizzard. She did not like to discuss his new status with him, and vaguely pretended to her friends at work that he was older than he was, properly retired, and that anyway his consultancies were wider and more frequent than was the case. Had she examined her own feelings she would have had to admit that actually she slightly despised the idea of a man living off his wife and organizing a house, however young his children.

But none of this was spoken of. Lottie paid immense amounts of money into a housekeeping account which Peter drew on. The only things she arranged and paid for personally were her clothes and their holidays; one of her PAs did the spadework and presented her with neatly typed options and itineraries.

Thus the Vernons' life, by and large, was now well regulated. Jocasta was an easy child, focused on her friendships and her two ponies, and extravagantly fond of the girl groom Kylie who looked after them and drove her to events. The even tenor of life at home – so different from the emotional rollercoaster of high-level fund management – was interrupted only by the periodic return of the boys from school. Lottie always suspected that her performance declined at work during the long, long weeks of summer when Eden was clumping and shouting with his friends and loosing off airguns in the grounds, and Damien was moping round the place with a Walkman clamped to his head, a silent reproach to a world that would never understand him.

During these periods she spent all the time she dared alone in Docklands, and when she did spend fraught summer periods at Moare Park or join the family on some hot luxurious beach, she left more decisions than usual to her ambitious subordinates. The dangerous season was coming up again soon: and the threat of economic recession scraped and rustled always at the edge of her thoughts. The prospect of another distracted trimester very much worried her.

'Hi, Mum,' said her small daughter at her elbow. She jumped. The child loved creeping up on people. 'Hello, possum,' said Lottie vaguely. She called all three children 'possum'. It saved confusion. 'School OK today?'

'It is Saturday, Mum,' said the child with a precision rather like her mother's. 'There-is-no-school. I've been at Ally's. We rode Punchinello.'

'How is she?'

'He! He's a gelding.'

'I meant Ally.'

'Same as usual. When I grow up, can I have a flat in Chelsea with pink fluffy carpets and turquoise fur cushions, and live there with Ally?'

'Perhaps.' Lottie finished her drink.

'I prefer Chelsea to Docklands. Ally says it's a better class of riverbank, and it's got shops. And I think I'll have a baby when I'm about nineteen.'

'Why on earth do that?'

'Get it over with. If you'd had me when you were nineteen, you wouldn't be a tired old mummy now. Your baby would be ever so old already. With a job.'

Lottie yawned. 'Run off and play, possum. Find Daddy.'

'He's talking to Maria about the Gelato Chef. He's invented a new pudding. It's cassata but with other stuff. I told him last night, I don't like baked bloody pears.'

'Don't say bloody.'

'Why not?'

'Go *away*,' Lottie snapped, and Jocasta, trying hard to whistle, sauntered off. She did not remember the days of her mother's real rages, and had no scars. If Damien had been there he would have cringed and flushed; Eden would have clumped and sneered. Jocasta merely wandered away from the source of irritability, to find someone mellower.

Lottie watched her go and thought of her friend's thin pallid Phoebe. Jock wouldn't go that way, she thought. No. Phoebe had been a rootless, confused little brat all her life, with that runaway father and Julia's high thinking and hippie living. She, Lottie, had done better in the end. She had earned all the financial comforts that her children needed, and by clever accident married a man who was prepared to stay home and provide the rest. That other mothers did more, or at least entangled themselves more closely, bothered Lady Vernon very little. Either you had the gift or you hadn't. Jules hadn't had it either, hence Phoebe; but she had never caught herself a Peter, and besides she had stayed poor for far too long.

No: when all things were weighed up Lottie had done pretty damn' well in organizing her life. She drained the last of her drink, tilted her Italian leather chair back luxuriously and wished Peter would hurry back to pour her another.

Julia Morrowack passed a restless evening after Alex left. She went into the garden, shivering in the cold, and stood for a long time among the darkling plants, breathing in their green benevolence. Mienke, observing her from the kitchen window as she crumbled the dried herbs into heaps for the evening drinks, said to Phoebe: 'I think your mother is worrying. Perhaps you should talk to her.'

'What's the point?' said Phoebe. 'She needs to be alone.'

'Nobody needs to be alone when they are sad. Go, see her.'

'Soppy Kraut,' said Phoebe rudely. 'Can't, anyway. I'm going up to Josh, read him a story.'

'I am not German,' said Mienke, stung into rare irritation. 'But yes, go, read your poor child a story. God knows he doesn't get much attention.' She slid the heavy kettle across the top of the stove to the hotplate.

'You cow!' Phoebe was roused from her sullen lethargy, and flung a slap at the Dutch girl's back. Mienke, with a grip of steel, whirled round, caught her thin wrist and held it, eyes flashing.

'I am not a cow, or a German. And somebody has to speak truth to the spoilt children.'

'Josh is not spoilt!'

'No, you are!'

166

'How dare you – I'll tell my mother – she'll sack you!'

'Do as you wish.' Mienke dropped the wrist, leaving Phoebe to rub it aggrievedly, and turned back toward the stove with an air of indifference. 'I am here to learn a healing art from a great lady. Not to be nursemaid to silly girls.'

The door swung open, and Julia walked in on the two glaring young women.

'Don't bicker,' she said. 'Phoebe, I saw you try and hit Mienke. You're too old for that sort of thing.'

'Christ! Mothers!' said Phoebe, and walked out. After an awkward moment Mienke put a tentative hand on her employer's shoulder.

'You OK, Julia?'

'No,' said Julia, sitting heavily down on a kitchen chair. 'That young man Alex has gone. He had a reason to be here, a reason he didn't come clean about when he booked, and he bearded me earlier tonight.'

'What? Is he from the council? An American, surely not?'

'No, no – not environmental health. Nothing like that. We had our surprise inspection only two months ago, anyway. Just before you came.' She smiled, then her face relapsed into gravity. 'No, the young man – Alex – he just knew someone I was close to years ago. He wanted to trace her.'

Mienke's silence was one of her gifts. Julia sat at the table, resting her elbows on it, and continued slowly.

'And I did something which might have been wrong.'

'Just might have been? Or *was* wrong?' asked the Dutch girl gravely.

'Was,' said Julia heavily. 'Yes, it was wrong.'

'Can you put this right?'

'It would,' said Julia, 'actually do more damage if I *did* put it right. I know that sounds mad, but it isn't.'

Mienke glanced at the kettle, which was barely beginning to steam, then sat down herself, opposite Julia, regarding her with big serious eyes.

'You told him a lie, yes?'

'Yes. But it was to protect another lie, which was a necessary one.'

'What can make a lie necessary?'

'If it is to save somebody. If it is to avert great unhappiness.'

'Who can judge such things?'

'Whoever is there, on the spot,' said Julia bleakly, 'has got to judge them, and it's sometimes a spur-of-the-moment decision.'

'Perhaps,' said Mienke, 'that is why we should always tell the truth. It is more simple, I think.'

'You're very young' said Julia. 'But then, so was I.'

'When is this?'

'When the first lie happened.'

The kettle boiled and the Dutch girl rose to make the infusions. 'I think,' she said, 'that it is just better always to tell the truth. Then you are not guarding the secrets of other people and making their decisions for them.'

Julia took her mug and cradled it, her pale face wreathed in the steam.

'I dare say you're right,' she said. 'But it's far too late now, anyway.'

<hr>

17

The plane, gleaming like a silver sword, dropped gently out of a brilliant blue sky. Janis, unbidden, had come to meet him at Logan Airport and stood hopping excitedly beyond the barrier, her bright curls jumping.

'Hey-ee! Was it great? Did you see the Queen? Did you sleep in castles? Did you find your long-lost Uncle Fester? Did you understand a word anybody said to you? Why didn't you take your other week? Johnny's worried you think he's riding you hard.'

Alex, who had been five paces away when this interrogation began, put down his cases and gave her a comradely hug.

'Yes, I saw castles, and it rained, and I am happy to say I have no long-lost British uncles. And I've had enough vacation, and if Johnny wants to be nice he can carry my time over to August.'

'Did you buy Isabelle's wedding present, at least?'

'Shit, I forgot. When is it?'

'Beginning of June. Marty bought her a vibrator with bunny ears but I'm not letting him give it to her.'

'Business OK?'

'Never better. Your Clobber.com's parent company is in ecstasics. They want you to train a coupla guys who are setting up an operation in Edmonton, and to talk to the Australians perhaps.'

'Same situation? Outworkers?'

'Yeah, and the protector program.'

'It doesn't work.' In the cab to the office they talked shop, happy and invigorated. The sight of familiar advertisements, shop-windows and lean, bright New England faces in the street filled Alex with absurd pleasure. Perhaps, he thought, you had to go abroad in order to see how much you liked your own place. A line stole into his head: *What can they know of England, who only England know?* He wondered whether Julia Morrowack had travelled much: arrogant witch!

The memory of her hauteur and contempt still smarted, and was beginning to roll up in his mind with all the other irritants of the past few days: the chilly stares, the averted eyes, the dead animals on the news, the late-night drunks, rain, nylon sheets and rubber-hose showers. Janis was reverting to the subject of his tour.

'Now, tell me where you went? Is Britain really cool? Did you go clubbing? Marty's crazy about some mix guy from Brixton who might be coming here, but only if he can get a visa and it's hard because of drugs . . .'

'No,' said Alex. He grinned, and the sensation of smiling widely again was in itself a relief after the last days. 'I guess I should have gone dancing. Apart from a couple of girls, I kind of mixed with some older people, mostly. I guess that was a mistake.'

Home now, he made no more mistakes. He told Grandad that it was all over, that he had satisfied his curiosity about his mother's country and that this was enough. He gave his technical report on Clobber.com to Johnny, telling him the full story of Doreen's piracy of the company computer and her small son's ingenuity in defeating the EcomGuard security program. Johnny, as he had expected, hooted with laughter and was happy to be complicit. 'And when the kid's sixteen, and I'm the new Bill Gates, we'll headhunt him for the team.' Marty – joining them to examine Alex's record of the child's system for getting round security – was equally charmed, but said sixteen was too late and that he had a good mind to fly over and grab the kid now. 'And I could bring you the mother, which by the sound of it you'd like.'

'No chance. Happily married to a dirt-poor farmer.' Alex laughed, content among colleagues.

In the following months he threw himself into the satisfactions of work, travelled into the Midwest on business and called on his grandfather, and spent a fortnight ironing out bugs in a new brokerage house at the World Trade Center in New York. There he met a smart young woman trader called Maddy, five years his senior, who showed him round the new bars and made him laugh and fully expected him to take her to bed.

It didn't happen. He did not, for the moment, want to be any closer to women; especially a woman whose fashionably gaunt features and dark eyes held an echo of Julia Tainton Morrowack.

He went with the gang to Isabelle's wedding, an immaculate and glossy production managed with the social pages in mind. Isabelle wore inappropriate virginal white with a medieval coronet and scolded him for not having made a properly scholarly investigation of his family history. Her husband, scion of as ancient a line as Boston could produce, grinned at everybody and said 'Ain't she just something?' like any hayseed. Johnny, in an extraordinary vivid pink tuxedo, smiled his most sharklike smile. Marty juggled five shot-glasses, ignoring the bride's tipsy shrieks of alarm. The sun shone. Alex met an old friend from Harvard and made holiday plans.

Together, accompanied by another classmate, they took off in August for the Alberta Rockies, and canoed a hundred and fifty miles down the North Saskatchewan River with a grizzled and taciturn guide. Digging his paddle in the churning rapids, drifting across lakes, sleeping under the stars with a pepper-spray aerosol and a gun at his side, Alex grew ever more content. The troubled spring and the chilly distant island meant ever less to him. Back in the Boston apartment, his father's diary lay gathering a thin film of dust at the back of his desk. Finding the red shawl one day while he was tidying, he had looked at it for a full half-minute before he remembered why he had it. Then, after the slightest of hesitation, he carried it downstairs to put it in the trash. It was, after all, Julia's.

When he got back upstairs – tired, because he had just flown back from Los Angeles – he hesitated again, then went down and retrieved it, because it also represented his dead father's anxiety to keep him warm. He folded it small, brushing off the ash from the can, and pushed it to the back of his least-used drawer. But that was the only moment of sentimentality he allowed himself all summer. The stupid England thing was over: over for good. He would go again, no doubt, on business or as part of a wider tour of Europe. But next time he would not go humbly, nor as a returning exile. He would go as an affluent, demanding American world tourist, and take no shit from any of them.

It was in August, while Alex was whooping and splashing through the ice-cold rapids with his friends, that Doreen Clark closed down the computer one evening and came through to the dining-room where Duncan was struggling with Ministry of Agriculture paperwork. Their eight hundred sheep had been slaughtered the month before, because of suspected contact with a lorry which had previously transported an infected flock. Duncan said little, refused to speak to the reporters on the doorstep, but become paler and more pinched in the face. The flock lay too long unburned, and for weeks the yard and the five acres around the farmhouse seemed to reek of death. The paperwork concerned compensation: he was late in completing it and Doreen had not the heart to nag him.

'Dunk?' she said tentatively. 'You want a cup of tea?'

'Yes. Thanks,' he said. He laid down the pen and put an arm out towards her. 'Give us a cuddle first.' She went to him and stood within his encircling arm, dropping a kiss on the top of his head.

'It's a bugger,' she said. The house around them was quiet, the children asleep. Jamie slept more these days: strangely, the arrival of the new computer and the teaching programmes had made him more physically active, not less, and he now swung around the house and farm on his crutches, chattering about the day's latest discovery. Doreen kept him out of school and had, so far, satisfied the inspectors as to his progress: her battle with the local education authority continued meanwhile. This improvement in their lot to some extent insulated her from the depression that hung around the lifeless farm.

'It's a bugger, but we'll come through it.'

'Yes,' said Duncan. 'I know. It's just the waste. They were good ewes. And the lambs.'

'Don't look back,' said Doreen. He glanced up at her, and his tired eyes smiled.

'OK. So how was your day?'

'Six hours for the company, two in overtime. But there's a bit of a problem with Alex van Hyden's genealogy thing.'

'Your nice American? I thought you finished that ages ago. When you did those trips to London.'

'No. I got hung up. I didn't talk about it because it was the bad time with the slaughtermen.'

He grunted. 'Mmm. So?'

'You know it was the English mother's family we were looking for? Well, I reckoned that since we had the facts off the birth certificate, the thing to look for next was her death certificate.'

He nodded, and yawned slightly. It was part of the marital pact that he listened sometimes to the detail of her work, and pretended it was other than vaguely meaningless to him.

'Only,' continued Doreen, running her hand distractedly through her already wild hair, 'there wasn't one.'

'Prob'ly looking in the wrong year,' suggested Duncan, his eyes wandering back to the Ministry forms on the table. 'Like with that other family, the whatsernames, Gavottes or something?'

'Gavorets. No, that was a wrong year because the grandmother confused two different air raids. Mr van Hyden – Alex – was emphatic that his mother died the same year he was born. Only a few months after he went to America.'

'But it wasn't there?'

'Nope.'

'Buried under another name, maybe?'

'Unlikely, in 1974. Very fussy. Very good record-keeping period, better than now actually. So anyway, just in case, I checked the years before and after. Then I went wider. No Graysons except a very old man in Scotland and a baby the year before. No sign of Moira Charlotte Grayson. I looked in *The Times* deaths page as well. Nothing.'

'So?' Duncan was interested now. 'Are you saying she isn't dead?'

'Could have died abroad. I've been caught that way before now. People going off to Marrakesh or whatever, dying there, no sign of it in the UK records, everyone too stoned.'

'Well, that'll be it then. The father will have got the wrong end of the stick. She'll have gone on the hippie trail and not come back, and then he gets the news and assumes it was in the hospital.'

'Yeah,' said Doreen. 'And I could tell him that. I've got the dates of the parents, and her brother Alexander who died, poor little toad, at only sixteen. And some nice Grayson ancestors, two hundred years nearly. I could give him the lot right now, in a red ribbon. Except for one thing.'

'What?'

'The trouble is – oh, shit, I've been so dreading trying to tell him this that I can hardly even tell you . . .'

'Oh, spit it out, girl!' Duncan's accent became broader, more West Country, when he was impatient.

'Dunk, I went on the magic website. You know the one, ukdata-hyphen-unchained-dotcom. The unofficial cross-index that Somerset House get sniffy about. And after a bit I found a reference, and checked it back by post, and got a copy. And there is a Moira Charlotte Grayson certificate after all.'

He looked at her blankly, unused to such circumlocution in his plain-spoken wife. Doreen paused, looking at him as if he were American Alex and she was about to unmake his world.

'Not a death certificate. A marriage certificate. December nineteen eighty-five. And it has to be the same woman. All the details match exactly.'

He gaped. Despite all his own troubles, the poignancy of

Alex van Hyden's story was still fresh in his memory from the evening they had all spent together round the kitchen table.

'So she was actually still alive – what – eleven years later?'

'Duncan,' said his wife despairingly, 'what I'm telling you is that she's still alive *now*.'

———•◆•———

18

'How'd you know?' asked Duncan. 'About now, I mean?'

'The usual way,' said Doreen a little impatiently. 'The trail goes on. Birth certificates. She's had three children in this marriage, the last one was only in 1995. And then there's this.'

From a folder she was carrying she produced a newspaper, not one normally afforded on the Clarks' frugal domestic budget but a broadsheet, with a second section for features and interviews. 'Look.'

Her husband looked uncomprehendingly at an oblique, artistic black-and-white picture of a sleek commanding wo-man in a tight dark suit, posed unsmiling against a stone portico above the legend QUEEN BEE. Doreen said patiently: 'The marriage certificate was with Rear-Admiral Sir Peter Vernon, KCMG. It made her Lady Vernon. More often known as Lottie Vernon – Charlotte, see? The middle name. She's totally famous, Duncan! I mean, A-list millionaire stuff!'

Duncan stared down at the article. 'You're sure it's her? I mean, you're sure it's his mother? It's not something to make a mistake about, girl—'

'This is August' said Doreen. 'I found out most of this before the end of May. I've spent six weeks worrying about it. I was like you, I thought it was just too fantastic. But I'm sorry, this is what I do: family history is what I'm trained for, and it all hangs together. And if you look at this—'

She turned the page, to a close-up portrait of Lottie Vernon in jeans and a sweater, pictured 'relaxing at her country home, Moare Park' with the tall white-headed Admiral, a couple of handsome boys and a small but modish daughter with a crop-top and a direct stare. Without her city suit and frown Lottie looked younger and more human, which was clearly the intention of the company public relations department which had arranged the photo session. In this picture of her face it was not at all difficult, once you had the clue, to find the slightly rearranged features of Alex van Hyden.

'You know I'm always wary of the Family Face, and all that stuff,' said Doreen. 'But I remember how he looked when he found out what James had done. A sort of sweet little smile, but anxious with it, because his boss was right there in the room. Normally he grins like an American, lots of lovely teeth – but that look was different. Now I look at her and I *know*.'

Lottie, anxious to smile and disliking the photo session, showed exactly the same quirk of the mouth and narrowing of the eyes as her son. Duncan – who had sat opposite Alex at supper and thought him a thoroughly decent young man – could almost have laughed at this eerie resemblance to the tight-faced lady financier. His wife's anxiety, however, trans-mitted itself too powerfully to him for any levity.

'Well, I'll be damned,' he said instead. 'You're right. Bit o' news for him, then? Not to mention her . . .'

'I don't know how to tell him,' Doreen said, tears springing to her eyes. 'He won't believe me, it's too fantastic. As for Lady Vernon, I think I ought to go and see her first.'

'Why?'

'She's got three more children, for God's sake. Her husband might not even know she ever gave away a baby. This kind of thing is dynamite. I can't blow a family to pieces.'

'It's the truth, though,' said Duncan, unconsciously echoing Mienke Haarlandt's advice to Julia. 'Once you know a solid truth, you might as well tell it. Saves confusion. Let them sort out the emotional stuff themselves. It's not your problem. You did a job, you did it very well. Send him the documents. Leave it to them.'

'She lives – well, her country house anyway – not that far the other side of the Dartford tunnel,' said Doreen slowly. 'I've a good mind to go there.'

'Before you tell him?'

'Yes. I owe it to her as a woman.'

'That,' said Duncan flatly, 'is a very, very bad idea and a very bad reason. Keep out of it. You'll make things worse. Just send him the papers. Like you did when you found out about that man being hanged.'

'That,' riposted Doreen in the same combative tone, 'was a hundred and ten years ago. People get over having stuff like that in the family, in a century. They think it's quite dashing. A mother and son is different. It's all raw.' She glanced at the ceiling, above which her James and Adam slept safe and rosy in their bunk beds. 'I can't tell him till I've warned her.'

Duncan gestured worriedly at the page before them.

'Doreen love, she earns, what, a million a year? She's got everything at her feet. She's hard as diamonds. She'll cut you off at the knees.' He looked with aching fondness and pity at his wife's dishevelled red hair with its streaks of early grey, at her darned jumper and the bags at the knees of her comfortable trousers. The woman in the newspaper terrified him.

'I have to go,' said Doreen miserably. 'Till yesterday I was managing to persuade myself I didn't. But I do. And that's that. So please, I need the car one day this week.'

'Well, make an appointment,' said Duncan. He shuddered. 'Or you'll have burned up all that bloody petrol for nothing.'

In the shining dove-grey city tower where DGB Investments roosted, Murray Harman and Adeline Cook were facing the wrath of their superior.

'It's fucking *madness*, what you did,' said Lottie Vernon, with cold fury. 'And it'll all come back to me, not you. Christ almighty! Are you morons or what?'

'Entomagic is a cutting-edge company,' said Murray sullenly. 'And in the general fund balance it's more than counterbalanced by the blue-chips.'

'Blue-chips! Oh, yeah, like Marks and Marconi?'

'We were never long in Marconi!'

'We are in BT and Marks. Honestly, I go away for a few days, and for the second time this year you go over your agreed quota and sink – she glanced down at the millions on the page in front of her – 'twelve point five per cent of one of our key client funds into a load of sodding insects. Which have been going down every day since.'

'It's the cutting edge of gene therapies,' said Adeline. 'There's going to be the most incredible killing on this. The human genome was only the start. Species diversity . . .'

'And you're a top scientist, suddenly?' snarled Lottie.

'I read the trade press,' said the girl sullenly.

She was twenty-four, and ambitious, and already earned eight times the national average wage. Lottie, whose young working life had been a bleaker business, often found that these kids set her teeth on edge. What could they know, these exhibitionist Docklands creatures of the wine-bar and the coke-spoon? For years – ailing and depressed and all but friendless, with the equally beleaguered Julia as her sole confidante in their icy flat in Palmer's Green – Lottie had commuted to work on a secretarial grade in the library of Neptunia Asset Management, the only job offered to her through a kind but brisk rehabilitation charity, TurnAgain. It was an initiative of the time: City finance houses reaching out to young offenders and recovering junkies. Lottie was one of its few successes.

Bored, afraid of relapse, loveless and stalked by shame and guilt about a dead baby, she had sunk herself in the secure neon-lit world of the company library to work long hours without overtime. It was warmer at the office than at the Palmer's Green flat, and Julia worked evening shifts as a waitress. Gradually Lottie's superior, a lazy old man called Chalmers, spotted that she had both native intelligence and – more rare – a certain quality of contemptuous arrogance which enabled her to make fast, sharp précis of company reports. He delegated to her; bored with her filing tasks, she enjoyed the job of cutting through the flannel of corporate brochures and reporting mercilessly in her small, neat handwriting on the real prospects of companies. She made, in the process, many a good phrase which lived on in City legend.

One day, Neptunia's Chief Executive barked with laughter over a particularly vicious observation about a leading hotel chain, and asked his assistant what on earth old Chalmers was on these days? When he discovered the ghost-writer he promoted her. By the time Neptunia sold itself to DBG, Lottie was not only worth a spectacular transfer fee but wielded sufficient clout to arrange the permanent loss of her Personnel record, with its reference to TurnAgain and her status as a rehabilitated person. Even in the late 'eighties any suggestion of a drug habit, however extinct, would have been bad news for the career of a major fund manager.

After all that, she could be forgiven a certain irritation at the spectacle of Murray and Adeline: overpaid, overconfident and openly recreational cocaine users. She tolerated them only because they were reasonably effective at their jobs and brought in useful gossip from the wine-bars, and because it was the done thing for fund managers nearing fifty to surround themselves with fashionably edgy young acolytes. But now, despite her specific warnings before the last visit to Julia's, the little clowns had used their few days of being in charge to plunge her most vulnerable fund even deeper into dangerous new territory. She looked again at the figures, then slammed the hard folder down on the desk.

'And now I have to pay the price for your leafing through the *New Scientist* in the jacuzzi. Get real, Adeline! Or get the hell out. As for you . . .' She turned to Murray. 'If the slide in Entomagic doesn't end today, get out of the fucking insects by Friday. I mean it.' She cut off his protests. 'We'll lose, but we won't lose the whole twelve and a half per cent.'

'You'll close the company down!' said Murray. 'We're the majority shareholder! At the very least it'll have to get a new CEO—'

'So?'

'It's not fair!'

'I am not a charity. There are clear distinctions between DGB and the Salvation Army. Check out the logos if you don't believe me. Now piss off and do what you're told for a change.'

The young pair left, their slim backs eloquent of contempt and fury. Lottie clutched the arms of her chair, bent her head forward and then shook it violently, and took a deep, steadying breath as she looked up. It might not be as bad as it seemed. The silly little tart might even be right about insect genomes.

But Lottie did not like the look of the FTSE index, nor particularly trust the Chancellor. She would take no risks until things steadied. The general election had not brought the resurgence of confidence she had bargained on. The country was nervous, the City fretful. Her instinct was to get back into retail stocks, on the likelihood of a consumer boom as the year ended. Let the kids ride untried broncos for fun: as far as she was concerned this was a time to edge back to the thoroughbreds.

The metapor made her think of Alan Mackinnon touting his racehorses at the kitchen table near Iver, and she almost smiled. Fat little creep, but amusing. Somehow, everything at Julia's was amusing and forgivable, even Phoebe. It was work that was hard; work, and home life in the dreaded school holidays.

The intercom on her desk buzzed discreetly.

'Yup?' she said to her cool, efficient PA. 'What?'

'A lady called Clark. Doreen Clark. Do you know her?'

'Nope. What's it about?'

'She says it's personal. Domestic, she said. Wants to see you at Moare Park for a few minutes.'

'If it's domestic, it's for Peter. Or Maria. Give her the tradesmen's number. Probably a nanny. I think Peter said ours was going back to New Zealand.'

'She did say she needed to speak to you personally.'

'They all do. Get rid of her.'

At the other end of the line, standing anxiously in her dark hallway after half an hour of struggling to get through layers of defensive professional rudeness, Doreen Clark received a cool refusal.

'At least tell me when she's home?' she essayed.

'We can't possibly divulge personal information,' said the voice at DGB.

'It's about one of her children,' said Doreen.

The secretary pushed a button on the console which automatically traced and recorded the remainder of the call. Ever since two frightening cases in the USA, Lottie Vernon had been given the company's Security One protection against possible kidnap threats to her children. This woman did not sound like a felon, but you never knew.

'Are you from one of the schools?'

'No,' said Doreen reluctantly.

'What is your connection with the family?'

'I can't say. I have to explain it to Lady Vernon.'

'In this case it is probably best to contact Sir Peter Vernon, on the number I gave you. He is resident at home full-time and manages the day-to-day detail of the children's lives.'

'Will Lady Vernon be home at the weekend?'

'Why,' asked the PA with thinning patience, 'don't you write her a letter? It's quite impossible for her to speak to you.'

Doreen put the phone down, and found that she was shivering. On the PA's desk, the buzzer sounded impatiently for the second time.

'Did you get rid of that call? Good. OK, come in here and take a memo to Bob Chediston.'

The DGB day went on, deals and calculations and illusions of profit shimmering through the heat-haze. Back on the farm, Doreen looked at the clock and called to Jamie to leave the computer and come to the car. It was their day for the physiotherapist. She took a pad and pencil and all the time she sat in the waiting-room, she scribbled drafts of a letter to Lady Vernon.

Dear Lady Vernon, I have some news which may shock . . .
Dear Lady Vernon, forgive me for intruding but . . .

Dear Lady Vernon, your son Alexander has asked me . . .
Dear Madam, I think you should know . . .

None of them sounded right, and the worst of them had a positively stalkerish ring of lunacy. Face to face she would know what to say, but it was clear that she never would get face to face. Stalemate. When Duncan met her that evening and asked which day she would be taking the car, she sadly replied, 'I won't. Can't get near her.'

'You're giving up?'

'Secretary told me to write a letter.'

'So, do that.'

'Can't. I couldn't read a letter like that without freaking out. I mean, imagine it!'

'She's got her husband there. Send it to Moare Park.'

'Suppose he doesn't know? Suppose he opens her letters?'

Duncan lost patience. 'Oh, for God's sake. Then just send Alex the papers and have done with it. It's his problem.'

'You're right,' said Doreen. Her sympathy for the aloof Lady Vernon had, in any case, lost its edge during the morning's rebuff. That night, she began assembling the file and a covering letter to Alexander van Hyden.

19

———◆•◆•◆———

It was a wet, tepid summer in Buckinghamshire; good for the herb-garden, thought Julia, but bad for the clients' morale. Footpaths reopened, and her regular health-seekers returned to their régime of infusions, meditation and rural rambling. Alan Mackinnon was absent for many weeks, so long indeed that she began to wonder whether the drink had finally killed him. Professionally, this gave Julia some cause for regret; personally, none at all.

Then he reappeared in July spry and malicious as ever, and made what was generally regarded as a quite unforgivable pass at Phoebe. What made it even less forgivable was that Phoebe, even more bored and discontented than usual, accepted his advances and vanished with him to a country hotel near Newmarket for the weekend. The weekend had stretched to a month, and the only postcard from the errant pair bore a picture of Deauville racecourse. Josh, left with his grandmother, showed little concern and appeared not to miss educational or maternal attentions at all. The school term had three weeks to run, but he informed his grandmother that it had already ended and began to lead a farouche outdoor life around the garden and the fields, coming in for meals and from time to time walking to the village shop to buy himself baked beans, his new passion.

But Mienke was shocked right out of her normal composure.

'This is strange,' she said. 'I do not understand English people very well, I think. Dutch people do not conduct their lives in this way. Particularly because I think she is not in love with him, at all.'

'She had better not be,' said Julia grimly. 'Horrid little man!'

'Perhaps,' said Mienke, frowning with the effort of grasping a charitable straw, 'he makes her laugh and is kind. She is lonely for a man sometimes, I think.'

'Not much,' said Josh, strolling in to the kitchen and swiping a carrot from the worktop. 'She had lots of men to stay with us at the flat when we were in London.' He crunched his carrot with something disturbingly close to a leer on his fresh little face.

Julia, who was rolling some wholemeal pastry, brought a sharp end to the discussion with a rap of the heavy wooden pin. 'Enough!' she said. 'Josh, I think Lottie's wanting someone to play chess with her.'

Lottie Vernon was back. She had missed her late-June visit, which gave Julia considerable anxiety. It seemed stupid at times, but even after twenty-five years she had nightmares in which her friend relapsed into the twilight world they had once shared. It was absurd, she knew it: the years had brought success, fame, love, and family; plastic surgeons had eradicated the track-marks from Lottie's arms and the old familiar nickname of 'Shark' had followed the childhood 'Moira' into oblivion. The treatment centre where they had both undergone their change advised clients to go through a symbolic discarding of old identities. But still Julia worried.

Ironically, she never gave a moment's thought to the possibility that she herself might go back on the needle; the very idea had seemed impossible for two decades at least. But she could never accept that Lottie was safe. Too much of Julia's life, too many of her lies, had been spent protecting her. The instinct was ingrained.

'I don't want to play chess,' said Josh. 'And Lottie doesn't want to either. She's reading the pink newspaper.'

Julia pursed her lips. Everything was just too much, these days: Phoebe absconding, sweet calming Mienke nearly at the end of her stay, Dave replaced by a gormless Australian girl with a diploma in horticulture but a heavy tread on the poor garden. There had been a particularly demanding run of new clients, and Lottie was preoccupied with the Stock Market and – Julia suspected – was forgetting to take her milk-thistle extract regularly.

'Your liver is never going to be strong,' Julia would say. 'You've got to keep up the boosters.'

'I do, usually,' said Lottie vaguely. 'But Jules, you've got to understand that my work is really stressful this year. We really are on the edge of a global recession. I watched the last one from the sidelines, but this time I'm in the firing-line. I have to make some very tough judgements.'

She had been in the newspapers the week before, forcing the resignation of the underperforming Chief Executive of a stores chain with the cool, contemptuous threat of withdrawing one of her funds' huge investments. 'Killer Queen' said the headlines, and the stories gleefully quoted her bitchy remark about headhunters not needing to bother with this particular man unless they were planning a remake of *Dumb and Dumber*. Looking at the fine lines of tension around Lottie's eyes now, and the faint liverish yellowing of her skin, Julia writhed with inward anxiety.

All this meant that it was not yet the time to tell her about Alex. After long wrestling with her conscience, Julia had promised herself to do it in June; but June had come and gone without a visit, and now such an air of crisis hung around her friend that she dared not add to it. She had no confidantes she could entrust with this terrible piece of dynamite, so a ceaseless, fruitless loop of conversation ran round inside her head.

Tell her! She has a right to know.

If she had a right to know, why did you lie in the first place?

I didn't lie. I told her the baby was gone. And he was. Gone to America.

She thought you meant he was dead. You let her think that.

That isn't the same as lying.

Isn't it?

It was the best thing. It made her start again. It made her detox. She needed a shock to turn her round. Like I had in that horrible court.

It was still her baby. You stopped her knowing the truth.

She couldn't have seen the kid again anyway. The Yank would have made sure of that. We didn't know where he lived, even.

The other lies, the ones she'd told to Christian and then Alex, bothered Julia not at all. Men were irresponsible, they scattered their seed, they rotted up women's lives and walked away. They deserved no consideration. Every woman knew that.

She shied away from the awkward circumstance that Christian had in fact resolutely walked towards his responsibility, and that Alex had come looking for his mother's grave and family halfway round the world and twenty-seven years on. The principle, she told herself crossly, still held good. Men should not be considered. Mienke, the gentle, logical and humane daughter of a post-feminist age, would have been very shocked indeed if she could have known the whole of Julia's reasoning in this matter.

★　　★　　★

190

So nobody warned Lottie Vernon at all, and Alex knew the truth before she did. When he breezed into the office, fresh off the 'plane from Edmonton, brown and fit and full of shaggy-bear stories, Janis plumped a pile of letters in front of him with one unopened brown envelope on top.

'It says PERSONAL,' she said. 'So I didn't open it. Probably full of lace panties from your Brit admirers.'

Alex took a moment to work out from the postmark and the round, schoolgirl handwriting what it must be.

'Aw, gee!' he said. 'I forgot she was doing this. It'll be my family tree. We'll all have a good look later.'

'See if you're descended from Robert the Bruce,' said Johnny Parvazzi, who had conceived an unlikely passion for Scottish history after seeing the film *Braveheart*. 'Now there's an IT troubleshooter in the making. I like a man who takes his cue from the patient spider.'

'It's other people's webs that cause the trouble,' said Marty from a laptop which he was balancing on crossed knees in the rocking-chair. 'But sticking an axe in their heads is a neat idea. Come and look at this, Al. Are these people morons, or what?'

The envelope lay forgotten until the end of a busy day. Alex stuffed it in his laptop case and headed for home, his mind on coming jobs. Candoo Solutions had been asked to take on some teaching at Harvard, and Johnny was enquiring tentatively whether he, Alex, might care to travel a bit less and take on a lecturing secondment. 'You'd scare the professors less than Marty.' The holiday had made him wonder a little about his life: both of his Harvard friends were talking about marriage. He had thought more about it himself under their influence, and realized with a faint, comforting warmth under his heart that truly, for the first time in his adult life, he now felt ready to look for that kind of long and steady love.

Not with a brittle New York girl like Maddy, though. Too strident, too demanding. Maybe he should look out for someone more like a younger version of his Grandma Marianna. Times had changed, sure. She'd want a job of her own and might not bake many cookies. But he hoped that this phantom wife of his would not want a butt-breaking, all-consuming, hysterical job like the New York brokers and lawyers and traders in Maddy's world, with their gym habits and shoe addictions and shrill imperious way with men.

One night in the tent, looking out through the mesh at a field of brilliant stars, he had admitted to himself that he was really thinking of Mienke Haarlandt at Iver. *Reverting to type*, he thought wryly. *Going for the Dutchwoman* . . . All the same, he liked to remember her halo of fair wispy hair and innocent goodness, the clear pale blue of her eyes and the soft tanned strength of her body as she bent over the green shoots of spring. He wondered whether she and Yoga Dave were an item, but thought not. He remembered Alan Mackinnon's gossip about her family wealth, and wondered whether it was true and how her girlhood had been spent. If she was a rich kid, it was all to her credit that she worked as a skivvy for Julia.

Then, remembering Mackinnon, it occurred to him for the first time to wonder what happened to his second bet. What was the horse called? *Dutch Courage!* He smiled. What a curse it was to have ancestors! Without that foolish omen he would never have taken the second bet. Or, perhaps, thought twice about Mienke. A man, he decided, ought to spring directly from the soil like the guy in the Greek myth. Antaeus, was it? Anyway, there shouldn't be the mess of ancestors and obligations and soggy parenthood. It led to no good. It had cost him sixteen hundred bucks in that second, presumably useless, wager.

At the apartment he emptied out his cases – for he had not been home after arriving on the early plane – rang for a pizza and casually slit open Doreen's envelope. A thick wad of photocopies and a folded newspaper came out, clipped firmly together; peering into the envelope he saw a single sheet of typing with the farm address on the top. He pulled it out, sat in his chair and began to read.

> *My dear Alex,*
>
> *I am sorry this has taken so long. We are all still feeling very grateful for what you did for us. The difference in Jamie is enormous, and he did so well in the last test which we got from the local authority chap that the school is talking about actually changing their policy and putting in a lift! They need Jamie – League Tables, you see.*

He didn't see, not really, but relaxed into enjoyment of Doreen's distant personality, and satisfaction at having helped the tough, crippled, bracingly cross little Jamie on his way. So the second paragraph hit him like a sledgehammer.

> *But to the point. I hope you're sitting down. Alex, I have to tell you that your father was perhaps misled. Your mother, Moira Charlotte Grayson, didn't die in 1974. She lived on. She's still alive and lives about fifty miles from here. She's married, to an Admiral, she has three other children including one who's only six, and she's a huge success and actually quite famous. I enclose the newspaper cutting which says it all.*

His hands shook uncontrollably. This was more shocking than the night he had spent with his father's diary; but then he had had Grandad snoring in the next room, a symbol of continuity and stability. Now he had nothing and nobody. The little room under the eaves began to spin, and he thought he would pass out.

An absurd thought ran through his head: *Thank God I didn't open it in the office.* Yet at the same time he longed for Janis, Marty, anybody. He had a mother living: he had three half-siblings and, for God's sake, a British Admiral for a stepfather. It did not occur to him to doubt Doreen. She had been slow, therefore thorough, and she was trained for this kind of thing. Besides, he thought, it had always been rather too pat – his mother dying just as he left, ending the story neatly. Even junkies didn't die so easily. Not always.

His eyes were swimming, and he blinked as he looked down at the next paragraph.

Her married name now is Charlotte Vernon. She seems not to use the Moira any more. Because of her husband, she is technically known as Lady Vernon. She's a big wheel in the City of London, some kind of investment queen. It's all in the newspaper article.

Alex scrabbled in the bundle of papers, and pulled the newspaper out. There she was: the familiar scornful face and smart suit, posed standing by some stonework hardly less yielding than the woman herself. It took a few moments before he fully understood that not only did he still have a mother, but that he had actually met her.

And rather disliked her. And – suddenly he was swept by the memory of Julia, pinched and tense in the kitchen that morning, listening for the car driving away – he had been extravagantly lied to about this woman, after actually sleeping under the same roof and sharing a meal table with her.

Pocahontas knew, the bitch! The two of them had conspired to keep the truth from him, not giving a toss about the fact that he had come humbly across the world to find traces of his genetic inheritance. He was an interloper, a bastard, a poor Colonial jerk they couldn't be bothered with. *Just, for God's sake, move on*, Julia had said.

He skimmed through the other papers, following Doreen's trail without difficulty. A horrid fascination drew him to the photocopied birth certificates of his half-brothers and sister, and to their photograph in the newspaper. Eden. Damien. Jocasta. Yeah, right!

Then he stood up, bundled it all together, and went across to the telephone. Employees of Candoo Solutions were well in the habit of ringing one another at home in the evenings.

'Janis? Something's up. I need to go back to England. Soon as possible. Can you fix it?'

———◆◆◆———

20

Johnny was concerned enough to drive him personally to Logan Airport. Janis had rung the night before, worried about their colleague's uncharacteristically shrill and vehement tone. The boss, standing in his sleek apartment with the towel still round his neck from the gym, had logged on to the company work schedule, methodically replaced Alex, sent out emails about subsequent delays and rung Janis back to tell her that he would personally pick up the errant employee at 8.30. He was outside the door at 8.25 in his neat yellow two-seater.

'You didn't have to do this,' grumbled Alex, who had been expecting a cab. He was pale, with dark rings under his eyes, his holiday tan of the day before almost unnoticeable amid the signs of strain. 'It's not your job.'

'Sure it is' said Johnny Parvazzi, 'if it gives me an hour to find out what the hell's going on. Janis thinks you've flipped. You came home from England a coupla months back, you were great, never seen you so cool. Yesterday you tell us you just had a great vacation. Now suddenly you're on some kind of elastic band to London.'

'OK,' said Alex. 'I'll tell you.' There would be, he had decided in the night, no more secrets of any kind in his life. He was going to begin telling everyone – well, anyone who showed the slightest interest – about his father's murder, about his junkie mother who didn't care enough to keep off drugs while she was pregnant, about the lies Julia told and the put-downs she delivered. Anyone could know everything. He was not going to be secretive and sneaky like a Brit, but open and straight like an American. He took a deep breath.

'You know how I had an English mother?'

'Yeah, you said,' said Johnny, cautiously easing into the flow of morning traffic. 'You were going to find some roots and stuff. You told us.'

'You might not know she was a junkie, who died on the needle?'

'Uh – Isabelle used to go on about it,' said Johnny apologetically. 'You know how it is. We reckoned you didn't like talking about it too much. I'm a bit the same. My dad drank. It's not something you tell people first-off.'

'Well, the point is she didn't die,' said Alex flatly. 'I found out last night. In a letter. She's alive.'

'Hey . . . wow!' Johnny made cautiously approving noises, and pretended to concentrate on a truck which was edging across the freeway ahead. 'I can see why you're all shook up!'

'To put it mildly,' said Alex. He was silent. Outside the car, the Boston waterfront glittered in the summer sunshine, and small sails darted to and fro off the club quay. Johnny turned right, and murmured encouragingly: 'Helluva shock.'

'Yup. She's alive. And she's not a junkie now, she's a banker or something. Bigshot. Millionaire. Titled lady.' Alex took a deep shuddering breath. 'And, Johnny, I actually *met* her, at the herb place I told you about.'

'The Addams family?'

'Yup. She's well up there with Fester and Morticia and goddamn Lady Macbeth. I went there because I knew that the herb woman had actually known my mother years back . . . it's a long story. But they all lied to me. The Morrowack broad

198

knew the whole story, and went on lying. Johnny, they are such *bitches!*'

'Hey, whoa – how'd you know all this?'

Staring out of the car window, head turned away from his friend, Alex told Johnny about Doreen Clark and her researches. 'She's good. I trust her. And it just explains everything about why the Morrowack woman was so goddamn' rude, and wanted me off the place as fast as possible. I can see her face now, listening to Lady Vernon's car on the drive! She was stalling for time!' The memory almost overwhelmed him again, then he recovered and blundered on with his new universal frankness. 'And, Johnny, I even told her some stuff I've never, ever told you or Marty or Janis. I told her about how my uncle Al killed my dad, after Vietnam, in some stupid drunk quarrel. I thought it would make her sorry for me, I suppose. What an idiot. She made a fool out of me.'

There was a silence. The morning traffic was thickening around them, and the car slowed to a halt. Johnny ached with pity for his friend. He had known there was something about the death of Alex's father, just by the gaps in what his friend said. But not this.

'Do you think,' he said hesitantly as the car began to move, 'that maybe your – um – mom also guessed who you were? I mean, the same surname and all that . . .'

'No,' said Alex reluctantly. 'I thought about that half the night. But of course they mostly use first names in that place. I only knew Lady Vernon's full name because of this creepy little scuttlebutt who was giving me all the biographies. She didn't pay much attention to me. I was just a Yank called Alex.'

'Well, maybe she'll be glad, hey? Do you think this Morrowack woman told her, after you'd gone?'

'Dunno,' said Alex. He had wondered about this too, in the sleepless night. 'I sort of don't think so. I reckon it's Julia's favourite power trip, keeping personal information from its rightful owners. Witch!'

'So you're going to go and tell your mother yourself?'

'Yeah,' said Alex.

'Well, that's good.'

Alex laughed, a sour unhappy sound. 'Don't go romantic on me, Parvazzi,' he said. 'She won't be pleased. Jeez, if you could see her, cold as ice, real rich bitch.' Johnny listened carefully for evidence that his friend was blustering to disguise a small simple private hope. He thought he found that evidence, but kept quiet. The hope was so small, so simple, that he could not bear to contemplate the moment of its quenching.

They were in the airport tunnel now, out of the summer glare, their faces lit intermittently by the pale lights on its ribs.

'Alex,' said Johnny seriously after a while, 'do you think you ought to do this all on your own? Shall I come along, or Marty, or Janis?'

Alex turned to look with gratitude at his friend's sharp dark Italian profile.

'No,' he said. 'It's OK. I have to do this on my own. Then it's all really over, and I can get on with my life.'

'We're all here,' said Johnny. 'At the end of the phone. Call us, big guy. Please.' Then, in a gruff rush of sentiment: 'I hope it comes good for you. I think any mom would be pretty damn' pleased to own you. Mine would swap you for me, any day.'

Alan Mackinnon stretched luxuriously on a plastic string lounger and glanced across at the pale, thin body of the girl beside him.

'OK, Phoebs?' he said. 'Want to come up and play black-jack?'

'I'm sick of gambling,' she grumbled. 'You are obsessed.'

'Ah, come on, you love it. And you're not sick of spending the winnings,' said Alan. 'For a scruffbag, you're bloody expensive to keep.'

'I want to go home,' said Phoebe. 'I ought to see Josh.'

'He's fine! He likes it in the country. Hayfields and stuff. He'd hate Deauville.'

'There's a beach!' She gestured towards the bright segmented umbrellas and the elegantly perambulating and heavily tanned French holidaymakers beyond the hotel fence.

'Nah, he's better off with Julia. Lots of healthy herbal drinks.' Alan sipped his Tom Collins, as debonairly as was possible for a man of his stoutness.

'You're going to die of drink unless you knock it off,' said Phoebe rudely. 'Anyway, I'm going home.'

'The end of the affair?' said Alan, rolling his eyes heavenward in parodic despair.

'Might be.'

She sounded sullen, defensive, not like the girl he had spent the past weeks with. He put down the drink and rolled on his side, wedging the towel under his ear, to look at her in comfort. Her pretty, sulky mouth was set into stubbornness and her eyes were distant.

Alan was, in fact, surprised and even mildly shocked at how long it had taken the young mother to insist on returning to her son. Since their joint defection he had made no conditions, enforced no demands. They slept together without overmuch passion, chatted amiably enough, giggled a lot, and kept company in the casinos and the racetracks. Phoebe had developed a taste for gambling faster than he'd expected;

women rarely shared his excitement, but she lit up and blazed with real glee at a lucky number, a leading horse, a near miss or a triumph.

'It's been fun,' he said lightly. 'You've brought me luck.'

Phoebe relaxed visibly in her chair. 'So you don't mind?' she said tentatively. 'I mean, me going home?'

'Dear Phoebe,' said Alan, yawning deliberately, 'we have had a good time. We will have other good times. When I have a particularly fine race meeting coming up, or a windfall brings me to an agreeable spot like this for a while, I shall call your number and Julia shall mind your brat.'

He sat up, and shook out his towel, continuing dreamily, 'I rather hope that one day we will do Vegas together. You would adore it. One can lean over and play fruit machines in between the *faîtes-vos-jeux*. Divine. In between times, you are you and I am I. End of story. OK?'

'OK,' said Phoebe. 'Hey, you're cool, for an old guy.'

'I have never understood,' said Alan loftily, smoothing the few spare hairs over his bald patch, 'why ordinary people make such a bloody song and dance about their so-called relationships. Ownership and duty are not concepts which harmonize, in my view, with affairs of the heart.'

Phoebe jumped up and raced towards the blue hotel pool by which they had been lying. There was a vast splash, which made two dozing French sunbathers sit up with elegant curses. When she emerged, vivid and dripping, she said to him in a lighter tone than he had heard all day: 'I've been feeling guilty about leaving Josh so long, you know. I'm not a Monster Mother. I just had to get a bit of life or I'd have topped myself or gone back on crack. But I do have a conscience. You can't grow up with Mum and not develop a conscience. *You* don't seem to have that problem *at all*, Fatty. Probably can't even spell it.'

'Oh, but I do,' said Alan. 'Where matters of sportsman's honour are concerned, I have the tenderest conscience imaginable. I am still fretting about our friend the vanishing Yank. Elmer, or whatever his name was.'

'Alex,' said Phoebe, who was standing over him, dripping insouciantly into his drink. 'Why?'

'Because I put a pony on a horse for him and won him a grand. Then I put the grand on Dutch Courage and won him ten K. And I never gave it to him.'

'And that's honourable?'

'He was gone,' said Alan plaintively. 'I didn't get the results till after supper, because Julia was on the phone for hours, and by the time I'd found out and had a little liquid celebration, he was gone. Haven't got his address. Asked Julia, and she bit my head off and said she didn't have it either. I reckon he did a moonlight flit. Even so, I owe him money and it troubles my sensitive soul.'

He struck an attitude of theatrical anguish, looking up at her with brown, untrustworthy spaniel eyes. Phoebe grinned.

'And you really want to pay it? It would make you happy?'

'Happy as only an honest man can be. But, alas—'

'OK,' interrupted Phoebe. 'One minute!'

She loped off into the hotel, her bikini pants so low at the back that he could look with affection on an inch of rear cleavage. As she cavalierly ignored the signs requesting patrons not to cross the marble foyer *en tenue de plage*, Alan lay back and contemplated the past weeks and their meaning, if any.

Julia would be, he decided, furious with them both. This was a problem: he had an almost superstitious reverence for his sessions at Iver, and had only missed the last one because Phoebe took the precaution of pinching some of his necessary milk-thistle infusion from her mother's store cupboard. Josh's attitude could only be guessed at. But although it was plain that peace must be made with Julia for the sake of his health, something about this skinny headlong brat appealed to him. He really did not want to lose her entirely to a bout of maternal conscience.

He wondered for a while whether he could stand to have the child trailing around with them, and reluctantly admitted that it was a possibility. He would not – perish the thought – offer to marry Phoebe. She would take off with a boy her own age eventually, as was only natural, and he had no intention of supporting her when that happened. But if he made it clear to Julia that his intentions were – hah! – *fairly* honourable . . .

Phoebe was back, with a small piece of paper; or rather six or seven small pieces stuck together with Sellotape, like an untidily done jigsaw.

'I picked this up off Mum's study floor, the night he went,' she said. 'I was looking for some money – well, never mind that,' she said hastily, blushing. 'Looks like she tore up his bill. I thought I'd grab it because I rather fancied him, thought I might look him up if Josh and I ever got to America. But it's got name, address, phone and email. So you can pay him.'

Her grin was malicious. Alan sat up and stared at the piece of paper.

'Bugger,' he said. 'So I can. We'd better get across to the casino then, my darling. Tonight's the night we win the rest of it back.'

———◆◆◆———

21

'I wish we could *know*,' said Doreen Clark for the twentieth time. 'I don't even know whether he got the letter.'

'Probably on holiday. Give it time,' said Duncan. He was almost as curious as she: time hung heavy on his hands with no sheep to tend. Nonetheless he felt it his duty to talk down her anxiety. For two weeks now she had jumped at the phone, run for the post and been so easily distracted from her Clobber.com work that official reprimands arrived every other day by email.

'Why not email him?' he said suddenly. 'Just to check it arrived?'

'I can't,' said Doreen. 'Suppose it hadn't?'

'Maybe he's just thinking about what to do. He can't have got in touch with her: it would have been all over the papers if Lottie Vernon had suddenly got a new-found son. Like when that Cabinet minister got traced by her long-lost baby.'

'Lady Vernon was in the *Telegraph* yesterday. I saw it at Miranda's, when I was picking up the boys. Apparently her funds are wobbling and one of the clients is kicking up.'

'Maybe – oh, I don't know. Look, forget it. We'll go mad, wondering.'

Doreen sighed, and went back to her work. Duncan wandered out to look at his desolate sheep-pens and dream about the day he could begin again. For a little while, Doreen had considered urging him to give up the tenancy and the heartbreak of farming and strike out afresh, looking for a regular job. He guessed this, and was grateful for her silence. He did not want an argument: he would begin again, and it would be different. Organic, perhaps. Rare breeds. A visitor attraction. He dreamed.

Minutes later Doreen ran out.

'I put the five o'clock news on,' she said, 'and she's on! It's a really big row now. One of the companies whose pension she's in charge of, or something, threatening to sue for negligence!'

'What – sue Lady Vernon?'

'Well, her company. Apparently it's in the air, there's other cases brewing, but this one's hit the news because the man who's complaining is talking to the papers. I heard him. He called her an overhyped commodity, and said that DGG or BCG or whatever it's called should have supervised her accounts or something.'

Duncan put sheep from his thoughts, and laid a hand on his wife's shoulder. 'Might be nothing,' he said.

'It might,' said Doreen, 'mean that the last thing she wants in her life is a strange American computer geek claiming to be her baby. Look, I think I *ought* to warn her.' Her cheeks flamed, her eyes were bright. 'Duncan, she's a woman even if she is rich. I know how I'd feel.'

Duncan was silent. Then he said, with finality and not without pity:

'Don't get involved. I know it's tempting. It's dramatic. Our lives are limited, you and me. We're back-lane, ragged-arsed farming people with not much future. Better to keep out. Anything we do will only make it worse. Especially for Alex.'

Doreen smiled thinly, then went indoors, sat at her desk and began to compose a letter.

★   ★   ★

Alex missed the news about the lawsuit, because after sleeping fitfully on the plane he arrived dog-tired on a bright London morning and went straight to his old hotel to sleep. He was so weary now that nothing much mattered except clean sheets; yet in the cab to the city he noticed that his feelings had somehow changed. The road in was almost familiar, and something in his mind was curiously pleased to recognize the idiom of the buildings and the freeway signs. England was no longer quite so foreign. London at least – where he had had his eerie, exciting moment on the moonlit Mall – held no bad memories.

Suddenly he remembered Brentwood, the ugly industrial estate, the restrained friendliness of Martin Sayeed and the flirtatious jokes of the office girls. He remembered Doreen, and thought that he must ring her soon and at least thank her for finding out the truth. He wondered whether to call in on young Jamie with some new games and programs, and to set him up an email address so Johnny and Marty could send him the teasing puzzles they devised.

He was still young, and fit from his holiday; his spirits began, in spite of everything, to rise. Hell, he would have it out with Lady V – as he defensively thought of her – and make sure that everybody in this mess knew what it was their business to know, with no lies and tacky secrets left. Then he would turn his back, see his real friends and get on with his life. He told himself sternly that he had not come to beg for acceptance. He had just come to set things straight, and stop that lying bitch Julia from having it all her own way.

He checked in at the Melbourne Court Hotel, glanced up with unexpected affection at its curly white balconies and down at its threadbare carpet, and took his luggage upstairs in the shaking lift. This time it was a far better room: higher, double the size, with a view across the rooftops towards the Palace. Up here, the sticky late-August air was thinner and cooler.

'I'm back,' he said to the roofscape. 'And this time, it's personal.' Then he slept, deep and unmoving, for nearly eighteen hours.

When he awoke, following long habit he plugged in his laptop and checked his messages. There was a 'Good luck' from Johnny and everyone at Candoo, and an extra 'Take care!' from Janis. Grandad, who occasionally visited the Internet café in town, had sent him a rhyme about fishing that he found amusing; Alex remembered with a pang that his grandfather did not even know he was abroad again, and sent a brief explanatory reply.

The others all looked like work: unfamiliar names, presumably clients or their agents. He would leave them for a while. One, however, drew his eye: *alanmk@outsider.demon.co.uk*. He opened it.

If you are who I think you are, and the beauteous Phoebe says you definitely are, I owe you ten grand. Dutch Courage, remember? Uncle Alan has all the best tips. Not everyone does a 40:1, 10:1 accumulator their first time out.

Can't send it. Suppose it wasn't you? If you are ever in UK let's do a face to face. Otherwise I'll message you when I next make it to Vegas. Alan Mackinnon (from Morrowack's Green Soupery)

Alex blinked in amazement. Hell! He keyed up the calculator on the screen and worked out that he had won some sixteen thousand dollars. Was that a good omen, or what? The sun shone in through the high hotel window and the London roofs glittered around him, paved with gold. 'Turn again, Whittington,' he said to himself.

He had left the computer plugged in, out of long habit which always proved disastrously expensive in foreign hotels. A low bleep alerted him to another incoming message, and he clicked on it without thinking. Glancing down, he saw that it was from Doreen, and rather guarded in tone.

Forgive me interrupting your work, but I'm just checking that you got the geneaological material and the letter I sent you. Please let me know straight away if you haven't. Maybe we could speak on the phone. It's OK to ring here when it might be night, I don't sleep heavily at all.

I wanted to tell you that the person you might be interested in, who I mentioned in the letter, is having quite a lot of rather public business trouble just now and that it might not be a good time to be asking questions. Also she's very well defended because of the press.

Sorry to be cryptic but perhaps it's better on the Internet.

He clicked the 'reply' button and wrote:

Thanks, I got the stuff and I'm actually in the UK briefly. I am going to see her. To hell with her troubles, she can give me ten minutes. Love, A.

He was angry again now. Doreen's sugestion that he back off because of the woman's business troubles infuriated him, and because he did not want to be angry with Doreen, he transferred his wrath to Lady Vernon. Who did she think she was?

Doreen, however, was probably right about the defences.

He began to reformulate his plans. The only hope was to catch his mother in a place where she could not evade him or have an underling fob him off. Alex knew enough about the business world to have a fair idea of how the Lottie Vernons of the world guarded their gates against tiresome outsiders, stalkers, aggrieved investors and general nuisances. It had been an extraordinary coincidence to get so close to her at Julia Morrowack's, a chance spoiled by his not realizing who she was. He knew she spent three days a month there, but had no idea when.

From an Internet search of articles he knew that she had a house in the country, called Moare Park, that her office was called DGB and that she kept a flat in Docklands. Neither addresses nor telephone numbers had been yielded by any of his searches: clearly, his mother guarded her privacy.

Moare Park, on the other hand, was plainly visible on an Ordnance Survey map of Surrey. The journalists who named the house in their articles had not thought of that. Or perhaps they had. Even so, he did not know how much time she spent there.

He considered for a while using a detective agency, but decided (indeed, hoped) that most reputable practitioners would be unwilling, in this age of violent revenges and plummeting pensions, to lead an unknown male from the land of the gun to the doorstep of a high-profile fund manager. However, after a little thought he realized that if he used it right his American-ness could play in his favour. Painstaking study of the media during his last visit had informed him that the British only envisaged two main kinds of American. If you were not a gun-crazed NRA freak with Jerry Springer reflexes, you were expected to be an immensely rich and powerful global magnate. There was little scope in the British mind, he thought, for any US citizen who was neither a trailer-trash lardass with a Bible and a gun, nor a George W. Bush crony with a trophy wife, ten billion dollars and a house on Martha's Vineyard.

Fine. He would play the latter. He would be rude and demanding and powerful and invincible. He would get through.

Five minutes later, still sitting on his hotel bed with the phone and waving an imaginary cigar in his other hand to help him project arrogance, he had cut speedily through the layers of DGB and was talking directly to Lottie Vernon's crisp assistant, the same one who had brushed aside Doreen a few weeks earlier.

'*She* called *me*, honey,' he said, in a heavy, patronising tone. 'Yeah, so maybe she doesn't tell you everything. Neither would I. Just put me through. We have a deal riding on this, and I fly out tomorrow. And between you and me, if she doesn't close this one, a little bird tells me that her own sweet ass flies West too. She needs to sign tonight, we made a deal.' It was a passable imitation of Larry Hagman as J.R. Ewing.

The assistant was conciliatory and clearly believed him. Alex smiled.

'I'm afraid' said the voice on the telephone, 'that there may have been some misunderstanding. I'm terribly sorry. She isn't in the office right at the moment. She won't be back till Monday.'

'So, it's Friday. I fly on Saturday. Do yourself a favour, sweetheart' – he pronounced it 'shweetheart' and hoped that he was not overdoing the caricature – 'tell me where I get her, right now?'

'I can't really—'

'Oh, can it, honey. My office here is in your Docklands. Ain't that where she lives? She told me—'

'Yes, but she's got a livery lunch, and then on Fridays she generally goes straight down—'

It was all he needed. She was in the country house, or would be by tonight. He cut roughly across the woman's voice, as if it had nothing to tell him.

'So she's on her ranch? Whyn'tcha say so? I'm visiting tonight with Lord Mackinnon from Deutsch-Invest. He's a neighbour of hers. I'll have him send a bike over with the papers.'

He put down the phone, repelled by his own fluency. Still, he knew where she was. Or would be, tonight.

Fifty miles away, Julia Morrowack was putting a spare skirt and blouse into an ancient and impractically heavy carpet-bag which had belonged to her mother. She then made it even heavier with a supply of small green and brown bottles, and a neatly twisted plastic bag of sachets. Phoebe stood beside her, docile and submissive, with an arm round Josh's shoulders.

'– so feed the guests tonight,' Julia was saying. 'It's all laid out on the programme, on the kitchen wall. And ask Mienke to lead the meditation tomorrow and get them working, and tell anyone who asks that I'll be back before Sunday. Tomorrow, probably. There's something I have to do. OK?'

'OK,' said Phoebe demurely.

'And, sweetheart,' said Julia, with sudden softness, 'I'm glad you're back. And though you mightn't believe it, I'm actually quite glad you had a break.' Her daughter's limbs looked not only browner but a little rounder; her face less sullen and haunted. Josh had been resilient and optimistic during his mother's absence, and made three friends among the village boys with whom he'd played violent Harry Potter broomstick games all summer. She could not be sorry at the turn events had taken. Maybe an older man was best for Phoebe. Even Alan Mackinnon. She suppressed a shudder, and smiled up at her daughter.

'Thanks,' said Phoebe. 'Come on, Joshie, let's go and make the supper. Or shall we wait till the old bat's gone and dial a pizza?'

Julia closed her carpet-bag, put a hand to her dishevelled dark head, and smiled. She was very tired, but peaceful in her heart. An old phrase from school religious instruction floated into her mind: *The truth shall set you free . . .*

———•◆•———

22

A football crashed against the smeared window, sending noisy tremors through the security glass and leaving a fresh fat muddy stain. Inside the big calm room, Lottie flinched and swore. Through the double glazing she heard confused shouts.

'Goal!' shouted Eden Vernon, catching his ball on the rebound.

'Bloody isn't!' yelled his brother, kicking it out of his hand with a Moulin Rouge dexterity. 'You're a cheater! Goal is if it hits the wall!'

'The window's part of the wall, dickhead!'

'It is not!'

Sir Peter came round the side of the house and caught the ball which Eden had kneed from his brother's grasp.

'For Christ's sake, you two! Mum's trying to work!'

'Da-aad!'

'No. Pack it in. Go and ride your bikes. Or do some bloody work, Eden, or I'll have to face another report like the last one. Term starts next week.'

'Which is why we're having some fresh air. You want us to be healthy, don't you?'

'Cut it, Den,' said the younger boy, who read his father's face more easily. 'Let's go and see the puppies.' Peter smiled at him, before his fine features fell back into an air of gravity. He glanced at the muddied window, and the vague hunched shape at the desk behind it. He had not seen his wife so stressed for years; never, indeed, since the day she gave up attempting the classic burden of working motherhood and handed the domestic reins to him. He had tried to plumb the problem earlier, but failed when she grew impatient.

'So it's not money actually lost?' he would say, frowning in his best simple-sailor manner. She did not like him to show overmuch understanding of her world. It was part of their silent pact.

'It's the Stock Market!' she had said. 'It's not my fault, but they're trying to load it on me because that little pillock Brian Ancaster keeps talking to the papers and waving his lawyers at us—'

'Aren't all that sort of funds down, though? What with the markets being low?'

'Yes, but this one – oh, for Christ's sake, Peter!' She had tipped over into petulant exasperation. 'Do I have to justify myself to you now as well? I might as well stay in the sodding office twenty-four-seven!'

So he gave up, with a placatory smile. He had a fair idea, though, of how the land lay. The accusation was that she had let this Mr Ancaster's company's fund slide by leaving its management to inexperienced subordinates, and had meanwhile given the benefit of her brilliance to more favoured pension clients.

It was not, in his view, the kind of case which could ever come to litigation. All investment was a risk, and Lottie could no more offer her clients a guarantee of unbroken success than a defence barrister or a sponsored athlete could have done. But the threat was being made, and in the volatile emotional atmosphere of high finance these things counted. Indeed, this phlegmatic and methodical man of war never failed to be amazed at how hysterical and prone to panic City institutions were. None of the silly buggers, in Peter's view, could have been trusted for ten minutes in charge of a ship. Anyway, if it went bad Lottie could certainly lose her job over it, and any chance of a similar job in the future.

For a moment, balancing the boys' ball idly from hand to hand, he allowed himself the daydream of a new life. Lottie would be at home, getting to know her children and enjoying the money she had made – travelling with him in termtime, perhaps – for even if they stayed in this great mansion, the price of the Docklands flat alone would keep them going for years. And there were investments abroad. Financially, it would be fine. As for their lifestyle, it would in many ways be better than now. Peter's eyes softened, thinking of how things might be if Lottie were not always so tense.

He shook his head and sighed. His wife, he knew, did not share that dream. Ever since she got back, having left a livery company lunch early and unceremoniously, she had been in her study hammering in short sharp bursts at her keyboard and leafing through files dense with numbers. Peter suspected that she was composing a dossier in her own defence. He took her in a tidy tray of tea, and winced with her when the football hit the window for the first time. He did not tell her that Maria, the housekeeper and cook, had left that morning to attend a week-long family funeral in Malta. He did not ring the agency, as Lottie would have told him to, but made a shepherd's pie with his own hands and – in the absence of the current nanny, who was having a week at the Edinburgh Festival – set Kylie the groom to devising a pudding and laying the table. A quiet family evening would soothe Lottie and remind her that there was more to life than work. On a good Friday night, she could even sometimes be persuaded to watch a film on DVD with the children.

At six o'clock Peter remembered that he had run out of vermouth. Lottie liked a drink at six-thirty. He jumped in his grimy little car – for the Admiral had no taste for ostentation – and sped down the driveway, opening the gates with the remote control which lay on the passenger seat beside him, tangled up in a spare bridle of Jocasta's. When he was through the gates, he pushed the 'shut' button and nothing happened. With a shrug and a curse, he drove on. He would be back in twenty minutes, fix it then. Silly affectation anyway, the gates. They had managed without for years, until some hysterical nanny started going on about prowlers.

In the village shop, he saw a back view which puzzled him in its familiarity. The tall, dark figure wore a long drooping cheesecloth skirt and a dark red shawl; he was struggling to find the association when she turned, and he realized it was Julia Morrowack.

'Hello!' he said with a rather forced joviality. 'Never thought to find you here! Come to see us?'

She was blushing; he wondered why, then his eyes travelled to the item in her hand. Sanitary stuff. Women's things. He averted his gaze and continued: 'Lottie never said – but that's splendid, splendid.' He was sounding like an old buffer, a comedy Admiral, Sir Bufton Tufton. It was the panty-pads which had thrown him off balance. Helpless to improve the situation, he turned and studied the row of drinks. No white vermouth. Only red. Hell!

Julia said hesitantly: 'She doesn't know. I'm not staying or anything. I just hoped to catch her for half an hour. Passing through. On business.'

She did not feel well. During the drive round the M25 motorway, Julia had found to her horror that a dampness was growing between her legs. Her monthly inconvenience, as she briskly thought of it, had ended with no trouble whatsoever two years earlier. She had dosed herself with Evening Primrose oil and sailed through the change unruffled. Why was she bleeding now? Was it the power of memory, a physical spring running directly from the grief and lies of distant youth? The last person she wanted to meet was a man, especially a man like Peter, who despite his domesticity was so very much all man.

Her head was spinning, her heart hammering. She wanted to lie down. The shopkeeper was tidying unconcernedly behind the counter, hoping to be able to shut the shop now that the evening commuters had flowed past from the station. Julia swallowed, and put her hand to her head. Peter was staring at her. Saying something.

'The thing is,' he said, 'if you really *are* just passing through on other business, tonight might not be the best moment. She's had a bit of trouble at the office. Nose down in figures.'

'I need –' Julia could not finish her sentence. Peter's face took on a look of real concern.

'Well, come on up anyway. Shepherd's pie. Or are you veggie? We could do –' he frowned – 'An omelette?'

'Do you mind' said Julia faintly, 'if I leave my car here? I'm a bit tired. Could I cadge a lift up the hill?' She did not think that she could drive.

'Of course,' said Peter, relieved to be able at least to keep control of this unscheduled visitor. 'Of course.' He could sit her in the conservatory, and tell Lottie only when she'd had a couple of drinks. Much better.

At some time during the transaction over the vermouth and the settling of Julia in the little car, Alex climbed out of the station taxi and walked unhindered through the open iron gates of Moare Park. By the time Peter got back with Julia and put a new battery into the remote control to close them, Alex was standing concealed in the shrubbery beneath the sloping lawn, looking up in blank amazement at his mother's house.

He had decided, during a thoughtful walk through St James' Park, that he would do it the traditional way: go down by train and arrive by taxi. He could have hired a car again, but to him that smacked of cowardice. He was stepping into a new world and delivering a well-deserved shock. To do so with a car waiting outside to take him away again would make the gesture somehow half-hearted. He still stoutly told himself that the Vernons would not want him there for long, and left all his overnight things at the hotel.

But hell! If they wanted him gone, let them at least have the trouble of ringing a cab to remove him. He would send his away, and arrive on foot. Simple, almost naked. Like a new-born.

The train journey left him quietly appalled: this was the prosperous, famous south of England, and these men and women crushed alongside him in the filthy carriages were presumably its wealth-creators. Yet the carriages smelt, and jolted, and were half an hour late without apology or, apparently, any new effect on the resigned and clearly habitual gloom of the train's passengers.

It made the surprise all the greater when he stepped out of this terrible conveyance into unparallelled rustic beauty: a pub more crookedly pretty than any Disney dream, a row of tidy limewashed cottages, a tangle of green shady trees, chestnut horses in a field. Even the lane was picturesque: a shining, patched and grooved tarmac fringed with soft green verges and shimmering cow-parsley. The commuters appeared not to notice any of this, any more than they had noticed the horribleness of the train. They merely scuttled out and climbed with noisy exclamations of relief into a motley fleet of waiting cars. The women drove themselves; the men were generally being met by a Volvo or Mercedes estate with a smart, slightly careworn woman in the front and a pair of grey-uniformed children or a well-tethered baby in the back.

The station taxi brought him rapidly to the gates of Moare Park, rolling, though he did not know it, right past his stepfather and Julia Morrowack as they emerged from the shop. But then quite unexpectedly Moare Park itself slowed down the headlong return of the native. Within seconds of glimpsing the house Alex became frankly afraid.

Its length, its foursquare golden Queen Anne solidity, its utter peace and symmetry, seemed to crush him. This was no grim castle or crouching Tudor farmhouse, living for the worst: this mansion, although it must have seen wars, did not expect invasions, alarums and excursions and horrid surprises. It was the physical expression of an uninvaded, unconquered countryside. It demanded politeness, dignity, a social harmony which might be superficial but which would always be graceful.

If his mother belonged here . . .

Alex could not finish the thought. If she belonged here, he did not. And he did not belong to her, nor to her people. There was no point pretending that he did.

He forgot that for two days he had been furiously rejoicing that he was not one of this deceitful, decadent tribe, but an honest truth-telling American. He forgot that he was, before anything else, angry with this woman who had cared so little that she had poisoned him with drugs before his birth and ignored him after it. None of this helped him: in this setting his shameful, hateful, inescapable instinct was to cringe.

The physical expression of this inward cringing led him,

despising himself all the way, to duck behind the avenue of trees and take shelter behind a small mound topped with a miniature maze. From there he moved in the lengthening shadows to the shrubbery below the lawn, and stood behind a pillared and domed folly of a summerhouse, frozen in a private sense of exile. Into his fearful silence fell the faint confident yells of his unknown half-brothers and the clatter of a half-sister's pony in the stableyard beyond the house.

Only the arrival of Peter's little car, crunching up the drive, brought Alex to himself. He would give the man a moment or two, then knock on the front door. Beyond that he could not think what he would do. But it would be a start.

———•◆•———

23

Lottie came out of her study into the hall as the door opened. She could wait no longer for her drink. She saw Peter, and beside him Julia. She gaped.

'Jules – what? Is everything all right? Is it Phoebe?'

'No. She's back. She's fine.'

Julia thought, through the haze and the increasing pains in her stomach and chest, how strange it was that when women of their age met, the first anxious question was about children. Even when the children were old enough to abandon their own children and run off to bang Alan Mackinnon in Deauville. She smiled weakly.

'Absolutely fine. The break did her good, I think. She's minding the centre with Mienke tonight, God help us.'

'Why? Oh, well, have a drink anyway. Peter?'

He clinked off to the kitchen with his bottles, glad to be away from them. His shirt was damp: there was a febrile atmosphere tonight. He hated these hot, late-August evenings with thunder in the air. The boys' shouts rang distant across the lawn as they romped with the puppies. They would be half an hour at least. He would leave the women with their drinks, and head off Jocasta from interrupting them.

In the study, where Lottie had drawn her in preference to the big sitting-room, Julia sat down on one of the chic white leather chairs and said: 'Look, I need to talk to you. Alone, without Peter or the children. It's very important.'

'After dinner?'

Julia breathed carefully. The pains, both of them, were worsening now. A fear suddenly struck her that she might not be able to speak later. Harshly she said, 'No. Now.'

Lottie crossed to the door, met Peter in the hall and brought the drinks in, closing the door again behind her. For all her visible perturbation she was still, thought Julia admiringly, every inch the decisive power woman.

'OK. Shoot.'

'Cast your mind back to London, after Cambridge,' said Julia carefully. 'Remember? The squat?'

'You know I don't look back,' said Lottie flatly. 'Ever.' She had been about to sit down, but instead stayed upright, roaming the room with her drink.

'Shark, this time you have to!'

'I don't use that name either. You know the rules. We've both lived by them. Cut off, look forward.'

'Please, please, listen. It's not looking back for the sake of it. You *have* to look behind you, if there's something there!'

The metaphor, disproportionately frightening, hung on the air between them. Lottie even glanced back at the darkening window, as if something might loom through it.

'What?' she said, turning back.

'The child. The baby you had.'

Lottie put her glass down on the desk and stood with her hands on her hips, threatening and defiant.

'I was ill. It was all a disaster. I've done my grieving, years ago. Don't go there. Please, Jule – I am just not up for this.'

'You thought he died,' continued Julia implacably.

'Yeah, you told me—'

'I let you think it. You were ill. It was better.'

Lottie walked to the window and peered out. She could see the boys by the kennel, closing it up; beyond them near the summerhouse moved another figure she could not make out. The gardener, this late? She turned back to her friend.

'What are you telling me?' Again the old nostrums of the clinic came to her: *Face the truth. Ask the questions. Listen to the answers. Then move on.*

'His father took him. Buddy. Christian. I gave evidence against you in court. Remember? Maybe not. You were so, so sick – she looked at her friend and in her eyes were tears of remembered pity – or was it, she wondered, self-pity? Julia shivered and went on. 'He took the baby to America.'

'And it died,' said Lottie flatly.

'No.'

The silence vibrated between them. After a moment Lottie said, in a small hard voice: 'You've just found this out? Is that why you came?'

'I knew all along. Not where he was, or anything. But I never heard he was dead. I made that up. So you'd forget. Not wreck your life chasing around looking for him.'

'So what you're saying is . . .' Lottie steadied herself on the desk, then sat down behind it, hands pressed flat to its surface to prevent them shaking. 'You're saying that – child – is alive now?'

'Yes.'

'And you know where?'

Julia looked at her hands, trembling in her lap like alien creatures. They seemed a long way away. She could not feel any pain now, only a lightness in her head. This was the hardest part, and it was nearly over.

'No,' she said. 'Not exactly. But I met him. He came to find me. He was there that weekend when you took Phoebe to the cinema. The American boy. I didn't know till after you'd gone. He'd found my name in a diary of his father's. His father's been dead for years.'

This additional revelation seemed too much for Lottie Vernon. She dropped her head on to her hands for a moment, then looked up and swivelled the chair sideways to stare at her friend.

'Buddy's dead?'

'Yes. He was shot, apparently. Years and years ago. Soon after he went back.'

Lottie's next question come like a lash.

'Who looked after Alexander?'

'I got the idea it was grandparents.'

'And they never,' said Lottie forcefully, 'even thought of consulting me, the mother? I mean, shit! The court said I was *unfit*, but nobody thought I might have changed? I was *nineteen*, Jules—'

'I know! I know! That was why I did it!' Julia was gasping for breath now, her lips blue. 'They didn't look for you because they thought you were dead!'

'What?'

'I told Christian van Hyden that you died in the hospital. Liver damage. You bloody nearly did,' she added, with an air of breathless self-justification which was almost comic.

Lottie exploded, jumping up again, almost shrieking.

'WHY?'

It was the loss of control she hated, the loss of her own right to run her life or understand its real shape. That, Lottie told herself later, was what she minded most in the heat of that moment. All these years Julia had been pulling bloody puppet-strings, lying, making the whole of her life a lie . . .

She remembered telling Peter, in their early days, the story as she knew it: her affair, addiction, the vaguely perceived baby, the dim shame of his loss and the grief of hearing about his death at a distance and later accepting, in hard sessions at the clinic, that it was probably her own needles which had dealt it. All their marriage had been founded on his forgiving her history, understanding and appreciating the balance between her present brilliance and her wicked youthful stupidity. All Lottie's relationships with her children were founded on the inward and certain knowledge that she had once been an unfit mother. She had done her best to provide a fit father and plenty of money instead.

But now it seemed that perhaps she had not been so wicked. Perhaps she had not really had so much to atone for, by work and self-discipline and success. Perhaps, she thought as tears pricked her eyes, it would have been safe to be more normal. All this rushed through her mind in a hot flood of feeling.

'Julia!' she said. 'You did this to me. Do you *know* what you did?'

'Yes,' said Julia. Her flat voice sounded far away, as if she was floating above herself in some more peaceful place. 'Wrong. See that now. So I came. To tell you.'

'Where is the boy – the baby – now?' Even as she asked it, Lottie realized that she did not truly want to know. She had always hated plays and films which ended in reunion: late Shakespeare, lost twins in soap opera, that thing with Bette Davis. They did not ring true, not to her. Nobody wanted a stranger barging into their life, making impossible demands for love and loyalty. She did not really want an answer, but had to ask or the story would be forever incomplete.

Julia was staring, vague and deathly pale, so Lottie had to ask the question again.

'Where is he now?' There was some commotion going on outside the door, male voices, scuffling. Locked in their separate anguish the two women barely registered it.

'I don't know,' said Julia's faint voice at last. 'I tore up his address, and when I went back to find it, it was gone.'

The door was wrenched open so hard that it crashed against the wall, jolting a small picture out of line. She could see Peter, his arms out, grabbing for the intruder's arms. A tall, dishevelled young man in a regrettable patterned shirt and crumpled pale suit stood in the doorway. Behind Peter, Jocasta stood in amazement, thumb in her mouth.

The young man did not come closer but stood glaring, shaking off Peter's hand from his arm, turning his head from one woman to the other as if he could not understand why there were two of them staring at him.

Julia spoke first.

'Oh, there he is!' she said almost conversationally, and slid sideways from the chair, crashing to the floor, her head hitting the polished boards with a horrid, inanimately hollow thud.

24

<hr/>

Peter was quick, trained all his life for emergency and disaster. He pushed past Alex and dived to the senseless woman. He bent his head to her white lips, pushed his hand inside her knotted shawl to feel her heartbeat, felt her skull cautiously where it had hit the floor, then laid her on her back and began, with frightening violence, to massage her chest.

Behind Alex, Jocasta screamed a name and began to cry. Her mother, torn by confusion, moved towards her, saying, 'It's all right, Daddy's just –' and Alex had to stand aside as she in turn pushed past him in the doorway to reach her child. Just then the two boys came from the kitchen end of the passage, running and skidding on the parquet.

'Whassup? Whozat? Da-aad!'

For a moment Lottie, pawing her way towards a shrieking, shrinking Jocasta, felt as if the whole world had tilted and would slide them all off the edge into oblivion. It was Jocasta's first cry which solved the immediate problem. Kylie the groom had been pouring herself some lemonade in the kitchen when she heard her name called: she appeared, glass in hand, and saw immediately that part of the situation which she could best alleviate.

'C'm on, Jockie,' she said. 'Looks like the lady's sick. Shall we go and make her up a bed, huh? Upstairs? Get a hot water bottle? And boys, you little bastards, two of the flaming puppies have got into the stableyard. Go round them up.'

Gratefully, the mother surrendered her small weeping daughter to the broad-shouldered Antipodean, and even in her distress made a mental managerial note to tell Peter to put up Kylie's pay and induce her to stay. Then she turned to Julia, who still lay lifeless on the floor, and watched Peter's attempts to revive her slow down and finally end, as he kneeled back on his haunches, panting.

'Dial nine-nine-nine,' he said. 'Better have an ambulance. But it's too late, I'd say.' He hesitated, felt Julia's pulse again and shook his head. 'Never seen one go so fast.'

'Can't we do anything? Massage her heart again, or – oxygen or something?'

'No. But we must get an ambulance. Quick.'

Suddenly they both became aware of a male voice speaking behind them into the study phone, in an American accent. 'Moare Park. Yes. Top of a road they call Station Lane. Up at the house.'

Peter turned to Alex as he put down the phone and said levelly: 'So you've done it. Good. I don't know who the hell you are, but if you want to be useful, run down to the gates with the remote control and open them for the ambulance. The gizmo's on the front seat of the blue Polo. It's not locked.'

'For the record, I'm Alex van Hyden,' said the young man. 'Your stepson.' He looked at Lottie, but her eyes were resolutely turned away from him, staring at what remained of Julia, sprawled on the study floor.

'Get him out of here,' she said flatly. 'Out. It's too much.'

'Do the gates. Please,' said Peter. Alex left them, and moments later they heard a car door open, then slam, and running footsteps receding on the gravel of the drive. The darkness seemed to crowd in fast now, with dark clouds obscuring the sunset. Soon a flashing light threw urgent beams

230

of blue across the empty hall, and kind professional hands laid Julia on a stretcher and took her away.

After a word from Peter, Kylie kept the boys and Jocasta busy for the next hour and fed them the shepherd's pie in the kitchen. They did not know Julia well, for only Jocasta had ever been to Iver, and that was as a newborn. Julia had visited once or twice, but briefly and without showing any particular interest in her friend's offspring. Eden, forking up a mound of mashed potato, said wonderingly:

'Imagine turning up on a surprise visit and dropping dead.'

'Shh!' said Kylie, nodding towards Jocasta, whose eyes were brimming again.

'Who was the tall guy?' asked Damien. 'The one in front of Dad?'

'Dunno. Really naff shirt,' said Eden.

'Dude, you are obsessed,' said his young brother crushingly, 'with looking cool. Fashion victim, basically.'

Eden flicked a piece of mince at him, as if it was an ordinary evening. Kylie was about to slap him down but reflected that perhaps it was best, after all, if they did carry on as if everything were normal. She had been at the foot of the stairs, ahead of Jocasta, and she alone had heard Alex's surprising claim. She saw him turn towards the door, got a good view of his face, and privately decided that he was no less than he claimed. The clues were not obvious until you were looking for them, but they were there: the set of the eyes, the width of the brow, something in the mouth. He certainly could be Lady Vernon's son. But Jeez, she must have been a kid when she had him! Anyway, for the moment her own task was to lie low and keep the Vernon children out of their parents' hair.

'OK,' she said, sweeping the last plates off the table, 'Monopoly. You said you'd teach me.' She was a socialist by inclination, and had spent months resisting Eden and Damien's attempts to make her play the game. But this was a night for personal sacrifices, and it was the one proposal they were bound to accept. Whooping, they did so.

Alex opened the gates, looked back at the house, and after a moment's hesitation carefully laid the remote control on the metal box which held the machinery. The guy Peter would find it there. Then he turned his back on Moare Park and began to walk in the gloaming down the pretty lane, towards the village and the station. To have killed Julia Morrowack, he thought, was enough damage for a man to do in one evening. Her last words, that faint surprised, 'Oh, there he is!' and the crack of her head on the floor kept replaying in his head. The sight of him had done for her. He brought nobody luck.

It took him half an hour to reach the deserted station, squeezing once into the hedge to avoid the speeding ambulance. None of his dark, sad thoughts on that walk inclined him to change his mind. A light drizzle began to patter on the rails as he waited on the platform, and by great good fortune one of the little trains arrived within a few minutes. He had a return ticket to London, and all the way there he leaned his head on the cold glass, watching the droplets of rain.

Peter did not let his wife stay in the study, but led her by the hand to the sitting-room and settled her on the long sofa. She was quiet, passive, and stunned: a new gentleness and vagueness seemed to soften the contours of her face, so that she looked both older and more approachable.

'Right,' he said. 'Phew. Poor old Julia!'

'Poor Julia,' agreed Lottie, mechanically. Then, remembering, she shuddered. She looked around for a glass, but Peter for once ignored her wish for a drink and asked carefully: 'What had she come about? I met her in the shop and she looked ghastly ill. Said she had to speak to you.'

'She came,' said Lottie, 'to tell me something I didn't know. About me. I rather think she knew she was going to die, and she had to put it right.'

'Ah,' said Peter. '*Stepson*, he said. Things begin to hang together. Do I take it that the American chap is yours? From another era?'

His bluffness gave her comfort and courage. She smiled.

'Oh, God, Peter. Where the hell would I be without you?'

'So he was? But you said the baby – the one you told me about – had died?'

'Julia told me he was dead. Or she let me assume it. But at the same time she also told the father that *I* was dead. I think she only came to tell me now because the boy turned up, in England. I actually must have met him – well, I did, briefly – at Iver. And she still tried to keep me clear of him.'

Peter gave a long, rather admiring whistle.

'Bloody hell. Julia! Always so upright and herbal and teetotal . . . talk about playing God – it's like something out of Shakespeare! You know, whoserface, Hermione. We saw it at the National.'

'That's what I thought. But I hate those plots. I never think people would feel the way they're meant to feel.'

He was silent, clasping his knees.

'So how do you feel?'

'Terrified,' said Lottie. 'Bloody terrified.'

'Yes,' said Peter. 'I can see that might be the effect.'

Lottie lapsed into one of the long, absent silences which had marked their marital conversations for fifteen years. She had always liked the way that Peter accepted this and did not intrude. Sometimes there were too many feelings swirling formless and inchoate for her to dare express them. Peter was too steady, too centred, too much on an even keel to hear some things. She loved him for his level kindness, but it made her wary of confiding her own worst instincts aloud, lest she shock and alienate this excellent man. The sentence which formed itself in her mind now, over and over again, annoyingly naive and quite unsayable, was, *I do not want a huge American.*

Alexander – she must start to think of him as Alexander – was taller than Peter, taller than Eden was likely to grow. He was broad-shouldered rather than slenderly elegant like her boys, dark rather than fair, brash in his manners – well, he had to be, bursting in like that. She remembered him only vaguely from Julia's as an awkward, negligible boy carrying pots around. He wore brightly patterned shirts with a pale ready-made suit, neither casual nor smart. He was – oh, hell, he was a great hulking American stranger who barged in.

Like Christian. He had actually reminded her of Christian, she remembered with a start, when he was hovering around shyly at Iver. She had told Phoebe so, more or less. Otherwise she had not thought about Christian for years. He was a memory, hazed at the edges: a great baseball-playing hunk, a Bill Clinton type, big bright grin and big teeth. She supposed she had loved him.

Well, fancied him. But his time was long ago, before the flood, before the heat and energy and desperation and squalor and shivering pains of the smack years. Charlotte did not think back into that time, or like acknowledging her old nickname of Shark; nor did she go back beyond it into the Moira time, the boredom and restlessness and suppressed anger of a dull country childhood. *Don't look back,* they had said at the clinic.

The risk is that, remembering your path into addiction, you'll relearn the feelings and take the path again.

Did other women look back? she wondered. Did other mothers who'd lost babies yearn for them always, enough to welcome them back in a new, unfamiliar adult form? One read of these things – cheap sentimental journalism – and the mothers always seemed thrilled. She searched her heart, as well as she could in the atmosphere of frozen shock, and eventually said aloud: 'Peter, I don't want to get involved with this.'

'No,' her husband said. 'I thought you'd say that.'

'Where is he anyway?'

Peter looked around, as if Alex might rear up from behind the sofa, and realized that he too had been in shock.

'Christ,' he said. 'He never came back from opening the gates, did he?'

He walked down the dark drive, and as the lights snapped on by the gate, saw the remote control placed carefully on the steel box. He buzzed the gates closed and looked out through their elegant swirling bars for a moment, but the lane outside was silent and empty.

———◆———

25

Alex sat on his hotel bed with the lights off, his face illuminated by the cold glow of his laptop screen. He needed to contact Janis, to get himself home and out of this nightmare. He connected, but before he could send his message the screen blinked and beeped.

alanmk@outsider.demon.co.uk had left another message on the email. Alex flicked the mouse to open it, and read:

> Flying to New York on 10 September. Got to stay in UK till then, doctor's appointment. Should we meet at JFK for dollar handover? Is this the right email Phoebe has given me? Or am I communicating with someone else entirely?
>
> Please respond. Anxious to placate conscience now it is aroused. Prolonged silence on your part will be taken as permission to put whole lot on England winning the World Cup.
>
> Alan Mackinnon

Alex's first instinct was to flick the message into his 'waiting' file. Through the sad, stunned confusion of the evening another sensation was worming its way to the surface: he felt humiliated. Beyond the drama of events he had seen a hasty snapshot of his mother's home life – affluent, elegant, achieving, surrounded by handsome, confident children and tall, patrician, white-haired husband. Even Julia, collapsed on the study floor, had looked somehow stylish in her long skirt and faded damask shawl. Despite the computer on the desk and the baseball caps on the children, it had all had the look of a Merchant Ivory film set.

He had a clear image of himself in that setting: gangling, crumpled, boorish, a bringer of disaster. Suddenly, for the first time since nervous adolescence, he was aware that his ears tended to stick out, poking stupidly through his hair when it was mussed.

And he had killed Julia. The shock of seeing him had sent her hurtling to the floor. She had said, 'There he is!' in that weak surprised voice, so maybe she had been in the process of telling Lady Vernon something about him. Perhaps his surmise was true: maybe she had lied as extravagantly to his mother as to his father.

He stared into the darkness. Maybe she had been putting it right, sorting it out, when he barged in. And she was, after all, the woman who had delivered him into the world, in whose shawl he had been wrapped. The pale screen reflected as a tiny glitter in the tears which gathered in the corner of his eyes. He blinked, and made himself look down again at Mackinnon's two messages.

. . . the beauteous Phoebe . . . I owe you ten grand. Dutch Courage, remember? . . . Is this the right email Phoebe has given me? . . . anxious to placate conscience . . .

Phoebe, thought Alex, was an orphan now. He remembered her thin pale face, her skinny provocative midriff, her bored advances, her mouthy frankness about her past. He remembered the kid Josh, frowning over the chessboard. What would happen to them now? The house, he supposed, would belong to them, but could Phoebe run it as a business? Never. She wouldn't want to. He had no idea of Julia's finances, but did not think she could be rich. Alternative therapists rarely were, unless they were crooks. She was no crook. She'd been harsh and arrogant towards him, but her expertise and sincerity were beyond question. She had cured the Mackinnon man.

An idea came to him, lifting the blanket of his misery a little. In its simplicity it made him think of Marty's favourite motto at work: 'Delete the crap and do the obvious'. He, Alex, had just won a totally undeserved and unexpected ten thousand UK pounds. He would give it to Phoebe, for Josh. He need not say that he saw her mother die, still less that he caused it. He could just hand the money over and vanish. It might cushion them a little in the first bewildering months. He remembered hearing – never from his grandparents but from Mary-Jo – how the Church had made a collection after the two van Hyden boys died, giving a thousand dollars to his grandparents to pay for the funerals and remove immediate financial worries over the child. It was an obvious thing to do, and his resolution made him feel so much better that soon a fresh wave of shame overwhelmed him. Boston carpetbagger, he thought. Think you can buy everything, even a clear conscience?

Well, nuts! If it did some good, never mind any of that. He would not stay to see the undoubted contempt in Phoebe's eyes. He would get the money, hand it over, and go. She might think it was a crass gesture, but she'd spend it all right, and perhaps be glad of it. He began to type:

alanmk@outsider.demon.co.uk
    Thanks for your email. As it happens I am actually in London. Could we meet as soon as possible?

He glanced at the date on the computer: it was now after midnight, and had flipped to 1 September. Alan, he supposed, might be out of town. If, indeed, he lived in London at all.

Monday would do. I could come to meet you. I haven't got a firm date for flying back yet but it will certainly be before your journey on the 10th.

He hesitated, then thought he had better try to echo the jocose tone of the original.

Thanks again for finding me, what a win!

He signed and sent it, and prepared to climb into bed. When he opened the window a blast of hot, damp air came in, with a distant roll of thunder. On the horizon sheet lightning flickered. Later, hard rods of rain pelted down on the roofs above and around him, and he had to get out of bed in the darkness and pull the window closed against the lashing, rumbling storm. Curling up again with his arms tight round the spare pillow, it seemed to him in his half-dream that he was adrift in a ship, foundering on a merciless Atlantic without succour or shore.

Alan Mackinnon, restless and liverish, yawned at his desk. He worked – insofar as he still worked at all – in the small study he had carved out of the hallway of his mansion flat in Maida Vale. The various consultancies and semi-sleeping partnerships with which he supplemented his betting income were slack; nor had he much enthusiasm left for them. The annual New York trip, usually a treat, bored him in advance. Today he had woken to a wet, stormy morning and nothing much to do, and admitted to himself after skimming through the papers that part of the problem was that he missed Phoebe.

Or maybe it was just that he missed Deauville and the fine weather. He switched on the computer and watched with idle interest while it 'warmed up' as he put it to himself. He was of the generation which still expected a television picture to shrink to a bright dot before vanishing. Connecting itself the machine purred, twanged and produced a dozen emails. The last was Alex's, and made Mackinnon's small petulant mouth broaden to a grin.

'Game, set and match to Miss Phoebe Morrowack,' he said aloud. 'Lucky we had those last two wins.' It had been a glorious final day at Deauville: the memory made him sigh. He pulled open the drawer at his side and began to count out banknotes. It was his habit to keep foolish sums of money in the flat, trussed bricks of wealth in neat flat orange rubber bands, and the fact he had never yet been burgled gave him a sense of invincibility. When he had stacked together two hundred fifty-pound notes in bundles of fifty and snapped the double orange bands round them two ways, he paused.

Then, with a giggle, he pulled out one note from the top bundle, tearing it slightly in the process, and put it back in the drawer. One must never be too honest. It was a bourgeois instinct. Anyway, well-brought up young people never, in his experience, liked to count the wad in front of you. At last, returning to the computer, he began typing with two pudgy fingers an invitation to Alex to meet him in the Savoy for lunch on Monday. Americans liked the Savoy, didn't they? It would pass an amusing hour. Perhaps he would pretend for a while that he did not intend to hand the money over at all.

He dealt with the other messages, then sat with his chin on his hands, wishing that Phoebe had an email address. A phone call would seem too pressing, and his tone of voice might be read too easily. A letter was old-fashioned and, again, too revealing. Email was perfect for these affairs: one short joking line, a flirtatious response, another line – none of it in real-time, none of it a commitment. Getting up, walking restlessly round the flat in his rather absurdly Cowardish velvet dressing-gown, Alan Mackinnon wondered with growing unease whether he was in danger of becoming a lonely and pathetic old man.

Phoebe, alone in the kitchen with Mienke after breakfast and resentful that her mother had not rung, decided to bury the hatchet.

'That was really good bread this morning,' she said, hitching up her bottom until she was sitting on the worktop. 'Even better than Mum's. Were they pumpkin seeds?'

'*Ja*,' said Mienke, accepting the underlying apology and olive branch. 'Your soup was good, also. Last night.' She smiled at Phoebe, who slid off the worktop and gave a little wriggle of satisfaction.

'Well, Mum mainly got the stuff ready. She hasn't rung.'

'I know,' said Mienke. 'And there is a booking, two ladies who want special baths and massage, and I do not know whether to say yes. I think Carl from Iver needs to be booked for the massage, and I do not know the number.'

'I wonder why she didn't ring? She was going to London. Some meeting or other.'

'Well, I think I must say no to the ladies,' said Mienke, and made a note on the pad she had taken to carrying around. 'In any case, I think Mr Mackinnon will be coming after the weekend and he will need the big room as usual.'

'He can share with me,' said Phoebe smugly. The Dutch girl looked at her, but with mild exasperation rather than dislike.

'He is quite old,' she said. 'Are you sure it is a good idea for a young woman to be like this with an old man? And he is not well, with his liver.'

'I'm not expecting him to *die* and leave me his money, you know,' said Phoebe virtuously. 'I actually like him. He's quite sexy in his way, and he makes me laugh, and we go gambling. Young men are selfish dickheads.'

'This laughing is important, and I told this to Julia,' admitted Mienke, smoothing her golden hair. 'But it is bad for you to leave Josh always. Julia is very kind, but she is not his mother.'

'We'll see about that,' said Phoebe. 'I guess Alan might not mind a bit of surrogate fatherhood, if I play my cards right. They could play chess. I think it sucks, and he's always wanting a game.' She looked dreamily out of the window, then turned back to Mienke, enjoying their newfound ease.

'But, hey, I always mean to ask – why don't you have a bloke?' She frowned briefly then added, 'Or a girl. I mean, I'm cool about it, whatever.'

'I am not gay!' said Mienke indignantly. 'But I wait.'

'You fancied that American boy Alex!'

'I think that was you,' said the Dutch girl primly, and pulled a handful of carrots out of the basket to slice.

'Well, whatever.' Phoebe abruptly lost interest in the subject and returned to her plaint.

'Mum hasn't rung!'

It was Peter who, over breakfast at Moare Park, reminded his wife that it was their job to notify Julia's family and colleagues. He had thought about it briefly the night before, but the hospital had not certified death until it was too late, and dark, to consider breaking such news. And his own focus, to his slight shame, had been on his wife's equilibrium. 'There's a daughter, isn't there? Patricia, is it?'

'Phoebe. Single mother.' Lottie had slept badly and risen early to struggle with her statement on the fund crisis. She had refused to eat, and drunk far too much coffee. A muscle jumped in her cheek. 'Got a little boy called Josh. She's a mess. Only just out of detox. I took her to the cinema a few months back.'

Peter grimaced. 'Oh, God. She has to be told. And that place Julia runs – ran – there are people working for her, right?'

'And she's on committees. Herbal things. She does lectures.'

In silence they contemplated the task before them. After a moment Lottie said tentatively. 'Don't the police usually . . .' She stopped.

Peter looked at her, his cup halfway to his mouth. He was used to, and indeed often complicit in, her habit of managing human relationships by remote control. But sometimes her willingness to delegate anything painful or messy took his breath away.

'You'd rather some strange policeman knocked on the poor girl's door?'

Lottie flushed. She did not like criticism, not from Peter, she could not bear it. There was only one way to respond.

'For God's sake! Police are trained for this sort of thing and I'm not! Can't you see the stress I'm under? Haven't I been through enough this last twenty-four hours without you sneering and criticizing and—'

'Lottie!' It was a warning note. Eden and Damien loomed in the doorway of the breakfast room.

'Dad, it's still raining. Can we put the ping-pong table up in the barn?'

'Sure.'

'Kylie says we can't, because she's going to be schooling Sycorax and Minty in there.'

'Well, the answer's no, then.'

'Kylie's not in charge round here, is she?' said Eden. 'We pay her, don't we?'

Peter erupted. 'Never, never, ever let me hear you say anything like that again! Kylie does a job, very well and conscientiously, and she has the right to be respected for it. Particularly by children who have yet to earn their own share of respect in the world. Money does not wipe out the responsibility to conduct human relationships decently.'

When the boys had ambled out, Damien throwing a reproachful look at his father, Lottie said in a low, nasty voice: 'And that was aimed at me, too, I daresay?'

'If the cap fits,' said Peter tersely, and for only the second time in their sixteen years of marriage, he walked out on his wife and slammed the door.

Lottie sat for ten minutes with her coffee, pretending to scan her folder of dates and investments through the wobbling tears in her eyes, until the breakfast room door opened again. It was Jocasta, who made it her daily business to go down to the gates and collect the morning papers and mail from the waterproof boxes embedded in the heavy concrete gateposts. She had once got into difficulties at nursery school when they had to play postmen, having never experienced the putting of letters through an actual front door.

'Post's for Dad, mostly,' she said, pulling a slightly soggy bundle from the front of her waterproof jacket. 'Except here's one for you, and the papers.'

'Did you give your father his post?' asked Lottie cautiously.

'Yup. He's in his study, writing something with *fu-ri-ous*

haste,' said the child precociously. She put the letter on the mantelpiece and glared at her mother. 'Are you *working* again?'

'Yes, I have to.'

'Will you come out and watch me ride Minty?'

'It's raining.'

'In the *barn*. We're turning it into an indoor school. So will you come?'

'Later,' said Lottie. She looked down at the figures, but her head swam. 'Oh, all right then. Now. For ten minutes. I'll get some boots on.'

Jocasta vanished, whooping, and her mother followed more slowly, pulling on a pair of canvas boots and a sweater and passing through the big, quiet kitchen to the glassed and covered passage which ran out to the stables. As she entered it, she heard a step behind her and Peter's hand fell on her shoulder. She turned and glared at him.

'Yes?'

'I wrote you a long letter,' he said. 'Explaining some things I feel should be said. But then I tore it up. Better to say them face to face.'

She was silent. On the manicured slopes between the upper and lower lawns the two boys were attempting to grass-ski on snowboards in the rain, leaving muddy gouge marks behind them. Had they looked up at the end of the house, they would have seen their parents facing one another, still as statues, inside the glass tunnel.

Peter said more gently, 'It comes down to something simple, anyway. So I'm going to say it.'

'That I'm a selfish cold-hearted cow, I suppose?' said Lottie. She opened her mouth again to continue, but he shushed her.

'No. I know you loved Julia. I know it's a shock. And there was the other shock, which we can think about later. But what I wanted to say was different. It's simply that you're not as much of an endangered species as you think you are.'

She waited, surprised. He continued.

'For years and years, you've carried on as if you'd only just left that drug clinic. You're careful of yourself. All your courage and energy is used at work, because that's only really game-playing and it wouldn't matter if you failed. It's at one remove from the important things. Meanwhile at home you've convinced yourself that you're a frail reed and if anything upsets you, you might go back on drugs and be in the gutter in a week. So you leave the children to me, and the staff and the house, and your secretary organizes your friends, and you go and spend three days a month being fed potions by Julia because if you don't take very, very good care of yourself in every way you might relapse. Correct?'

'It's something you learn,' said his wife, a little huffily. 'A recovering addict has to know her areas of weakness. You're never free. Stress is dangerous.'

'You've made it into a religion,' said Peter, tersely. 'I've wanted to say it for a long time, and this is the moment. You're a tiger at work, but then you convince yourself you're a feeble rabbit away from it. An invalid. And you're not. You're about as likely to go off the rails as I am. You're forty-six years old, with three children and money in the bank and me in love with you. You haven't touched anything worse than a third martini since you were twenty. You aren't a mixed-up kid, Lottie. Any more than I'm a spotty little boy buffing up my shoes at Dartmouth.'

'What are you telling me?' said Lottie, but her voice was calmer.

'I'm telling you that I'll drive you to Iver this morning, so you can break the news to Phoebe, privately, because you were her mother's best friend. And if she wants, we'll bring her and her child back here and look after them, and you will do what a friend does, which is listen to her and take over some of the pain yourself. And it won't tip you over the edge. There is no edge, sweetheart. It's bloody miles away.'

Lottie could hear Jocasta mounting her pony, with cheerful cries of encouragement from Kylie. She glanced towards the stone arch of the stableyard.

'I'll go and watch Jock,' she said. 'For ten minutes. Then I ought to do some work – on Monday morning I've got to present the board with a complete answer to Ancaster's accusations. Then, perhaps—'

'No,' said Peter. 'Watch Jock while I get the big car out. Then we're off. You can't leave little Phoebe to go on with her day while her mother's lying dead. It's always the first thing people need to know: when it happened, and what were they doing at the time themselves? They need to know that whatever they were up to doesn't seem callous.'

Lottie nodded, and raised an uncertain hand as if in greeting or farewell. To accept defeat, she thought numbly, brought a kind of peace. She glanced down: this sweater, blue with a faint green fleck, was sober enough for the occasion. She need not even go back indoors to change. What must be, must be.

Then she walked slowly towards the archway, the barn, and her daughter's squeaks of glee.

———◆◆◆———

26

Waiting in the big Mercedes, Peter checked the details about undertakers and transport which he had written in his note-book, and the phone number of the hospital mortuary. He was glad of the moment alone: his hands, he noticed, were shaking slightly. Friction with his wife had been a rare thing, largely through his efforts. In his professional life, despite its under-lying warlike purpose, he had always been a soother and a conciliator: deliberately upsetting applecarts went against his nature. Probably, he thought, it had been disgust at his son's adolescent arrogance which had provoked him into confront-ing Lottie during that dramatic breakfast. Her unwillingness to take responsibility for telling Julia's daughter, her instinct to ask some underpaid copper to do it – he winced in real pain for his wife's crassness – was too close for comfort to Eden's careless, 'We pay her, don't we?'

The wealth and ease of his children's upbringing often worried him. He would make damn' sure that when it came to gap years before university, they did something hard and eye-opening and preferably fairly squalid. He hoped that Lottie would agree. If not, he realized to his surprise, he would be willing to pick another fight with her. Their life, almost without anybody noticing it, had become too artificial and protected to be tolerable.

She came out to the car sooner than he had expected, in the

same blue slacks and sweater, with a big leather bag over her shoulder he had not seen before. Normally, like royalty, she carried the minimum: tiny telephone, credit cards, lipstick. Her assistant would scuttle after her carrying anything else. She got into the car.

'I grabbed an album,' she said, tucking the bag down by her legs. 'Some pictures of Julia in it. When we were both living in Cambridge. I haven't looked at it for years, but it came under my hand. She was really beautiful, you know.'

'That's good,' said Peter. 'Good idea. Celebrate the life, that sort of thing.' He eased in the clutch, and the big car moved off. 'We'll be there in an hour and a half, at this time on a Saturday. The cones are off on the M25, I heard.'

Despite this tacit offer to leave the subject, Lottie went on.

'Jules saved my life, you know. I was angry last night, about the lies, but she saved me. I came out of that hospital really low, and I was all for going back to Neville's place. The squat. But she told me the house had been raided and repossessed. Come to think of it, that was probably another lie.' She almost laughed. 'Oh, Jules!'

'She took you to a hostel, didn't she?' Peter asked, voice neutral, his eyes on the road. He was genuinely curious: Lottie had sketched her life for him honestly enough when they were first courting, in the stilted therapeutic language she had learned at the clinic, but had never returned to it or given it any colour.

'Yes. It was horrible. She'd decided to try cold turkey at first, but I was on methadone. So were a lot of the others. There were fights. There were some terrible hag-women there who stole stuff from your bed while you were in it. Then she got some money from her dad – or my dad, I was never sure which, probably both, but mine was ill already. Mum had died that spring. I never saw her again after I moved in to Neville's. Anyway, the money. That was how Jules got us into Melford Abbey.'

'Which did the trick?'

'Yes.' Lottie was silent, remembering the strong peace and strict certainties of Dr Su's clinic, the gentle, bespectacled, intelligent face of the Burmese director, the hateful cleanliness and neutrality of the nurses, the twice-daily circles where addicts of all kinds absorbed the rules: don't look back, don't be that person, don't be soft on your old self, and watch yourself forever.

'It was a very strong, kind place. And they were good people. I don't think Jules paid them anything near the going rate.' She paused, staring straight forward at the windscreen wipers. 'But I remember Dr Su saying, 'Never trust yourself again,' and wondering, even then, whether that was the right thing to say to people.'

'Wrong, I'd say.' They were out of the lane now, and gathering speed on the main road. 'You have to trust yourself, or you're crippled.'

'Well, it was in a particular context. The substance context. We'd all proved we couldn't be trusted. Even Jules had problems later on, till Phoebe came along. Some people had been in and out of their habit for ten years. There were disgusting stories. They'd robbed their parents, everything. Actually, I think that was one of the things that helped me, hearing how horrible they were. That, and nearly dying.'

'Liver, you said?' Peter marvelled, rejoicing in the car's smooth speed and his wife's unaccustomed mood of reminiscence. It was like being new lovers again, wanting to hear every detail. 'You said you had liver failure?'

'Not that bad. Nearly. That's the other thing Jules did for me. I think it was because I went on having problems, going yellow, that she started studying herbalism. I was her first patient really.'

'Well, it turned into a success for her. So you did her some good, too.'

'She was amazing,' said Lottie. 'A one-off. I wish I hadn't shouted at her last night.'

'Did you?' He knew she had: he had heard it while he was arguing with the big young man in the hallway.

'It was such a shock. That she'd told me the baby – and Christian dying –' suddenly, quite unexpectedly, her composure left her and Lottie Vernon began to cry. 'Oh, shit.'

Peter reached into the pocket in the driver door and passed her a packet of tissues. She cried all the way to the M25 motorway intersection, and was still sniffing when they left it, heading northward into Buckinghamshire. The rain had eased off, and the sun glinted occasionally through gaps in the greyness.

'Not far now,' said Peter. 'OK?'

'Stupid,' said Lottie. She crumpled the last tissue and pushed it into the door pocket. 'And, Peter, I still don't want to get involved with the American boy. I know you probably think that's wicked, but I just don't. It's all over. I have to shut the door. I was crying about *then*, not now.'

'It's a start,' said her husband. Leaving the main road for the lanes leading to Julia's, he marvelled silently at how he, a simple chap who had loved more ships than girls in his first forty years, had ever got involved with such dense female complication. Love played odd tricks. He had sat next to Charlotte Grayson at an otherwise grindingly tedious City dinner for a seafarers' charity, had looked at the melancholy puzzling beauty of her profile all through the speeches and resolved that night to marry her. Sixteen years later, she still surprised him more frequently than he liked.

The lane forked. 'You'll have to direct me now,' he said. 'I don't know these byways the way you do.'

Fifteen minutes later Josh wandered into the kitchen and observed, 'There's an ace car outside. A Merc.'

'Oh, no!' said Mienke, who was making a large, dark-green salad. She dusted from her hands the tiny, sticky seeds she had been sprinkling and peered through the window. 'I hope it is not those ladies, come anyway. If Mr Mackinnon is coming on Tuesday—'

'Mum's still in bed,' said Josh. 'I woke her up but she says she's got a headache.'

'Oh, shoot!' exclaimed Mienke. 'I cannot do everything. We have the new clients here – asking for Julia, complaining she's not here – and now these women, and we *must* finish the picking for drying or everything will rot—'

'It's not the women,' said the child. 'It's Lady Vernon. Cool. I hope she's got that fox coat.'

'She's not booked, it's not her week,' said Mienke. 'Who is that man?'

She ran out on to the drive and, moments later, came back looking grave. Josh had spent the intervening time eating all the sunflower seeds he could find and ripping up the rest of the parsley into individual trees for a plate garden he was making. Ignoring the mess, Mienke said in a kind but un-defiable voice, 'Josh, please ask your mother to come down now. In a dressing gown would be fine. Give her mine, from my room, if she likes. There is something Lady Vernon needs to talk about with her.'

*   *   *

Lottie, hours later, told Peter that she had never seen such shock. He had waited in the kitchen with Mienke, talking quietly about practicalities. The little boy had gone outside to jump in puddles: they watched him nervously through the window, wondering when would be the right time to tell him.

Lottie drew a yawning, truculent Phoebe into Julia's little study and pulled the door shut. She tried to remember their last conversation, back in the spring. They had gone to the cinema, and the kid had mentioned her drug treatment and laughed about Lottie's fur coat. She tried to drag herself back to that night, to that brief moment of friendliness with this farouche little creature.

'Phoebe,' she began, and longed for Peter to come and take over the difficult conversation, as he always had with their own children. When Eden got thrown out of Charterhouse, or Damien had tried to run away from St Edward's, or Jocasta's first pony died of colic, Peter had led the discussion and protected her from the wildness of their feelings. Now, alone with the trouble, she took a deep breath.

'Phoebe, there's some bad news.'

Phoebe stared. The dressing gown was pink candlewick, clearly not her own; her lank spikes of hair hung incongruously over the satin collar, and the silver stud in her eyebrow sat strangely with its prim mother-of-pearl buttons. 'What?' she asked with rude abruptness, rubbing sleep from her eyes. 'I was *asleep*.'

'Your mother came to see me last night, and she wasn't at all well. Phoebe, I'm terribly sorry, but she died suddenly. We think it was a heart attack. Peter did everything he could, he's a trained first-aider, but the hospital—'

Phoebe came wide awake and screamed. Lottie had expected silence, weeping, trembling, anger, shock, but not this.

The screams turned to doglike whimpers, forming the same word: 'No . . . no . . . no!' The girl's shoulders shook, and then she began to walk around, doubling up like a wounded animal, furious in her pain. 'No! Mmmh! Not Mum, mmmh, no!'

Lottie stood helpless, but when Phoebe banged her head hard against the door with another scream, she moved forward and took her by the shoulders: at first gingerly, then as the girl tried to twist away, more forcefully. You were meant, she thought, to slap hysterics. But how on earth could you lash out at somebody when you had already dealt such a blow?

'She'll want to know all the details,' Peter had warned, but Phoebe seemed not to. Trembling in the older woman's grip, she just said:—

'Why? Why? Why Mum? I need her. Josh needs her. She can't just be *gone!*'

Lottie stiffened, suddenly confused. Another high wailing voice had said something like that, long ago. *Gone! Can't be!* Hollow loneliness rose in her, and ruthlessly she quashed it. On the wall a grave portrait of Julia looked down, and Lottie found herself staring at it, asking for strength, even as she held Julia's broken daughter by the shoulders.

Another twist from Phoebe recalled her attention. She began to soothe, to use words dredged from some memory of her own early childhood.

'It'll be all right . . . it'll be OK . . . you'll be fine. You and Josh. You'll be looked after. Julia's watching, she'd want you to be brave . . . come on, sweetheart . . .'

'But I was a crap daughter! I was nothing but grief! I was going to be better to her, I was just thinking yesterday—'

'Hush. She loved you, whatever. Mothers do that. She was proud of you.'

In the kitchen, Mienke and Peter exhausted the practical-ities and fell into silence. Josh walked through once, asking, 'Whassappening?' but to their relief, was gone before they could frame an answer. They heard him clumping up the stairs, and caught each other's eye with a guilty sigh.

'Phoebe will not be able to tell him, I think,' said Mienke, jerking her head towards the direction of the screaming and whimpering which was only just dying away. 'Maybe Lady Vernon?'

Peter bit his lip. He could not say that it was amazing, almost a miracle, that his wife was even facing up to telling Phoebe. And he was increasingly troubled by something else. She had mentioned that this American boy – her son – had been at Iver. This nice, even-tempered, competent Dutch girl must have met him. Peter found, to his annoyance, that he was both fascinated and repelled by the idea of his children having a half-sibling. He had known about the baby ever since he and Lottie began courting, because on their first date she had laid out the bones of her past before him with clinical, unemotional precision. She had, he suspected, been told by Dr Su's clinic that this was a necessary ritual. He did not mind then: he pitied her from the bottom of his heart, and vowed to make her life easier and safer thereafter.

But in those days the baby was dead. So they all thought, except the secretive Julia. Would it, he wondered, have made a difference if he had known that an adopted adult might come back suddenly into their lives?

He shivered at his own selfishness. Of course it wouldn't. He loved Lottie, brave tough brittle Lottie Grayson who needed him and always would. All the same, he was unsettled when he thought about the scuffle in the hall with that tall, intent young alien. Alexander had a prior claim on Lottie:

prior to his, to Eden's, Damien's, Jocasta's. And between DGB Investments and Julia, his mind added treacherously, they had little enough of her as it was. There was no room in the fragile balance of their family for a returning prodigal from Idaho or Texas or wherever it was.

Mienke had lapsed into silence opposite him, and abruptly, to counteract the unworthiness of his own train of thought, Peter said: 'Did you have a young American called Alex here for a while, lately?'

'Yes,' said the girl unhesitatingly, and he thought for a moment that her cheeks became pinker and her accent a little more foreign. 'A nice boy. Well, not a boy, middle twenties, I'd say. I think he was from New York.'

'Did Julia and he – talk a lot?'

'Oh-oh!' said Mienke. 'Do you know about this? I have been wondering – they were in the study one evening for a while, then he left very suddenly. Even his car sounded angry, if you know what I mean. And there was no bill. I thought perhaps there was some trouble with Phoebe.'

'Ah,' said Peter, unwilling to ask what sort of trouble with Phoebe might be envisaged. He could guess. 'But there was nothing else you noticed?'

'Only,' said Mienke, 'that he was very attractive.' She twinkled at him now, then stood up and swept the teacups from the table. 'Most of our clients are not attractive at all.'

'I suppose he went back to America?' tried Peter.

'No idea,' said the girl. 'And no address. Why?' She started, and looked closely at him. 'You do not think that her death—'

'No, no, no,' said Peter hastily. 'It's just some admin stuff – something of his that she had – oh, you know.'

A while later, Lottie came through from the study, with a

tear-stained but quiet Phoebe improbably clutching her hand like a child.

'Peter,' she said, 'I'm going to stay here tonight with Phoebe, and we're going to talk to Josh together after lunch. Perhaps you'd better go back to Moare Park and see to the children.'

'Kylie can cope. I can ring her,' he said defensively. 'I'll stay with you.'

'No. Please. Go.'

'Do you want me to come back and just drop off your laptop?' He was almost pleading to be needed, and Lottie hesitated. It was the first time in a decade that she had been away from home for the night without her portable computer, access to world stock market figures and all her working life in summary. And on Monday she had to face the Board over the Ancaster allegations.

She thought of the papers on her desk and the half-finished statement on her computer; remembered the torrid afternoon and the grubby, infuriating thud of the football on the window. She thought of her sleek smug underlings who would come out of this mess unbesmirched, having got her into it in the first place. Then she felt the damp warmth of Phoebe's hand in hers, remembered Josh playing upstairs and Julia's long years of almost maternal solicitude, and said:

'No. It's OK. I'll catch up.'

27

Josh took the news more calmly than his mother, but with far more questions. Phoebe rallied a little to answer them, with Lottie never far from her side.

'Who killed her? Was she sick? Why didn't the doctor come? Do grownups often just *die*, like that?'

'Hardly ever,' said Lottie firmly. 'It's very unusual.'

'And is there heaven?' asked the boy. 'Will she be there now?'

Phoebe turned stricken eyes to the older woman, who after minimal hesitation said, 'Yes, she deserved every kind of heaven. A lovely rest, with no more work to do.'

'She liked working,' said Josh. 'Messing about with herbs . . .'

'Well, imagine how good heavenly herbs would be,' said Phoebe with a flash of inspiration.

'Shall we go and pick some of the late ones for the drying-shed?' said Lottie. 'She'd be pleased with that. She'd like us to keep things tidy.'

'OK.'

Under the direction of the Australian student – who was, according to Mienke, finally getting efficient just as her time drew to a close – they spent the afternoon in the damp green beds, cutting the best specimens, laying them out on the muslin trays and slotting them into racks in the long, quiet, warm, headily fragrant shed. It was almost a ritual, thought Lottie with a rare flash of poetry, almost as if they were tending and embalming the body of Julia herself, or folding clean linen to embrace her in the grave. Sometimes a tear dropped from her eye; sometimes she put out a hand to the thin, bent back of Phoebe alongside her, or smiled at the child who, by now apparently unconcerned, grubbed semi-usefully around beside them. It was ironic, thought Lottie, that her first long family afternoon in years without work in the background should be spent with someone else's family. She thought with a pang of Jocasta, her most familiar child. Would Jock ever weep for her as desperately as Phoebe for Julia? Or was there something special about a single mother's effort and devotion?

Mienke – who had miraculously got rid of the two remaining paying guests – brewed a soporific infusion at bedtime. A cold wind was blowing off the distant hills, and all three found rubber hot-water bottles waiting in their beds. Lottie fell into a deep, unconscious sleep and woke refreshed on Sunday morning, to find Josh perched on the end of her bed.

'Mum is *not good*,' he said. 'You'd better go and see her. I'm going to have my breakfast.'

Bleary-eyed, Lottie stumbled into the bedroom and found Phoebe sitting upright, pallid, truculent and trembling.

'It's no good,' she said. 'I'm going to London.'

'No!' said Lottie, who had a very good idea what London meant to one with Phoebe's history. 'Don't waste all that effort now! Don't go back! Don't be that person!' Dr Su spoke through her.

'I can't stand it. Not without Mum,' said Phoebe. 'And I was horrible to her, I ran off and left her with Josh and only sent one postcard. I'm calling a cab now. Will you look after Josh?'

260

'Phoebe, you *can't*,' said Lottie. 'And no, I won't.'

'Mienke will,' said the girl angrily. 'I just need some space.'

'You are lying! You'll go straight back to the first dealer you can find.'

'So? Whose life is it, huh?'

The soft, weeping child of the night before had vanished, replaced by this hard-nosed combative punk. Lottie thought with sudden admiration that the late Julia had dealt with Phoebe for over twenty years, and got two degrees and a certificate in herbal medicine while doing so.

'Have you got any *other* friends?' she said, purposely stressing the word. 'People you could just chill out with? Who aren't on that scene?'

There was a moment of hesitation, then Phoebe said, 'Nope,' and began looking around for her clothes.

Downstairs, Lottie said urgently to Mienke: 'Phoebe wants to go to London. I think she's heading back towards the drugs. You know she's just out of detox? A year ago?'

'*Ja*, Julia told me. She worked very hard, I think, to stop Phoebe taking crack. It is sad if she begins again.'

'Has she got any friends – or boyfriends – who might do instead? I mean, someone who might come over and steady her a bit?'

'She went off for a while,' said Mienke, 'with one of our regular clients, Mr Mackinnon. You know him. He is quite old and a gambler and not approved of at all by Julia, but when Phoebe came back I think she was better. And Julia saw this, I think.'

'Can we get him?'

'I asked her last night,' said Mienke surprisingly. 'Because I thought this might happen. She does not have a very strong will.'

'And what did she say?'

'She forbids me to tell him. She says they don't have that kind of relationship, and that they stay cool, and just have fun, and no strings, and end of story.'

'Hmm,' said Lottie. This was not entirely her business. Phoebe was over twenty-one. The habit of corporate command, however, was strong in her, and after a pause she said, 'Give me his number.'

'Good,' said the Dutch girl, and handed it over. 'I have cancelled her taxi already. And I have taken away all her jeans so she has no clothes. And the hop drink I made, which Josh took up, will make her sleep for a while.'

'I wish you worked in my office,' said Lottie. Mienke told Kath the Australian gardener later on that it was the first time she had seen a proper smile on Lady Vernon, ever.

Alex slept late, drank too much black coffee and rang his grandfather as soon as it was reasonable to expect Iowa to be awake.

'Hey, boy,' grated the familiar voice. 'I'm still in bed!'

'Sorry. I'm in England,' said Alex. 'Grandad, I wanted to tell you something. I found my mom.'

'You found the grave? Ah, boy, are you OK?'

'Not a grave. She didn't die. I've sort of met her.'

'Sort of?'

'The first time, neither of us knew. The second time – it was kinda confused.'

'So is she pretty damn' pleased? I should think so?'

'Umm – pass on that one.'

'And you?'

'Pass also.'

'Jeez, boy,' said the crackling old voice down the phone, 'I guess you'd better come home, if that's as far as England gets you.'

'Yeah,' said Alex. 'Just one job left, then I'll be glad to be home.'

But the sound of his grandfather's voice galvanized him out of apathetic self-pity and made him resolve to get some benefit from his final British weekend. He could not get the money until Monday lunchtime, but after that he could send it to Phoebe Morrowack and vamoose. He called Janis when the office opened and asked for his flight to be confirmed for Monday afternoon, then went down to the hotel reception to ask about secure courier systems. Unsatisfied with the reply he studied his map for a while, then rang Janis again and asked for a later flight. She expostulated ('I've earned a damn' good present, Alex') but went back to her screen. He would go to the airport, drop his luggage, and then deliver the packet by taxi. It would take only a couple of hours.

So that was fixed. He felt a brief pang at disposing of the largest sum of money he had ever got for no effort, but sternly told himself that it must be so. He had barged in on Lady Vernon and Julia, and shocked Julia so much she dropped dead. Worse, he had done all this with real malice in his heart towards them. He had called them bitches. He wanted to get home and tell his grandfather about it, and eventually Johnny and Janis and Marty as well. But for the moment this small piece of unfinished business must be achieved, alone and expensively by cab, as a penance.

Meanwhile he would learn London. Maybe he had left the capital too precipitately last time round. He bought a guidebook and studied the subway map with interest. He rather liked it being called the Underground: it had an elvish, Tolkien ring to it. Leaving the hotel at noon he spent a couple of hours rattling along its grimy tunnels, popping up to look at new districts, and changing eventually on to a surprisingly new line in the East. He emerged, as much by chance as by design, into the empty spaces of the Millennium Dome station at Greenwich. He wandered round the eerie ghost station, looked at the rows of silent deserted turnstiles and struck up a conversation with one of the guards.

'It's a helluva space,' he said. 'Must have cost a bit.'

'Five hundred and nine million. Pounds, not your dollars,' said the man with a kind of perverse pride. 'Then twenty-one million to close it down, and the papers say it's lost a million a month ever since.'

'Since the millennium? For nearly two years?' asked Alex, fascinated. For the first time in his day's tour he was jolted out of his gloomy preoccupation with his own troubles. There was something perversely cheering about this proof that others, older and wiser and more powerful, could screw up even worse than he had. 'A million sterling lost every month for two years? What's it actually used for, now?'

The man grinned. 'I'm not supposed to let you see,' he said teasingly. 'But since you've come all the way from America to check it out – c'mon!' He led Alex to the edge of the structure and opened a door, just a crack. Inside lay a vast grimy emptiness, with a few pieces of litter blowing lazily around the floor in the draught. 'It's used for – nothing!'

Alex craned in, bewitched by the lunatic uselessness of this vast space in a crowded city. He took a step further than the man wanted, and was pushed back.

'Awright, mate, I'm not supposed even to show you. You're not from the newspapers, are you?'

'No, no – I'm a tourist. But, please,' he begged, 'just tell me, what's that sort of pants-leg, just a bit offcentre, like a tunnel from the top to the bottom?'

The guard closed the door, glanced around to see if any colleagues were watching and said, 'Issa air vent. From the Blackwall Tunnel, the road tunnel under the river. They built the Dome on top of it, see. And they found out, and put that thing in to let the fumes out.'

'*They built the Dome on top of it?*' said Alex. 'On top of a poison vent? Like, a five-billion project? But there's room over the other side, there, it could have moved over a bit.'

'S'right.' The guard seemed perversely pleased. 'And there's more poison underneath it, in the earth. And so they can't sell it. Million a month! Good, eh?'

'Depends what you mean by good,' said Alex. A curious affection was rising in him for this man, with his dull crazy job and his ironic grin. '*There'll always be an England,*' he thought suddenly, '*Where there's a useless Dome . . .*' He laughed. 'OK, I give in. It's pretty good. As a joke.'

''S' giving me a job,' said the man. 'Who's complaining?'

'Hey, can I walk to the old bits of Greenwich from here?' asked Alex.

'Nah,' said the man. 'Well, you can, but it's a horrible walk. There's a problem with the footpath, know what I mean? What you can do is, get the Tube back across the river to Canary Wharf, walk across to the Docklands Light Railway, it takes about five minutes through the shopping centre, then take the DLR back across the river again, down to Cutty Sark Gardens.'

'But it's only about a mile on the map! I thought you Brits walked more than us Americans?'

'Please yourself.'

Alex walked, through traffic and across howling round-abouts, and eventually found himself back among older buildings. He knew what they were from the guidebook, but did not expect the pleasure of seeing the graceful colonnaded Museum, the domed Naval College and the Disneyish brick Observatory on the hill, all stacked together in one view. He did not feel inclined for a museum, as the sun was out again, but climbed the green hill to the Old Royal Observatory and stood athwart the Meridian Line with a group of giggling children doing the same.

The children dispersed, and Alex was left alone to look down at the sweep of eighteenth-century grace and the curve of the river; and, shining beyond it, the towers of Canary Wharf. A few more of those little skyscrapers, he thought, and this spot would be a miniature metaphor for the two English-speaking worlds: graceful old Greenwich with its fabulous buildings, grimy streets, pointless Dome and ironic world-weary voices; then a stretch of water like a miniature Atlantic, and across it a vision of bright new towers, fast-moving bankers and technophile geeks like Marty and himself. Old world, new world.

He also supposed that DGB International, with his mother at its heart, must have a home across that river, among those towers. Well, never mind. Her voice rang in his ears: 'Get him out of here. Out!' OK, lady, he said inwardly. To be honest, you're not my type either. He shivered, because the rain was beginning again and he had no coat. One more blank day, then he could leave.

On Sunday, he took the train to Brighton, went on the pier, played slot machines with a surprising amount of pleasure, and was propositioned by a prostitute with candyfloss hair and – with rather more grace – by the male antiques dealer who sold him a beaded Victorian handbag as a present for Janis. The sense of rueful reconciliation and closure which he had found in Greenwich was still with him, but he itched to go home. Already the scenes around him seemed insubstantial and dreamlike – small green fields, chalk downs, slow grimy trains, resigned humorous British potato-faces. He didn't belong here, he never could have done. It was best to go home, and let them get on with it.

———◆◆◆———

28

Alan Mackinnon, propped on four pillows, yawned into the telephone and then sat almost upright in surprise. He was still in bed, a litter of racing pages spilling off the dark-green duvet on to the floor to join an upturned coffee-cup and a piece of toast which he had dropped, butter down, when he went back to sleep earlier. His cleaner was lavishly (if irregularly) tipped and hence expected to refrain from grumbling. His girlfriends were summarily thrown out if they complained. One of the assets of Phoebe had been her infinite tolerance of mess.

'Lady Vernon. What a pleasure,' he said, smoothing his thin hair. 'How can I be of help to you?'

The voice at the end of the phone was terse and informative. He squinted down at the receiver, incredulous.

'But she was so healthy! Are you sure? My dear, she radiated wholesomeness – none of us had the right to outlive that *paragon*.' And: 'Her heart – well, yes, I see. Oh, dear.'

Lottie Vernon was standing in Julia's study looking at the portrait, of which she grew more fond every time she saw it. It was no pleasure to her to talk to the weaselly Mackinnon man – a waste of space, if ever there was one – but if Mienke thought he might protect Phoebe from the perils of her grief, he was a necessary evil. She put her proposition.

'Oh,' he said, disconcerted. He rubbed his grey stubble. The lover had genuinely forgotten, in his surprise, that Phoebe was

Julia's daughter. He thought about her a great deal, but not in a filial context. 'Yes. Poor kid. And yes, of course, there's the boy. Hmmm. Oh, dear. Well . . .'

He reached for the diary on his bedside table and riffled the pages. There was something on Monday, surely?

Oh, yes. Settling up with young Alex. He had been half-intending to wriggle out of any involvement in this boring, female mess of grieving and children, but suddenly he saw an image of Phoebe, scrawny in her bikini beside the Deauville pool. He could see, as clearly as on video, her dark eyes dancing with mischief as she handed him the Sellotaped paper with the American's addresses on it.

'She's very, very low,' said the clipped voice on the phone. 'I don't know whether you know, but she does have a history with drugs. We're afraid that without a good friend near her, she might be tempted . . . she's talking of London, and apparently that's always meant bad news, with her.'

Alan grimaced. He tried to dismiss the image of Phoebe, happy and starry-eyed with soaking wet hair, but it refused to leave him. Another image rose beside it, of a 'very, very low' version of his companion. It was not difficult; over the years he had seen her often in the background at Iver, sullen and depressed with her brat in tow and her mother shooting her anxious glances. It was only back in April, when he had spotted her flirting with the American, that he began to take notice of her allure.

'OK,' he said. When he made his mind up, he did it quickly: it was a gambler's knack. 'I'll get down there today. I have to be back in London on Monday, but perhaps I'll bring her too.' He silenced a worried quack from the phone. 'No, she won't go anywhere near any dealers, I'll see to that. To be honest, I don't think it's as much of a danger as you clearly do.'

He rose from his bed more cheerfully than on any morning since his return from Deauville. Within an hour he had locked and left the flat, only pausing at the last minute to scoop the American's winnings into his briefcase lest he should not have time to come home before their meeting. Hailing a taxi in Maida Vale, he sped to the garage where his own car waited, kept washed, waxed and serviced for him as one of the many small bachelor luxuries he favoured. Heading for the house he had always called 'Julia's' but which now, he supposed, would get another name, he wondered for the first time who would dispense his herbal remedies. He did not see Phoebe as a natural heir. Poison everybody, probably. Perhaps one of those holy-looking foreign girls who were always drifting round the place would take over.

He made such good time that Phoebe opened her eyes at two o'clock to find him hovering in her bedroom doorway.

'What the fuck . . . ?' she said. 'What you doing here?' She struggled upright, revealing that she wore a frayed old Snoopy T-shirt in bed. 'What d'you want?'

He and Lottie had agreed, when they had met downstairs, to perpetuate the Morrowack tradition of benevolent lying.

'I was booked in. Then, when I got here, I heard what happened. It's terrible. Poor sweet! Do you want a cuddle?'

Phoebe was unconvinced. 'Lying bastard. You were *not* booked in till Tuesday. Who called you? Mienke? I told her not to, Dutch bitch – I can cope perfectly—'

Tears welled in her eyes, and Alan, old enough after all to be her father, moved swiftly to the bed and took her in his arms.

'Wasn't Mienke. Never you mind, I'm here. Look, Phoebs – we're mates, aren't we? Mates come round when someone's had a shock. A mate just comes round and has a drink with you, no strings. It's all right.'

271

Her heart beat against his, and a fierce surprising joy surged in him as she pushed her ruffled head against his shoulder. 'Shhhweetheart,' he said into her hair. 'Everything will be all right.'

She said something so muffled he could only just make it out. It was, 'Dirty old man!' He smiled and laid his cheek on the top of her head.

By Sunday teatime, Lottie Vernon at last felt that it was safe to leave. Insouciant of cost as always, she summoned a bewildered local taxi to drive her to Moare Park.

'You'll stay with her?' she said to Alan Mackinnon in a low voice, as they looked out at Phoebe and Josh walking across the lawn. 'You won't leave her to wander off? For a few days at least?'

'We're all going to London in the morning,' he said. 'Going to take Josh to the Science Museum. I've got one very quick meeting, then we'll all have lunch, stagger round the sights a bit and probably come back here.'

'Peter rang last night. Apparently they can't release Julia's body. A post-mortem has to be done so the funeral has to be delayed a bit. It might be a week.'

'I'll keep Phoebe with me. Just, for God's sake, don't ask me to arrange any funeral stuff. Gives me the creeps. Never got over having to fix up my mother's. Ugh!'

'Peter's doing that,' said Lottie. 'He's already got numbers for her Herbalist Association, people to ring in the morning. And the green funeral people. Julia was into all that.' She shuddered. 'I know what you mean, though. Peter's best at that sort of thing.'

'Good old Admiral Sir Peter,' said Mackinnon flippantly. 'The Nelson touch. Splendid.' The Admiral's lady attempted a haughty glare, but for once did not quite pull it off.

So Lottie went home in a taxi, and worked until three in the morning on her presentation to the DGB Board. Meanwhile the bundles of nine thousand nine hundred and fifty pounds won by Alex van Hyden, having travelled up to Iver, travelled back to London again and were handed over without ceremony in a Harrods' carrier bag in the foyer of the Savoy Hotel. Alex was startled by Mackinnon's briskness.

'Can't do lunch, sorry,' said the little man, grinning with his usual air of knowing malice. 'Something came up. It's all in the bag. Enjoy! I must fly.'

And he was gone, like Rumpelstiltskin in the story. Minutes later he rejoined Phoebe and Josh in the pizza house opposite, leaving Alex, rather sheepishly, to collect his cases from the Savoy cloakroom into which he had booked them only minutes before. He stashed the carrier-bag of money in with his laptop and headed out into the Strand to make his way to Buckinghamshire.

Phoebe and Josh were still in the Science Museum, abusing the interactive exhibits, when the American's taxi finally rolled up to Julia's house. There Alex entrusted to the Australian girl in the garden a bulky brown envelope marked FOR PHOEBE.

'It's nothing important,' he said, to minimize any dangerous curiosity from this stranger. Mienke, worn out by the weekend's emotions, was taking a half-hour nap.

The Australian girl, who was in the middle of unblocking an irrigation pipe and whose hands were filthy and wet, put the packet on the topmost drying-shelf in the shed and promptly forgot about it.

29

On Monday 3 September, after one of the hardest and strangest weekends of her life, Lottie Vernon went before the main Board of DGB Investments and failed to convince them of her professional competence. Her handling of the Ancaster pension fund, they ruled, had been inadequate. The panicky atmosphere in the City could not fail to colour their judgement: around them in that early autumn lay every kind of evidence that these were hard times to be a fund manager. Equitable Life had left furious policyholders facing enormous losses, shares in blue-chip companies like Marconi, Marks and Spencer and BT had plummeted alarmingly during the year, and the new technologies had seduced and then tripped up countless investors, from corporate giants to cheeky individual gamblers. On every side fortunes were crumbling, lawsuits pending and reputations peeling.

Compared to many, as one financial journalist observed, Lady Vernon's management had in fact been reasonably canny. Her other funds were in good heart. The disaster of Entomagic – whose shares had plunged more steeply than any firm in City memory – could not fairly be laid at her feet. If Lottie had allowed a certain leeway to her young team that was surely a forgivable flaw, wrote the journalist: particularly as DGB made so much of the responsibility it entrusted to the rising generation.

But their bet had not paid off. The company preferred a rapid settlement of the Ancaster claim to a long and embarrassing lawsuit, and the can was Lottie Vernon's to carry. As another more excitable journalist observed, 'A bloodletting was overdue. Few women reach the top of a City organization without leaving some unsettled scores. So when they fall, they fall hard.' Murray Harman and Adeline Cook met their former team leader on the stairs, wearing unconvincing expressions of concern, and she said coolly, without pausing as her heels clicked on the marble: 'Don't worry. *You're* all right. Too far down the food chain for anyone to bother eating you. Your time will come to be shafted. If you get that lucky. *Ciao*, then.'

By noon she was gone. Peter had wanted to drive up and wait for her with the car, but Jocasta had been having nightmares about people dropping dead, and was so pale that he decided to stay home. Lottie was brisk, as she generally was in matters concerning work.

'I'm all right,' she had said. 'Truly, I am. Even if it goes the wrong way, I'll be fine. Don't fuss.'

So she came home alone, and rather than ringing from the station decided on a whim to walk up the lane to Moare Park. She had done this only once since they moved there, preferring to take her exercise on her own acres where no curious villagers could point her out and offer sly, disingenuous greetings. But today, with nothing to carry but a slim briefcase on a shoulder strap – she had never kept distracting family pictures or mementoes in her office – she walked up the deep green lane in solitude.

A weekday quiet hung over the commuter village. The leaves had not begun to fall; the trees made a dappled tunnel overhead and a few birds twittered. Lottie breathed deeply: the earth was damp and fragrant with a sharp edge of wild garlic which reminded her of Julia's garden. She walked slowly in her high hard heels, and for a moment she fancied that the whole world had slowed down to the pace of a dream sequence in a film.

Slowed down? she thought drily. Speeded up, more like, and thrown me off the edge. The row of stern faces and dark suits in this morning's kangaroo-court rose before her, but the dreaminess of the quiet lane overwhelmed them and like wraiths they vanished. She was off the edge now, out of the loop.

So what? She shrugged, trying to turn her lingering sense of humiliation into nonchalance. The birds still sang, the weak sun edged cleverly round the clouds to shine through the green arch overhead. She tried out this so-what feeling, and found that it fitted her real mood surprisingly well. Why wear yourself out, handling risk for ungrateful bastards too stupid or afraid to choose their own investments in a slippery world? Why not turn your back and let them all get on with it?

And she was walking home. Jocasta would be pleased to see her. The boys, too, in their way; but little Jock was the one still young enough to cuddle up artlessly, and to demand what she wanted from her mother whether she got it or not.

The boys were older, and had learnt, thought Lottie sadly as she walked, only to ask for things which experience told them they would get. Sharp clothes, holidays, mini-scramble bikes, computer games; detached material benevolence from her, and their father's constant interest. Damien seemed sometimes to look at her with big-eyed reproach when she left the family table early to go back to her work, but Eden had never wanted to be a mother's boy. Peter thought Damien was troubled, not fit for boarding school. She had wanted him to be easy, independent, like his brother. Perhaps she had let down her second son.

Her third son. Lottie's step faltered. In her shock, grief, anxiety over Phoebe and apprehension about DGB, she had pushed aside the revelations of Friday night. The storm of tears in Peter's car had calmed her, and enabled her to forgive Julia's lie and wash the whole ancient disaster away. She had briefly been afraid that Peter would take a high moral line and tell her it was her duty to welcome the lost son into the family, or some such horror, but he had been silent on the subject. Her own feelings seemed clear. She shrank from the strangeness and embarrassment of the situation, and was not attracted to what she had seen of the pushy young man himself. He was no son of hers. She had other responsibilities; he was a strange adult, no more. A high profile like hers would always attract people wanting something. He was just another of those. Fortune-hunter, maybe. Possibly he was not even her real son, but some impostor who had stolen his identity to exploit her, and fooled poor Julia.

But in the peace of the lane her conscience gnawed at her. Nearly home, skirting the ripe brick wall of the estate, she kicked off her shoes and stepped on to the smoothly mown verge which edged it. She would have his identity checked, obviously, but if he was real she owed him something. If they ever heard from him again, with an address, she could settle some money on him: there was enough. Fifty thousand, maybe. The deposit on an apartment, or a bit to set himself up in a business partnership, get married or whatever he was up to. Peter would approve. In her new softer mood, it seemed to Lottie important that Peter should approve of her.

She would not see this Alexander again, but write to him formally, wishing him well and asking for an account number to transfer the money. Not every adopted baby got such a windfall in his twenties, nor such an undemanding birth-mother.

The idea of herself as undemanding and unselfish in her detachment gave Lottie back some of the tranquillity of the moments before. The grass beneath her feet was soft and damp, and the sensation of being barefoot, despite her muddy stockings, produced an irresponsible holiday feeling. She reached the iron gates, fished out her remote control from the briefcase, and almost skipped into Moare Park. Peter was on the lawn with Jocasta, directing the child's attempts to climb a spreading beech tree. Lottie waved, and ran towards them.

'You look way better,' said Johnny Parvazzi. 'How'd it go?'

He had met Alex at the airport and was driving him straight to the office, with a flurry of shop talk: 'Want you to meet Microsoft Abby, now re-designed as Candoo Abby. He's been in Alaska. We are now in the oil business, man. And the teaching contract looks like happening, too.' He chattered deliberately about work and left the main question until they were almost out of the tunnel.

'It went – OK,' said Alex. 'I found her, in this kind of palace she lives in, but someone dropped dead on the floor at that moment. And after that she kinda threw me out, and I decided to cut my losses and run for it.'

'You didn't talk?' said Johnny, thinking of his own small idolized Rudy at home, nestled up to his pretty mother. 'Not at all?'

'You wouldn't ask that if you'd seen her,' said Alex. 'Bonding is not her thing. Chip of ice. Look, I'm OK. I satisfied my curiosity, that's all. I got an idea of what sort of country it is, and I've actually seen my birth-mom. So I guess I can let go now. I'm an American. End of story.'

Johnny glanced sharply sideways, but his friend appeared tranquil, even nonchalant.

'And the other dame? The one who told your dad she was dead?'

'Uh – it was her who dropped dead. I called the ambulance. So I never spoke to her again either.'

'Wasn't there a question,' asked Johnny, 'about whether she'd also told your *mom* that *you* were dead? I mean, if your mom never knew you were alive, that makes it kind of more OK?'

'I don't know,' said Alex, and for the first time a crack of misery opened in his voice, so that Johnny wished he had not probed so far. 'That's the one thing I don't know. I reckon it's likely enough the Julia woman lied to everyone in the whole damn' planet. I'm surprised she hasn't come back from the grave already to tell us all that George W. Bush is dead, also Oprah, Jerry Springer and Little Jimmy Osmond.'

Johnny laughed. 'So you're really OK.'

'Yeah. It's over. I am not going to try and find anything else out. I am through with goddamn' roots. England is now a mere tourist destination in my life: official. Will you tell the others, and tell them I've had it with the whole subject? No secrets about anything, but let's move on, huh?'

'Sure,' said Johnny. 'OK, here we are. Work to do!'

'Great,' said Alex. 'That's what I need.'

Two days later, waiting in the New York office of a British magazine company whose layout program kept crashing and freezing, Alex looked idly through the UK newspapers and found a single-column obituary in *The Times*.

JULIA TAINTON MORROWACK

Julia Morrowack, who has died at the age of 46, was widely regarded as a leading practitioner in the field of herbal medicine. Although she published no books under her own name, and was notably reticent about public appearances, her contributions to symposia and to all the major scientific journals were well received, and did much to enhance understanding among the mainstream medical establishment, of cures often dismissed as purely folkloric.

Julia Tainton Morrowack was born in 1955, the daughter of Professor Antony Tainton Morrowack and the Italian-born Marina Frascelli. In a rare interview she recalled that her interest in herbalism began when she herself was diagnosed with chronic heart disease at 22, and a close friend suffered liver damage as a result of heroin addiction.

A brief marriage to the late John Menthorpe and the birth of her only child Phoebe delayed her formal studies, but after separating from her husband she took degrees in pharmacology and biochemistry through the Open University, at the same time pursuing her researches into the growing and preparation of medicinal herbs. Her small, informal treatment centre in Buckinghamshire quickly developed a loyal following, and some remarkable medical results have been recorded. Rather than expand, Ms Morrowack chose to use it as a training centre for herbal practitioners, often from Continental Europe, and to keep her clientele small and closely supervised. 'I am a healer,' she said in the interview, 'not a business person.'

Her own health was never strong, although colleagues cite her formidable determination not to be slowed down; she died on 31 August of a heart attack caused by her lifelong condition. She leaves a daughter, Phoebe, and a grandson.

Alex read it through, then re-read it, and did not hear the secretary who stood by his chair repeating, 'Morris can see you now, Mr van Hyden.' When she broke through his concentration he looked up, confused, and said: 'Hey – sorry – do you think I could take a copy of this page?'

'Take the newspaper,' said the girl. 'Nobody much reads them. It's for the image.' She grinned. 'All yours.'

'Thanks.' With an effort, he pulled his mind back to the job in hand and followed her through to the meeting.

All day, though he tried to keep his mind on the vagaries of the company J-peg routings, he kept pulling out the page and glancing at it again. His feelings were confused. On the one hand it seemed that he need not blame himself overmuch for Julia's death. It sounded as if the combination of a lifelong heart condition and overwork could have carried her off any time at all. The relief was immense: he had not realized how deep his guilt ran, and how large a component of his unhappiness it was.

On the way back to the office, which was only three blocks away, he dived into a Starbucks and read it through again. Another feeling came over him: this woman he had called Morticia Addams, who had given him such a hard time and been so arrogant in her dealings with him, was highly distinguished in her own field. She must have been brilliant and dogged, to take two distance-learning degrees, study herbalism and bring up a child alone. She was respected. She had an obituary in the London *Times*. Perhaps she could be forgiven for her haughtiness.

He read it again, ever more interested: the Italian mother accounted for the dark Pocahontas looks, and the apparent haphazard eccentricity of the centre at Iver clearly disguised an international reputation. Talk about British understatement! On the other hand, she obviously didn't bother about making money, so he was glad he had given his winnings to Phoebe.

He found himself feeling lighter, brighter than he had done since it happened. At the end of a literary tragedy, he thought, there always came a death and a reconciliation. Here was the death. The reconciliation lay in the ending of his rancour towards Julia. She was dead, rest her soul, as Grandma used to say. She had done what she did for the best. He was now prepared to believe that she had really gone to confess her lie to Lady Vernon, and anxious to believe that the stress of that confession was what had killed her.

Perhaps she had even been right to lie. She had, after all, engineered a clean break between the desperate, drug-addicted Moira Charlotte Grayson and the baby who might have died in her care. Her ruthlessness had enabled Moira Charlotte to lead another life, and metamorphose into the dazzlingly successful Lady Vernon behind her stately iron gates. And she had meant him no harm, either. For all she could know, Alex had a good and strong young father to guard him while he grew.

It was not Pocahontas' fault, thought Alex wearily, that Christian died when he was two. It was not Julia Morrowack's fault that so much was missing in his life. Tears sprang to his eyes. Nobody's fault: none of it was wicked, only sad and survivable. You could not forever condemn, down the arches of the years, a nineteen-year-old pregnant drug addict. You could not hold a grudge against a dead woman who told lies to smooth an impossible situation, and who at the end tried to tell the truth.

He finished his coffee and considered for a moment, hands flat on the newspaper in front of him. He could not know for sure that Julia had gone to Moare Park to tell the truth; but still ringing in his ears were her last words: 'Oh, *there* he is!' So yes, yes, she had definitely been talking about him. And, moments before, while he was arguing with Sir Peter, he had heard raised voices.

He was almost sure. Equally, he was sure that Lottie Vernon had thought him dead these past twenty-seven years.

Which made all the more painful, all the more unbelievable, the equally strong memory of the way her hennaed head had twisted away from him. She had not even wanted to look at him. *Get him out of here. Out! It's too much.*

Alex sighed, and carefully closed and folded the newspaper. He would put Julia's obituary in the red box with the shawl and the diary. One way or another, she had done more for him than his mother ever did. As he glanced down at the front page, he saw another item: FALL OF CITY'S ICE QUEEN AS FUNDS TUMBLE. He read that too, then shrugged and thrust the paper in his computer case. To hell with her.

30

Julia's body was released at the end of the week, and Sir Peter, with unaccustomed assistance from his wife, set about organizing a 'green' funeral according to Julia's reputed wishes. Friends and colleagues in the alternative medicine world made contact after the obituary was published, and Mienke, left in charge of the house and garden, was grateful to be able to refer them to Moare Park.

Phoebe and Alan Mackinnon came back to Iver after three days, and helped desultorily with preparations for the funeral tea, now set for the following Monday. Alan spent most of his time being beaten at chess by Josh, not always intentionally. Kath, the Australian student, informed them apologetically that she had booked her flight home for the tenth, and only now realized that it was also the funeral day.

'I can't change it,' she wailed. 'It's a cheapie. I am so sorry, Minky.'

'No problem,' said the Dutch girl resignedly. 'Sir Peter has offered to hire somebody to help with the food and drink.' She had, like all of them, been stunned to find that Julia had so many friends and admirers. The phone rang constantly, with people demanding the funeral time.

'I suppose,' said Lottie Vernon, surveying the lengthening list by the phone at Moare Park, 'that people in these alternative-y trades don't believe in memorial services.

They'd want to be there for the full monty, wicker basket and all.'

The wicker coffin was a cause of great interest to the children: it was having to be procured from a green funeral store, lined with biodegradable plastic to meet public health regulations, and would be quilted with fragrant herbs, on which the body would lie in a simple shroud. Peter, who had seen more deaths than the rest of them, was intensely worried about the aesthetics of this, given the week which had passed since her death, but the boys were fascinated.

'Is she going to be buried in a wood, then?'

'Yes. It's a woodland burial site. It's not too far, thank goodness.'

'I heard you on the phone to the undertaker. Is he arguing about the wicker hamper?'

'Not hamper, coffin. Yes, he is. We're not using that undertaker in the end. I've arranged otherwise.'

'Cool! When I die, I'm going to cause all the trouble I can. That way people don't forget you.'

Peter laughed at Eden's cheek, but felt increasingly nervous. He kept glancing at Lottie, who although she seemed un-usually calm and benevolent, had after all been bereft within a few days of her oldest friend and her job, and who must (he silently presumed) still be wrestling with the question of what to do about the young American.

His own feelings on the subject were mixed. Natural justice demanded that they find him and make him welcome; emo-tional instincts told him to let sleeping dogs lie. That the young man had vanished was surely a blessing. They had no idea where he lived: Julia was the only one who knew anything at all, and she had torn up and thrown away his address. He had asked Mienke, but she knew nothing. It did not occur to him to ask Phoebe. It very rarely occurred to well-organized, reputable people to assume that Phoebe knew anything useful at all.

On the day of the funeral, the five Vernons drove over together in the early morning, and found the household tolerably ready for invasion. Peter had delicately broached with Phoebe the question of Julia's business effects and records, offering to look through them, and Phoebe agreed.

'Only I want to know everything,' she said. 'I know I carried on a bit last week, but I'm not that big a baby.' Peter looked at her: she seemed indeed more adult than the punkish, sobbing creature he had left in his wife's care. The stud, he noticed, had vanished from her eyebrow, leaving a faint pink scar, and her hair was smoother. The abominable Mackinnon man was clearly being some help.

Julia's accounts and records were simple and straightforward; her desk notable for the absence of personal records or souvenirs. There was one photograph of Phoebe as a small child, clutching a cat and displaying her familiar sullen stare, but most of the files were professional, full of correspondence with pharmacologists, botanists and fellow-herbalists, and of careful records of treatments.

After a time he found what he was looking for, a will: again it was a model of simplicity. Her working records were left to a university medical school, whose representative had already rung to announce his interest and intention to come to the funeral. Her existing season's stock was to be sold 'at a fair and current price' to one of three potential practitioners, listed with addresses and also likely to appear at the funeral. Whoever bought the stock took on the responsibility for providing, or finding, treatment for a named list of long-term patients which included Moira Charlotte Vernon and Alan Brownlee Mackinnon.

The proceeds of this small transaction, together with the house, belonged to Phoebe. There were no additional bequests, nor any sign of further investments or savings. Peter had hoped, sentimentally, that some souvenir would be left to his wife, but it seemed that souvenirs had no place in Julia's austere world.

With a sigh, he set the desk in order and took the will to Phoebe, who listened gravely to his explanation of it and then thanked him with curious formality. 'I am grateful to you for doing the things I'm no good at,' she said. 'And I'm sorry I went so ape last week.'

'Fine,' said Peter, embarrassed.

'The only thing is,' said Phoebe, 'if I want to live here, with Josh, do you think I can afford it?'

'I looked at the bank book,' said Peter. 'It all rather depended on the income from paying guests. Would you carry that on?'

'No, I couldn't. Christ, no. So I've got to sell it pretty soon? Alan says houses like this eat up money. He's going to help me a bit, but his money sort of comes in and out, in big lumps, when you least expect it. His income isn't that great.'

'Hmm, well . . .' Peter grimaced. 'The house is worth at least half a million, with the gardens,' he said. 'You could buy something smaller for you and the boy . . .'

Phoebe's eyes welled with tears. 'I grew up here. How much would it cost just to stay?'

'Outgoings . . .' Peter thought back to the neat bank records. 'Council tax, oil for the Aga, electricity . . .'

'I mean, have I got a year's worth? I mean, with food and stuff?'

'Probably not,' said Peter with great gentleness. 'Not after inheritance tax. Which is another thing I am afraid will affect you. Property in this part of the country is almost all over the threshold.'

'Ah, shit,' said Phoebe. 'So that's it, then.'

'Lottie and I will want to help,' he said diffidently.

'I couldn't take help,' said Phoebe. 'Mum would be pissed off if I did.'

'Will you get a job?' asked Peter.

'I can't do anything,' said the girl simply. He was about to contradict her, but as he looked at her the words died in his throat. Luckily, Alan reappeared, and took her off his hands.

The woodland funeral was a simple service, with a short and moving oration from a distinguished consultant physician and a message from the Prince of Wales. To Peter's surprise, few of the crowd looked like witches or hippies; there were more cardigans than suits, and most people were quietly spoken. A song about worms and dissolution into earth was sung by a vast blonde woman in a kaftan, which startled Peter a little; but Lottie was amused and told him that she had met the singer several times during her stays at Iver, and that she was a respected Song Healer. Peter began to see that his brittle, businesslike wife had stepped during her absences into another world entirely. He rather respected her for it. Most other rich businesswomen in her circle merely went to health farms, to rest in chic pampered insulation among their own kind.

Back at the house, drinking the inevitable green teas and nibbling at Mienke's brown scones, the Vernons stood aside from the general professional conversation. They were soon squashed into the end of the hallway, and when the telephone rang at his elbow Peter, absent-mindedly, picked it up.

'It's Kath!' howled a voice, half-drowned by singsong airport announcements. 'Look, I forgot something and my plane goes in, like, ten minutes. They've let me get off, but they're not happy—'

The upward lilt and the pronunciation of 'heppy' gave Peter the clue. 'Oh, you're the girl in the garden?' he said. 'Have you forgotten something? Do you want it sending on?'

'No . . . I forgot to tell Phoebs she's got a parcel. It's in the drying-shed. On top of everything. A guy brought it. I was cleaning the drain and I forgot to give it to her. Could be there for years, up on that top shelf.'

The announcements echoed again behind her, menacing. 'Ah, Jeez, I gotta go.'

Peter replaced the phone and thought with longing of the cool garden. 'Eden,' he said to his bored elder son, 'there's a packet for young Phoebe in the shed. The Aussie girl just rang. Tell your mother I've gone to get it, if she asks.'

But Lottie was engaged in conversation with a Professor of Pharmacology with long, white hair like the wizard Gandalf. Peter slipped out, got the bulky brown envelope, and brought it indoors. As luck would have it, Phoebe was sitting at the top of the stairs with Alan Mackinnon.

'When will they all *go away?*' she asked plaintively. 'I got a headache.'

'Got a parcel,' he said. 'Australian Kath forgot to tell you about it. It's been in the shed for days.'

'Parcel? Oh,' said Phoebe. She looked very tired now, with rings under her eyes, and was leaning her head on Alan's shoulder. 'I don't know how much more of this I can stand.'

'Me neither,' said Alan. 'God, why are funerals so bloody *noisy?* Affirmation of life, or what?'

'Let's go upstairs.' The two of them climbed up, arms over one another's shoulders, and Peter turned away with a smile. Unlike his wife, he rather approved of this pairing.

Alan sat on Phoebe's sagging bed, and watched her idly as she ripped the envelope open. Inside was a letter, and another envelope.

'Chinese boxes,' he said. 'What's it say?'

'It's not signed,' said Phoebe. 'Look.'

The note, in neat bland handwriting, said: 'This money is for Phoebe Morrowack and her boy Josh to use for anything they need.'

'Bloody hell!' said Phoebe, ripping open the second envelope. 'Get a load of this!'

Alan stared. On to the bed fell four fat bundles of fifty-pound notes, each neatly snapped together with criss-crossed orange rubber bands. He blinked.

'Whoo!'

'How much is that?' said Phoebe, dazzled.

'About ten K,' said Alan.

'Trust you to know.'

'I could tell you something else, if you let me count it.'

'All I want to know,' said the girl, riffling a stack of notes, 'is who the hell goes around sending me thousands of pounds anonymously? I feel like a *dealer*. All I need now's a BMW with blacked-out windows.'

'Well,' said Alan, 'if you let me count, that's exactly what I can tell you. Maybe. I have an eye for rubber bands and their origins.'

He picked up the first stack, pulled off the longitudinal bands and counted fifty notes. In the second, there were also fifty. The orange rubber bands, four per stack, neat and symmetrical, made him almost sure of what he knew, but he counted the third stack and stopped at forty-nine. Then he counted it again. Forty-nine. He pulled from his pocket a wallet, and eased from it a half-ripped £50 note, which he inserted under the shorter rubber bands before snapping the lengthways ones back on.

'This money,' he said dreamily, 'has a piquant history. It began life back in spring as a pony on a runner at Newmarket. Little horse of mine called Something of the Night. Forty to one, and it skipped home like a gentleman. Then the brave little wad took its chances on the 4.10 at Kempton, on that same lovely spring afternoon, riding to victory aboard Dutch Courage. Ten to one. And thus does the price of a bottle of decent Scotch transform itself, by the miracle of horseflesh, into the price of a family car. It's almost enough to turn a man to religion.'

He looked affectionately at the money on the duvet. 'I had to count it, to make sure it was the authentic Mackinnon rubber bands, but I knew them as soon as I saw them.'

'You mean it's yours?' said Phoebe. 'Why the fuck did it end up in the drying-shed with my name on it? You don't give me *money*, I'm not a tart.'

'Not mine. You made it clear to me in Deauville that this particular money is not mine. It's the winnings of your American fancy-man, Alex van Hyden, courtesy of my magnanimous double tip. The special relationship, you see, aren't I wonderful? It was a very good day. I won forty thou, he won ten. That's because I am not a cautious born-again Yankee but an English gentleman, and I gave Something of the Night a full hundred quidsworth of my love and trust.'

'So why's he sending me all this money? Anonymously?' said Phoebe. She squinted at the letter. ' 'Cos it is anonymous, he can't have known you'd be hanging around me identifying rubber bands.'

'God knows. But you know the old saying: "We regret we have no administrative mechanism for returning money". It'll give you a breathing space. You can stay in this heap for a while anyway. You deserve it, after the shocks you've had lately. Who knows? A few more tips and trips to the casino with Uncle Alan, and you could be as rich as Lottie Vernon.'

'I can't take it!' said Phoebe. 'I don't even know him.' She was very, very tired; her thumb crept to her mouth.

'Oh, for God's sake!' said Alan. 'If I thought you were a girl with scruples I'd never have taken up with you! Now lie down, and sleep on it.'

31

━◆━◆━

On the day of Julia Morrowack's funeral Alex was in New York, talking about problems in photographic transmission. The British magazine company was still screaming for attention, and Marty was out of town. Alex, with a hangover, had driven down the Interstate through a clear and lovely autumn dawn, to beg some advice from a former Microsoft designer at the finance house where he worked. On the way out through the vast foyer of the building he ran into Maddy. She was with a strikingly handsome and Nordically blond man, and her body language towards her companion became exaggeratedly flirtatious when Alex drew near.

'Al-ex!' she said, draping herself over the fair man's arm with purposeful affection. 'Hey! This is Jay!'

'Hey, Jay,' said Alex, and raised his hand in a neutrally friendly greeting. 'Great to see you, Maddy. You're looking totally sensational.'

You had to say these things to women whenever you met them, in her world. Not to do so would have been an act of positive hostility. Was it, he wondered as he walked on, his churchy Midwest upbringing or his recent British sojourns which made it seem so damn' ridiculous?

But seeing the pair together, sexy and fond, lowered his mood. He found himself thinking again of the Dutch girl at Iver: sweet-faced, busy, unassuming Mienke. It was high time he found another girlfriend. Not, perhaps, in these high-octane surroundings: New York girls made him feel like a permanent outsider. But then, so did Isabelle's Boston friends. He had been to dinner with her and her new husband in their inordinately grand waterfront house the night before, which brought on something of the same despair which had gripped him at Moare Park. The house was like a stage set, perfect and smug. Isabelle had pointedly fixed him up with a sleek brunette with huge eyes and a job on *Vanity Fair*. Layla had talked about her job the whole way through dinner, dwelling at length on the brilliance and flair of the editor, Graydon Carter. When she remembered to ask about Alex's job her eyes glazed over at the answer, and she looked past him, longingly, at a fashionable British actor who Isabelle had selfishly sat at her own right hand.

Finally, having had more drink than usual, Alex had broken into Layla's flow and said abruptly: 'I'll tell you a story. I was in Britain last week. Do you know what I did? I won sixteen thousand bucks on a racehorse, and gave it away to a girl I only met once.' Layla stared at him with distaste. Only later, on the way back to Water Street, did he realize that she had thought he was boasting about a prostitute.

But none of that was any excuse for sentimental thoughts about Mienke, who probably saw him as no more than another soup-plate to be cleared in the witch's cave of Julia Morrowack's kitchen.

Back in Boston that night, tired from the Interstate, he found a letter.

Dear Alex,
  I hope it went well. I wish I had been able to do more to help. It must have been a bit traumatic all round, but I hope

*it was a happy trauma. I think of you a lot, and hope that
next time you're in the UK you'll come and see us. Duncan
is talking about re-stocking before the spring, and Jamie is
teaching Adam to use the Internet on your wonderful
computer.*
  Your friend,
  Doreen Clark

He sighed, and put the letter carefully on his desk to be
answered when he felt strong enough. The time was not yet.
He did not want to think, speak, or write about Moira
Charlotte Vernon for a long, long time. He flicked on the
television, opened his laptop, put a book within reach just in
case, and sat down alone to pass the hour until bedtime.

Some hours earlier Lottie Vernon, equally jaded, got home
from the funeral. It had been somewhat marred at the end by
the flat refusal of Alan Mackinnon to let anyone wake up
Phoebe to say goodbye to the guests. Lottie had done the
honours instead, and hated it. Shrugging off her jacket, she
found Jocasta brandishing a letter in neat, unfamiliar handwriting.

'It came ages ago,' said the child self-importantly, handing it
to her mother. 'I brought it in with the papers after the lady
died, and it's been lying under the clock in the breakfast room.
I've been doing good tidying, but the boys have made ever
such a mess. When's Maria coming back?'

Lottie looked at the letter with mild curiosity. The envelope
was greyish and cheap, but the handwriting looked educated.
Begging letters and hate-mail rarely reached her at Moare
Park, tending to arrive at the office to be dealt with by her PA.
Not a friend, nor a request for an interview, by the look of the

stationery. Wandering into the sitting-room, she slit it open with Peter's silver paperknife, engraved with a tribute from his Falklands officers.

> *Dear Lady Vernon,*
>   (wrote Doreen)
> *I have tried to contact you by telephone to arrange a meeting, but it proved difficult. I would prefer not to raise this matter by letter, and you must forgive me for not giving you my address, but . . .*

'Oh, God, a loony,' said Lottie to Peter, who was contemplating the drinks cupboard. She put the letter down. Peter brought over her martini a moment later and glanced down at it, for he worried a little about the nuisances who wrote to his rich and famous wife. Then a word caught his eye and he frowned, stiffened, and picked it up.

'Hey,' he said. 'Not a loony.'

'Give, then.'

Peter would not let it go, but held it before her while they both read on. It was the second paragraph that had taken his eye.

> *. . . I am a professional family historian and met, some time ago, one Alexander van Hyden from the US. We met because he helped my family very considerably at a hard time (we are farmers and my son is disabled). In return for his great kindness I offered him help in tracing the family of his mother, who he believed to have died in 1974 in the UK. However, my researches indicated that he was wrong in his belief, and that his mother is in fact still living.*

Peter glanced at his wife's white face, waited for her nod, then turned the page over.

I have given him all the details of my research. You will understand that this means he will probably try to contact you directly. I feel great responsibility over this, as I am a mother myself and would have wished to spare you the shock. Unfortunately I could not get through to your office when I tried.

Please believe that I wish you only joy from this strange discovery. And forgive me for not identifying myself; my husband is strongly against my writing this letter and I do not wish to add to his anxieties in this difficult year. But I felt that I must write. I wanted to reassure you, before you have the shock of meeting Alex, that we have come to know him reasonably well, and found him a most extraordinarily kind, intelligent, gentle and likeable young man.

I would be very proud if he were my son.

There was no signature. Lottie was shaking. Peter put his hand on her shoulder.

'He probably is,' she said after a while. 'He probably is all those things. Oh, Christ, Peter. He's probably a nice chap.' She looked up, her face older and softer than he had ever seen it. 'I've been a lost soul, haven't I, these last few years? I think I just lost touch with the idea of ordinary nice people. I mean, that poor woman, still worrying about my feelings after getting the DGB brush-off . . .'

'Should we try and find him, do you think?' said Peter quietly.

'How? Julia said she didn't know.'

He grimaced thoughtfully.

'New York telephone book?'

'He's definitely from New York?'

'Mienke thought so.'

Later, while Lottie combed through the New York online directory, dismayed by its wealth of A. van Hydens, Peter rang Mienke to check that they were combing the right city. He came back pale-faced to his wife's study.

'Phoebe's woken up,' he said. 'And informed the household that your long-lost son Alex has just given her and Josh ten thousand quid, anonymously.'

She stared. 'What d'you mean? How do they know it's him?'

'Because he won it on a horse, courtesy of Alan Mackinnon. Mackinnon recognized the rubber bands, according to Phoebe, from handing it over in some hotel before the chap left. He also recognized the fact that there was fifty quid missing, which she says is his trademark little joke. She was shrieking with merriment, I have to say. They're all a bit tiddly by the sound of it. Reaction after the funeral.'

Lottie stared, trying to take it in. Peter shook his head and went on, for once too surprised himself to notice the effect it was having on his wife.

'But what an amazing gesture. He can't have known they'd pin it on him. I'd like to meet this chap properly. How's the search?'

'There are hundreds of van Hydens,' said Lottie tightly. 'And we don't know he's in the book. Or even in New York. I can't even remember which state Christian came from, I never listened much in those days.' She gave a shuddering sigh. 'Peter, he's vanished. I told him to go away, and he did.'

'We'll find him,' said Peter reassuringly. 'We could get a detective on it.'

'No,' said Lottie bleakly. 'I feel it. I had my chance and I blew it. He's really gone this time. And Peter . . .' She began to cry. 'I've just remembered how he stood there so quietly and rang the ambulance for Julia. He's a decent boy. What have I done?'

32

Three days later, Peter and Lottie Vernon walked unnoticed up the Mall to stand at the back of a quiet, pale throng. Like thousands of others, their small story had collided with history.

A friend had rung, quite unexpectedly in the early afternoon of Tuesday, and said in an odd strained voice: 'Lottie, turn on the television.' Wrenched from her private preoccupations and the hopelessness of her search, she turned from her computer screen to watch with the world, hour after hour, into the next grim day. When the shock and incredulity subsided a little, she began firing off emails to contacts who worked in or alongside the fallen towers of Manhattan.

The financial world, Peter reflected as he watched her, was actually just a village like any other: these brittle million-makers were, in their fickle way, as closely bound together in disaster as any Navy. He made his own enquiries, quietly, about his own acquaintances; and walked alone in the garden as he assimilated the worst of it.

On the second day Lottie's answers began to trickle in: five familiar names from one DGB partner company confirmed dead; eight or ten missing colleagues, some of them friends. It could have been more, and closer, thought Lottie; Adeline had been due for a secondment to New York. It was a jolt, but somehow a cleansing one, to realize that she would have mourned the annoying Adeline's death with all the shocked sincerity of the rest.

On the Wednesday evening a circular message passed on by her old PA at DGB confirmed a worse blow for them both. The Vernons' most recent New York hosts and their child were aboard one of the planes. From the Surrey darkness Lottie sent messages into the bright New York afternoon, and until midnight sat at her desk, talking quietly on the telephone, passing on bad and good news around the world.

Only Peter knew what other agony underlay her sad composure. On Wednesday morning, at her instigation, they made a rare visit to the village church. A service had been arranged by Americans living locally. Outside, talking to the vicar who had been preaching about the pain of uncertainty, Peter heard her say: 'I know, I've a son in New York.' The vicar made sympathetic noises, for he was new; but a neighbour turned her head in puzzlement. The Vernon boys, surely, were little chaps at boarding school?

On the way home Peter said, 'Were you telling the vicar about Alex?' and she answered quietly: 'Not deliberately, no. But he mentioned people with relatives out there and I knew that I mustn't deny Alex. Not again. The cock's crowed three times now.' Then she murmured, almost too low for her husband to catch: 'He's dead, isn't he? I sent him away, and now he's dead.'

It was after hearing the radio news on Thursday that they had come here to the Mall for the Changing of the Guard. 'I ought to be there,' said Lottie. 'I have an American son.'

Ahead of them on the wide avenue the crowd of expatriates stood quiet and intent and seemingly numberless. Several carried flags, one touchingly home-made with each star and stripe painstakingly coloured in. At last the moment arrived which, by the modern alchemy of rumour, email and text-messages had assembled this sombre group of mourners at the Palace railings. The band of the Coldstream Guards struck up the familiar tune, and faltering at first but then growing, around the memorial and back up the Mall came the sound of singing.

    . . . by the dawn's early light,
    What so proudly we hailed at the twilight's last gleaming . . .

Peter put his hand on Lottie's shoulder. Unlike her he knew the convoluted words of the anthem. He had learned them out of politeness, for joint ceremonial events on distant quarter-decks. At least one of the men he had sung alongside was still missing in the Pentagon rubble. He thought of the waste and the chaos and the shadow of war to come, and his heart was too heavy to sing. But the voices around him grew stronger with every line, and when the music rose and slowed Peter could at last join in softly with the living and the dead:

    O! say, does that star-spangled Banner yet wave,
    O'er the Land of the Free, and the Home of the Brave?

A ripple of applause, growing to a storm, swept the crowd and was followed by a deep silence. More music played, and gradually the Americans dispersed, quiet and grave.

'Never seen anything like it, ever,' said Peter that evening. 'I'm glad we went up.'

Lottie nodded. She was pale and composed; he thought she had never been more beautiful. Peter knew what she believed about her eldest son and had stopped trying to reassure her. But how, he wondered, would they ever know?

'Drink?'

'Thanks.' He picked up the bottle, but in his own study on the far side of the hallway the phone rang; he grimaced in apology, put down the vermouth and went through. It was Phoebe's voice.

'Isn't it all just awful? Alan's got two friends he can't get in touch with. One of them runs a bar next door to the tower thing. Alan was actually meant to be flying out there the day before it happened, he was talking about taking me and Josh. I mean, Jesus!' He could hear her voice crack, excited and appalled at once. 'But the thing is, Peter, we were wondering if Lottie might have a fast track to finding stuff out about people? It's chaos apparently—'

'I don't know any fast track,' said Peter, cutting into her flow. 'Lottie's been struggling like everybody else. I'll ask her for you, though. But look, while you're on, do you think I could have a word with Mienke?'

'She's not here,' said Phoebe. 'She went home early. Apparently her father's got contacts out there and was really upset, and her mother called her to come home'.

'Oh,' said Peter. Once again, the vision of a whole world shaken and transformed by the attacks overwhelmed him. At that moment it seemed that Lottie was probably right, and that Alex van Hyden had vanished for good into this black chaos. He steadied his voice with care and said: 'I just wanted to check if she knew what city that young American chap lived in, who won the money on the horse and then vanished. Long shot, but she might just know.'

'Oh, Alex, you mean?' said Phoebe. 'My phantom sugar-daddy? Boston, I think. Alan's still got the bit of paper—'

'What?' Peter could not believe his ears. 'You've got his *address?*'

"The address got a bit ripped, but we've got the email, and that worked for Alan last time. I've been dickering about whether to send him a thank-you for the money, but when people want to be anonymous it's sort of rude, innit? But it definitely wasn't New York. Alan!' she yelled, and in the background a brief exchange took place.

'Here it is,' she said. 'AVH two zero one, at aol.com.'

Peter wrote it on a scrap of paper and carried it through to his wife. When he had explained, she looked at it with huge, pale eyes and without a word, went alone to her study and began very carefully to type.

Epilogue

———◆◆◆———

The world was not the same again, thought Alex, turning round a cardboard cup of airport coffee in his hands, but then it never is. Eventually, as the planes began to fly again, the flurry of grief and confusion resolved itself into just another strand in the greater pattern of national and personal histories.

Maddy was alive because she had been at the emergency dentist; her new friend Jay was dead. Johnny Parvazzi's cousin was a New York fireman, and was lost. Marty and Janis lost a dozen friends in one company, but both drove straight to New York with Mahmood to support a joint Jewish-Muslim prayer group set up by Janis' brother. Abby from Microsoft took three weeks' leave to be with his terrified Arab-American grandparents, who had seen the whole thing from their window and couldn't sleep for the smell of ash. Ellie wept, and found she could not bear to be apart from her babies, so began bringing them into the office with a collapsible playpen. Alex rang his grandfather, who flatly forbade him to do anything so damn' silly as drive a thousand miles home: 'just to prove to me you're alive. I can hear you, boy. Get back to work.'

At Candoo, though, work came almost to a halt for a time. Alex answered the phone, gave clients succinct advice, comforted Ellie and played with the twin babies while she tried to work. He thought a great deal about his young father and uncle, the new tragedy stirring up the embers of the old.

Recovery work went on, rumours ran wild, poison scares streaked through a nervous nation. After weeks of limbo and uncertainty a kind of war began on the other side of the world. Johnny, Marty, Janis, Mahmood and Abby came back to Boston and picked up the threads of the business. Janis organized a benefit concert in Boston one weekend for the fire service orphans, then, at Marty's instigation, another for famine relief in Afghanistan.

Against this background certain private words crossed and recrossed the world in the artfully casual medium of email. Alex stored them on printed sheets which he carried in his pocketbook. He pulled out the last one now, and re-read it as his family's plane circled Logan Airport in the last moments before landing.

. . . 1520 your time. It was going to be just me and Peter, but the boys and Jocasta are coming too because they insist. Perhaps it's just as well we'll be a crowd. I shan't know what to say. I'm too English for this kind of thing.

I hope you'll forgive me, and believe that what I really mean is everything that I have written to you in the last few weeks.

Peter says hi, and to tell you that Mienke from Iver says she's glad you're OK. Her email back in Amsterdam is going to be mikk2100@diamant.nl. He rather thinks she'd want to hear from you.

The only thing left to say is hello. That'll be soon. For the moment, forgive me if I sign off just as

Lottie

The screens above him winked; the London flight was safely down. Alex folded the paper, stowed it carefully away, and walked lightly towards the open gate.